# THE DESCENDANTS

# THE DESCENDANTS

## Kaui Hart Hemmings

First published 2009
by Vintage
This Large Print edition published 2012
by AudioGO Ltd
by arrangement with
The Random House Group Ltd

Hardcover     ISBN: 978 1 445 82711 7
Softcover     ISBN: 978 1 445 82712 4

British Library Cataloguing in Publication Data available

Printed and bound in Great Britain by
MPG Books Group Limited

*For Andy*

For Andy

# Contents

# Contents

# PART I.

# The Minor Wars

# 1

The sun is shining, mynah birds are chattering, palm trees are swaying, so what. I'm in the hospital and I'm healthy. My heart is beating as it should. My brain is firing off messages that are loud and clear. My wife is on the upright hospital bed, positioned the way people sleep on airplanes, her body stiff, head cocked to the side. Her hands are on her lap.

'Can't we lay her flat?' I ask.

'Wait,' my daughter Scottie says. She takes a picture of her mother, a Polaroid. She fans herself with the photo, and I press the button on the side of the bed to lower my wife's upper body. I release the button when she is almost flat on her back.

Joanie has been in a coma for twenty-three days, and in the next few days I'll have to make some decisions based on our doctor's final verdict. Actually, I'll just have to find out what the doctor has to say about Joanie's condition. I don't have any decisions to make, since Joanie has a living will. She, as always, makes her own decisions.

Today is Monday. Dr. Johnston said we'll talk on Tuesday, and this appointment is making me nervous, as though it's a romantic date. I don't know how to act, what to say, what to wear. I rehearse answers and reactions, but I've nailed only the lines that respond to favorable scenarios. I haven't rehearsed Plan B.

'There,' Scottie says. Her real name is Scottie. Joanie thought it would be cool to name her after Joanie's father, Scott. I have to disagree.

I look at the photo, which looks like those joke

3

snapshots everyone takes of someone sleeping. I don't know why we think they're so funny. *There's a lot that can be done to you while you're sleeping.* This seems to be the message. *Look how vulnerable you are, the things you aren't aware of.* Yet in this picture you know she isn't just sleeping. Joanie has an IV and something called an endotracheal tube running out of her mouth to a ventilator that helps her breathe. She is fed through a tube and is administered enough medication to sustain a Fijian village. Scottie is documenting our life for her social studies class. Here's Joanie at Queen's Hospital, her fourth week in a coma, a coma that has scored a 10 on the Glasgow scale and a III on the Rancho Los Amigos scale. She was in a race and was launched from an offshore powerboat going eighty miles an hour, but I think she will be okay.

'She reacts nonpurposefully to stimuli in a nonspecific manner, but occasionally, her responses are specific though inconsistent.' This is what I've been told by her neurologist, a young woman with a slight tremor in her left eye and a fast way of talking that makes it hard to ask questions. 'Her reflexes are limited and often the same, regardless of stimuli presented,' she says. None of this sounds good to me, but I'm assured Joanie's still holding on. I feel she'll be okay and one day able to function normally. I'm generally right about things.

'What was she racing for?' the neurologist asked.

The question confused me. 'To win, I guess. To get to the end first.'

*       *       *

'Shut this off,' I tell Scottie. She finishes pasting the

4

picture into her book then turns off the television with the remote.

'No, I mean this.' I point to the stuff in the window—the sun and trees, the birds on the grass hopping from crumb to crumb thrown by tourists and crazy ladies. 'Turn this off. It's horrible.'

The tropics make it difficult to mope. I bet in big cities you can walk down the street scowling and no one will ask you what's wrong or encourage you to smile, but everyone here has the attitude that we're lucky to live in Hawaii; paradise reigns supreme. I think paradise can go fuck itself.

'Disgusting,' Scottie says. She slides the stiff curtain across the window, shutting all of it out.

I hope she can't tell that I'm appraising her and that I'm completely worried by what I see. She's excitable and strange. She's ten. What do people do during the day when they're ten? She runs her fingers along the window and mumbles, 'This could give me bird flu,' and then she forms a circle around her mouth with her hand and makes trumpet noises. She's nuts. Who knows what's going on in that head of hers, and speaking of her head, she most definitely could use a haircut or a brushing. There are small tumbleweeds of hair resting on the top of her head. *Where does she get haircuts?* I wonder. *Has she ever had one before?* She scratches her scalp, then looks at her nails. She wears a shirt that says I'M NOT THAT KIND OF GIRL. BUT I CAN BE! I'm grateful that she isn't too pretty, but I realize this could change.

I look at my watch. Joanie gave it to me.

'The hands glow and the face is mother-of-pearl,' she said.

'How much did it cost?' I asked.

5

'How did I know that would be the very first thing you said about it?'

I could see she was hurt, that she put a lot of work into selecting the gift. She loves giving gifts, paying attention to people so she can give them a gift that says she took the time to know and listen to them. At least it seems like that's what she does. I shouldn't have asked about the price. She just wanted to show that she knew me.

'What time is it?' Scottie asks.

'Ten-thirty.'

'It's still early.'

'I know,' I say. I don't know what to do. We're here not only because we're visiting and hoping Joanie has made some progress during the night, reacting to light and sound and painful jabs, but also because we have nowhere else to go. Scottie's in school all day and then Esther picks her up, but this week I felt she should spend more time here and with me, so I took her out of school.

'What do you want to do now?' I ask.

She opens her scrapbook, a project that seems to occupy all of her time. 'I don't know. Eat.'

'What would you usually do now?'

'Be in school.'

'What if it were Saturday? What would you do then?'

'Beach.'

I try to think of the last time she was completely in my care and what we did together. I think it was when she was around one, one and a half. Joanie had to fly to Maui for a shoot and couldn't find a babysitter, and her parents couldn't do it, for some reason. I was in the middle of a trial and stayed home but absolutely had to get some work done,

6

so I put Scottie in the bathtub with a bar of soap. I watched to see what happened. She splashed and tried to drink the bathwater, and then she found the soap and reached to grab it. It eluded her grasp and she tried again, a look of wonder on her small face, and I slipped out into the hall, where I had set up a workstation and a baby monitor. I could hear her laughing, so I knew she wasn't drowning. I wonder if this would still work: putting her in a tub with a slippery bar of Irish Spring.

'We can go to the beach,' I say. 'Would Mom take you to the club?'

'Well, duh. Where else would we go?'

'Then it's a plan. After you talk and we see a nurse, we'll check in at home, then go.'

Scottie takes a picture out of her album, crushes it in her hand, and throws it away. I wonder what the picture was, if it was the one of her mother on the bed, probably not the best family relic. 'I wish,' Scottie says. 'What do I wish?'

It's one of our games. Every now and then she names a place she wishes we were besides this place, this time in our lives.

'I wish we were at the dentist,' she decides.

'Me, too. I wish we were getting our mouths x-rayed.'

'And Mom was getting her teeth whitened,' she says.

I really do wish we were at Dr. Branch's office, the three of us getting high on laughing gas and feeling our numb lips. A root canal would be a blast compared to this. Or any medical procedure, really. Actually, I wish I could be home working. I have to make a decision on who should own the land that has been in my family since the 1840s. This sale will

7

eliminate all of my family's land holdings, and I desperately need to study up on the facts before the meeting I have with my cousins six days from now. That's our deadline. Two o'clock at Cousin Six's house six days from today. We'll approve a buyer. It's irresponsible of me to have put off thinking about this deal for so long, but I guess this is what our family has done for a while now. We've turned our backs to our legacy, waiting for someone else to come along and assume both our fortune and our debts.

I'm afraid Esther may have to take Scottie to the beach, and I'm about to tell her, but then I don't because I feel ashamed. My wife is in the hospital, my daughter needs her parents, and I need to work. Once again I'm putting her in the tub.

I see Scottie staring at her mother. She has her back against the wall, and she's fumbling with the hem of her shirt.

'Scottie,' I say. 'If you're not going to say anything, then we may as well leave.'

'Okay,' she says. 'Let's go.'

'Don't you want to tell your mother what's going on in school?'

'She never cares about what's going on in school.'

'What about your extracurricular activities? Your schedule's fuller than the president's. Your scrapbook, show her that. Or what did you make in glassblowing the other day?'

'A bong,' she says.

I look at her closely before responding. She doesn't appear to have said anything remarkable. I never know if she knows what she's talking about. 'Interesting,' I say. 'What is a bong?'

She shrugs. 'Some high school guy taught me

how to make it. He said it would go well with chips and salsa and any other food I could think of. It's some kind of platter.'

'Do you still have this . . . bong?'

'Sort of,' she says. 'But Mr. Larson told me to make it into a vase. I could put flowers in it and give it to her.' She points at her mother.

'That's a great idea!'

She eyes me skeptically. 'You don't have to get all Girl Scout about it.'

'Sorry,' I say.

I lean back in my chair and look at all the holes in the ceiling. I don't know why I'm not worried, but I'm just not. I know Joanie will be okay because she always makes it out okay. She will wake up and Scottie will have a mother and we can talk about our marriage and I can put my suspicions aside. I'll sell the property and buy Joanie a boat, something that will shock her and make her throw her head back and laugh.

'Last time you were the one in the bed,' Scottie says.

'Yup.'

'Last time you lied to me.'

'I know, Scottie. Forgive me.'

She's referring to my stint in the hospital. I had a minor motorcycling accident. I crashed at the track, soaring over the handlebars into a pile of red dirt. At home, after the wreck, I told Joanie and Scottie what had happened but insisted I was okay and that I wasn't going to the hospital. Scottie issued me these little tests to demonstrate my unreliability. Joanie participated. They played bad cop, worse cop.

'How many fingers?' Scottie asked, holding up

9

what I thought was a pinky and a thumb.

'Balls,' I said. I didn't want to be tested this way.

'Answer her,' Joanie said.

'Two?'

'Okay,' Scottie said warily. 'Close your eyes and touch your nose and stand on one foot.'

'Balls, Scottie. I can't do that regardless, and you're treating me like a drunk driver.'

'Do what she says,' Joanie yelled. She's always yelling at me, but it's really just the way we speak to each other. Her yelling makes me feel inept and loved. 'Touch your nose and stand on one foot.'

I stood still in protest. I knew something was wrong with me, but I didn't want to go to the hospital. I wanted to let what was wrong with my body run its course. I was curious. I was having trouble holding up my head. 'I'm fine.'

'You're cheap,' Joanie said.

She was right, of course. 'You're right,' I said. I could just picture it: 'You're injured,' a doctor would tell me, and then he'd charge me a thousand dollars, at least, and do unnecessary things and give me unreliable, overly cautious advice to avoid a lawsuit and then I'd have to deal with the insurance companies, who'd purposely lose documents to avoid paying, and the hospital would send me to collections and I'd be dealing with all of this over the phone with people who didn't even have a GED. Even now I'm skeptical. The fast-talking neurologist and our neurosurgeon say they just need to maintain oxygen levels and control the swelling in her brain. It sounds pretty easy; keeping someone suffused with oxygen should hardly require a surgeon. I relayed my thoughts on doctors to Joanie as I rubbed the right side of my head.

'Look at yourself,' Joanie said. I was looking at a painting on our wall of a dead fish, trying to remember where we got it. I tried to read the artist's name: Brady Churkill? Churchill?

'You can't even see straight,' she said.

'How am I supposed to look at myself, then?'

'Shut up, Matt. Get ready and get in the car.'

I got ready and got in the car.

Turns out I had damaged my fourth nerve, a nerve that connects your eyes to your brain, which explained why things had been out of focus.

'You could have died,' Scottie says now.

'No way,' I say. 'A fourth nerve? Who needs it?'

'You lied. You said you were okay. You said you could see my fingers.'

'I didn't lie. I guessed correctly. Plus, for a while there I got to have twins. Two Scotties.'

She squints, assessing my subterfuge.

I remember when I was in the hospital, Joanie put vodka into my Jell-O. She wore my eye patch and got into the hospital bed and took a nap with me. It was nice. It was the last truly nice thing I have done with her.

I have a nagging suspicion that she is, or was, in love with another man. When she was first admitted to Queen's, I went through her wallet looking for her insurance card and found a note written on a small and stiff piece of blue paper that seemed designed for clandestine messages. The note said: *Thinking of you. See you at Indigo.*

The note could be years old. She always finds faded receipts from ancient vacations, business cards for businesses that no longer exist, movie stubs for *Waterworld* or *Glory*. The note could also be from one of her gay model friends. They're

11

always saying lovey shit like that, and the color of the small card was a feminine Tiffany blue. At the time I dismissed my suspicion, and I'm trying to forget about that note, even though lately, I find myself thinking of her deviousness and flirtatiousness—the way she can drink and drink, and what drinking leads to, the many nights spent out with the girls—and when I think of things this way, an affair seems possible, if not inevitable. I forget that Joanie is seven years younger than I am. I forget that she needs constant praise and entertainment. She needs to be wanted, and I am often too busy to praise, entertain, or want. Still, I can't imagine her actually having an affair. We've known each other for more than twenty years. We get each other and don't expect too much. I like what we have, and I know she does, too. My suspicions aren't convenient right now.

Scottie is still narrowing her eyes at me. 'You could have flat-lined,' she says.

I'm wondering what my accident has to do with anything. Of late, Scottie's been pointing out my flaws, my tricks and lies. She's interviewing me. I'm the backup candidate. I'm the dad. She and Esther are trying to prepare me for the role, I guess, but I want to tell them that it's okay. I'm the understudy, and the star will be back soon.

'What else do you wish?' I ask.

She is sitting on the ground with her chin resting on the seat of a chair. 'Lunch,' she says. 'I'm starved. And a soda. I need soda.'

'I wish you would talk to her,' I say. 'I want you to do that before we leave. I can get you a soda. I'll give you some privacy. You can talk in private.' I stand up, putting my arms over my head and

12

stretching. I feel bad as I look down at Joanie. I have so much mobility.

'You want a diet something?'

'Do you think I'm fat?' Scottie asks.

'No, I don't think you're fat, but Esther loads you with sugar, and I'm going to put you through a little detox, if that's okay. Things are changing around here.'

'What's detox?' She lifts her stringy arms over her head and stretches. I've noticed her copying things I do and say.

'It's what your sister should have done,' I mumble. 'Be back in a flash. Don't go anywhere. Talk.'

# 2

I walk into the hall, which is quiet. At the central reception area, there are nurses and receptionists and visitors waiting for the nurses and receptionists to look up and acknowledge them. Every time I pass the other patients' rooms, I tell myself not to look in, but I can't help myself; I look in the room next to Joanie's. It's the popular patient's room, and it's usually filled with family, friends, balloons, leis, and flowers, as though he's accomplished something by ailing. Today he's alone. He emerges from the bathroom barefoot and holding his hospital gown together. You can tell that on the outside of the hospital, he's a tough sort of guy, but the gown makes him look delicate. He looks at a card on the table, then puts it back down and shuffles to bed. I hate get-well cards. It's like telling someone to have

13

a safe flight. There's really not a whole lot you can do.

I continue toward the central area and see Joy and another nurse walking toward me. Joy personifies her name beautifully.

'Mr. King,' she says. 'How are you today?'

'Wonderful, Joy, and you?'

'Good, good.'

'Good,' I say.

'I saw you in the paper today,' she says. 'Have you made your decision? Everyone's waiting.'

The other nurse nudges her and says, 'Joy!'

'What? Me and Mr. King, we're like this.' She puts her middle finger over her pointer finger.

I continue walking toward the store. 'Mind your own business, young lady.' I try my best to sound carefree. It's embarrassing how much strangers think they know about me, and how many people, my cousins especially, are waiting to see what I'll do. If they only knew how little thought I've given the matter. After the Supreme Court upheld the trust's distribution structure, making me the largest shareholder, I just wanted to hide. It's too much responsibility for one man, and maybe I feel a bit guilty, having so much control. Why me? Why does so much depend on me? And what did the people before me do in order for me to have so much? Maybe I subscribe to the idea that behind every great fortune is a great crime. Isn't that how the saying goes?

'Bye, Mr. King,' Joy says. 'I'll let you know if there's anything in the paper tomorrow.'

'Great, Joy. Thank you.'

I can tell that other patients are wary of this banter I have with Joy. Why do I get

14

acknowledged? My name probably augments their jealousy—the way it sounds: Mr. King, as if I've requested they call me this at Queen's Hospital as some kind of joke. Patients don't like that I'm somebody, but don't they realize that you don't want to be somebody in a hospital? You want to be nobody, in and out and forgotten.

*     *     *

The small store is filled with things that show we care: candy, flowers, stuffed animals. These are the things that make us feel loved. I go to the fridge in the back to get the diet sodas. I feel proud of my no-sugar-soda rule. I've never had a rule so specific with my children besides 'No, you can't have that.'

Before I check out, I flip through the cards. Maybe there's one that Scottie can give to her mom that will do the talking for her. *Get well. Wake up. I love you. Don't leave me with Dad anymore.*

There are postcards, too, and I look at scenes of Hawaii: lava shooting out of rocks on the Big Island, surfers shooting out of a wave at Pipeline, water shooting out of a whale surfacing near the coast of Maui, fire shooting out of the mouth of a dancer at the Polynesian Culture Center.

I turn the wire rack and there she is: Alexandra. It's a picture I've seen before. I look around as if I'm doing something I shouldn't. A man walks behind me, and I move so that I'm blocking the picture of my daughter. When Alexandra was fifteen, she did shots for Isle Cards, whose captions said things like *Life's a damn hot beach.* One-pieces became string bikinis. String bikinis became even smaller, dental-floss bikinis. She and her mother

15

told me about these shots only after they'd been published, and then I put an end to her little modeling career, but every so often I'll see one of these cards in Longs. Mainly they're in Waikiki shops where no one I know goes, so I forget the fact that my daughter's body is still out there being sold and stamped and sent off to people in places like Oklahoma or Iowa—*Wish you were here* on one side, Alex on the other, blowing kisses or soaking up the sun in unlikely positions.

I look around for the shopkeeper, but I'm the only one here. I look for more cards with her on them, but there are just five copies of this one shot. She's in a white bikini, straddling a surfboard and getting splashed by some unseen person, using her hands to block the water. Her mouth is wide open, laughing. Her head is tilted back. Her torso is lithe and glimmering with beads of water. It's actually my favorite, if I had to pick one, because at least she's laughing and smiling and doing something someone her age would be doing. In the others she looks old, sexy, and exasperated. She looks like she knows all there is to know about men, and it makes her seem pissed off but lustful at the same time. It's a look that you don't want to see on your daughter's face.

When I asked Joanie why she let her do them, she said, 'Because it's what I do. I want her to respect what I do.'

'You model for catalogs and newspaper ads. What's not to respect?' I found immediately that this wasn't the best thing to have said.

\*       \*       \*

A chinese woman enters the shop and stands behind

16

the register. 'You ready?' she asks.

She is wearing a muumuu over navy blue polyester pants. She looks like she has escaped from an asylum.

'Why do you sell these?' I ask. 'At a gift shop. For people to get well. These aren't get-well cards.'

She takes the postcards from my hand, flips through them. 'They all the same card. You like buy all the same card?'

'No,' I say. 'I'm asking why you sell these at a gift store in a hospital.'

I can tell that nothing will come out of this conversation. It will be a confused and combative verbal, pidgin verbal, match.

'What, you no like girls or something?'

'No,' I say. 'I like women. Not underage girls. Here.' I pick up a card that says, *Get well, Grandpa.* 'This is the kind of card that's appropriate.' I hold up my daughter. 'This is not appropriate. It's not even a card. It's a postcard.'

'This my store. And people in hospital are haoles, too. They get hurt here, then they get better and want souvenir for mainland.'

'They want a souvenir of their trip to the hospital? Look. Never mind. Here.'

She takes the postcards and starts to walk back to the wire rack. 'No,' I say. 'I'm buying them. I want all of them. And these two sodas.'

She pauses. She looks confused, as if she has imagined our entire exchange, but doesn't say a word and won't look at me as she rings me up. I give her money. She gives me change.

'I need a bag, please,' I say. She hands me a plastic bag, and I use it to cover my daughter. 'Thank you.'

She moves her head but doesn't look at me. She busies herself at the register. I always seem to get into fights with old Chinese women.

I walk back to 612, to my other crazy daughter. It feels strange carrying copies of Alex in my hand, and strange to think that she has been here all this time and only now have I rescued her.

Joanie and Alex have issues with each other. That's how Joanie phrases it whenever I ask. 'She'll grow out of it,' Joanie says, but I always thought it was something Joanie needed to grow out of, too. They used to do everything together, and I imagine that Joanie was a fun mother to have because she was young and cool and fashionable, but around the time Alex stopped modeling, their closeness came to a halt. Alex retreated. Joanie became more involved in racing. Alex started to sneak out. Then she started to do drugs. It was Joanie's idea to send her to boarding school this past school year, but then last January, Alex was going to come home and go back to her old school. Something happened over Christmas, a fight of some sort with her mother, and all of a sudden she liked boarding school and returned of her own accord. I've asked them both what this fight was about, why Alex went back, but they never have a clear answer, and Joanie has always made the decisions about school and everything, really, concerning our daughters, so I let it go. 'She needs to get it together,' Joanie said. 'She's going back.'

'This is it,' Alex said. 'Mom is out of her mind. I don't want to have anything to do with her, and neither should you.'

So much theatrics and tension between the two of them, and it's sad because I miss Alex and

18

the relationship we once had. Sometimes I think that if Joanie were to die, Alex and I would make it. We'd flourish. We'd trust and love each other as we had so easily before. She could come home and she wouldn't be screwed up. But of course I don't really believe that if my wife died, our lives would be better—what an awful thing to think— and of course I don't think Joanie is the root of all of Alex's problems. I'm sure I have something to do with them as well. I haven't been the most available parent. I've been in a state of prolonged unconsciousness, but I'm trying to change. And I think I'm doing a good job.

*         *         *

I stand in the doorway of my wife's room and see Scottie playing hopscotch on the linoleum, marking her place with wooden tongue depressors.

'I'm hungry,' she says. 'Can we go? Did you get my soda?'

'Did you talk?'

'Yes?' she says, and I know she's lying because whenever she lies, she answers in the form of a question.

'Fine,' I say. 'Let's just go home.'

Scottie walks toward the door, not even glancing at her mother. She grabs her soda from my hands. 'Maybe we'll come back later,' I needlessly assure her. I look at my wife, and there's a slight smile on her face, as though she knows something I don't. I think about the blue note. It's hard not to think about it.

'Say goodbye to your mom.'

Scottie pauses, then keeps going.

19

'Scottie.'

'Bye!' she yells.

I grab her arm. I could yell at her for wanting to leave, but I don't. She pulls her arm out of my grasp. I look up to see if anyone is watching us, because I don't think you're supposed to aggressively hold children these days. Gone are the days of spanking, threats, and sugar. Now there are therapy, antidepressants, and Splenda. I see Dr. Johnston at the end of the hall, walking toward us. He stops talking to the other doctors and gestures for me to wait. He holds up his hand: Stop. His face is eager yet unsmiling. I look in the other direction then back at him. His steps quicken, and I squint, for some reason pretending I don't recognize him. And I think: *What if I'm wrong? What if Joanie doesn't make it out of this?*

'Scottie,' I say. 'This way.'

I walk in the other direction, away from Dr. Johnston, and she turns and follows me.

'Walk quickly,' I tell her.

'Why?'

'It's a game. Let's race. Walk fast. Run.' She takes off, her back-pack jiggling on her back, and I follow her, walking quickly then breaking into a slow jog, and because Dr. Johnston is my friend's dad and was a friend of my father's, I feel like I'm fourteen again, running from the patriarchs.

I remember egging Dr. Johnston's house as a prank on his son, Skip. The three of us—Blake Kelly, Kekoa Liu, and I—ran off only to be pursued by Dr. Johnston in his truck. He practically ran us down, and when we cut into an alley, he got out and hoofed it, eventually cornering us. He had a Foodland bag in hand, and he said we had a couple of choices: He could either call our parents, or we could help him dispose of his wife's tofu surprise. We chose the latter, and he reached in the bag and gave us a taste of our own medicine. We walked away, tofu surprise in our hair, ears, everywhere. To this day he calls us the Soy Boys, laughing hysterically and yelling 'Boo!,' which still causes me to jump a little. Not lately, though. He hasn't done that in a while.

I run down the hall with my daughter, feeling like I'm in some other country. All around, people speak pidgin English and glare at the two of us like we're crazy white fools, even though we're Hawaiian. But we don't look it, and we don't count as true or real Hawaiians because we don't talk right, either.

Dr. Johnston said Tuesday. That's when we've scheduled our date, and that's when I'll show up. I don't want to know anything just yet. I have too much to take care of right now. I take a good look around. Twenty-three days. This has been my world: the people looking at one another trying to guess what they're here for, the magazine covers featuring the healthiest people alive. I see the model train in its glass case making slow laps around a model coast with model citizens stiffly sitting on beaches. I run from the diagnosis. I'll be ready for it tomorrow.

# 3

I tell Esther she should ease up on the lard. There's no need to mix lard in with Scottie's rice, chicken, and beans. I tell her she hasn't read the blogs. I've read the blogs. I know what Scottie should eat.

I've gotten the hang of home. I help run the household, help decide what Scottie eats, when she sleeps, what she's allowed to wear, watch, do. I say things like 'time out' and 'full circle,' and I tell her to check the Chore Door, an invention of mine: It's a door in the den that posts her weekly duties. It's sort of fun, these responsibilities, and I think Joanie will be impressed.

'Is good fat,' Esther says. 'She so skinny. This good fat.'

'No,' I say. 'Some fats are good, but not that fat.' I point to the white substance in the pan, melting slowly like wax. On parenting websites, I've learned that corn syrup, nitrates, and hydrogenated fats are bad and that soy is good, as well as organic produce and whole grains. I've also learned that Scottie needs a booster shot for whooping cough, meningitis, and that there's a vaccine for HPV, which causes genital warts and can lead to cervical cancer. It's recommended as a preventive measure for tweens before they become sexually active. When I read this, I was so appalled that I participated in the online vaccination chat, only to be severely reprimanded by Taylorsmom. *Why not protect them as best we can?! Yes, Scottiesdad, I would give them a vaccine for loneliness and heartache if it were available, TYVM, and it's not the*

22

*same! Genital warts are not emotions! They're warts, and we can put a stop to them.*

I had to ask Scottie what TYVM meant, because now that I've narrowed into her activities, I notice she is constantly text-messaging her friends, or at least I hope it's her friends and not some perv in a bathrobe.

'Thank you very much,' Scottie said, and for some reason, the fact that I didn't get this made me feel completely besieged. It's crazy how much fathers are supposed to know these days. I come from the school of thought where a dad's absence is something to be counted on. Now I see all the men with camouflage diaper bags and babies hanging from their chests like little ship figureheads. When I was a young dad, I remember the girls sort of bothered me as babies, the way everyone raced around to accommodate them. The sight of Alex in her stroller would irritate me at times—she'd hang one of her toddler legs over the rim of the safety bar and slouch down in the seat. Joanie would bring her something and she'd shake her head, then Joanie would try again and again until an offering happened to work and Alex would snatch it from her hands. I'd look at Alex, finally complacent with her snack, convinced there was a grown person in there, fooling us all. Scottie would just point to things and grunt or scream. It felt like I was living with royalty. I told Joanie I'd wait until they were older to really get into them, and they grew and grew behind my back.

\*  \*  \*

Esther, as usual, is humming. Our kitchen is a good

23

size, yet it feels small whenever I'm in it with her. She's a short ball of a woman and has no awareness of her body; her stomach is always brushing me on the hip or abdomen. I'm slicing carrots and celery that Scottie can dip into a bowl of ranch. I realize Esther and I are in a sort of food battle, *Iron-Chef*ing my child's lunch.

'Have you talked to your family yet?'

'Not yet,' she says.

Just a week ago I told Esther that we won't need her anymore, even though I feel terrible about this, but she claims her family is away from their home in San Diego and she doesn't have the keys to her house.

'They still on vacation?' I ask.

'Yes,' she says.

'The Jersey Shore, you said?'

'Yes. Jersey Shore.'

'How lovely.' I bend over to pick up shreds of vegetables I have dropped, and Esther walks behind me. I feel her stomach brush across my ass.

'You're not ready anyway,' she says. 'There's much I haven't told you.'

She has been using her years of experience with Scottie as power, dishing it out slowly to extend her stay. I allow it because I can't deny how helpful she is and how much she loves Scottie. Her method is genius—I truly do need her to teach me more things before she goes. I feel like I'm taking the bar again—I'm cramming, stuffing myself with rules, learning the logic and the language of girlhood. Esther teaches me what Scottie loves: Xbox, dance, *SMART* magazine, almond butter, hamburgers, Jay-Z, Jack Johnson, making playlists on her iPod, text messaging, and I tell myself I need to know

24

this because Joanie may be weak for a while, out of sorts; she may not be herself mentally or physically for a long time, but I never tell myself that I need to learn the habits of this creature because Joanie may die.

'Should we continue?' I ask.

Esther sighs as though this is tiring, but I know she enjoys our study sessions. She gets to be the teacher of her employer, she gets to show me the girl she knows so well, and she gets to create the girl she wants Scottie to be.

'She like for read *Jane* and listen to music,' Esther says as she stirs her pot of fat and beans. The kitchen smells like a heart attack. 'She used to like MySpace, but now she does the scrapbook. She like *Dog the Bounty Hunter*. She like back rub.'

'Back rub?'

'Yes, when she was baby, I rub her back until she sleep. I still do this now when she wake up with nightmare.' She pokes the pot with a wooden spoon.

'Nightmare? What is she having nightmares about?'

This is a stupid question. Her mother is in the last state before death, the brain on the last and lowest level, but I don't want to admit this has a profound psychological effect on Scottie.

'I don't know,' Esther says. 'I haven't yet told you about child nightmares. Is common thing. We go over it next week.'

I really like Esther and don't want her to go. It's just that the idea of her, a Mexican nanny, doesn't sit right with me. I never thought Scottie needed a nanny, since Joanie didn't really work, and I don't like spending the money on someone to care for my

25

kid. It also makes me feel like some kind of colonist to have Esther around. Especially now that I have stepped in and she's doing mainly housecleaning and cooking. Ever since we've been spending more time with each other, she has acquired quick retorts and smooth comic timing, so now she's the sassy Mexican maid, sitcom-ish and wise. But I need to think about what's best for my family instead of how others perceive my family, something I've been guilty of all my life, trying to prove I'm great and not just a descendant of somebody great.

I have inheritance issues. I belong to one of those Hawaii families who make money off of luck and dead people. My great-grandmother happened to be a princess. A small monarchy decided what land was theirs, and she came in to a lot of it. My great-grandfather, a haole businessman, was doing pretty well himself. He was a good land speculator, good banker. All of their descendants, as well as Hawaii's missionary descendants, sugar plantation descendants and so on, are still benefiting from these old transactions. We sit back and watch as the past unfurls millions into our laps. My grandfather, my father, and I rarely touch the money we've made off the trust. I've never liked the fact that how much I have is public knowledge. I'm an attorney, and I use only the money I earn from being an attorney, not what I have inherited. My father always said it was the right thing to do, and in the end I'll have more to pass down. Anyway, I don't like legacies. I think everyone should start from scratch.

I think of Joy, her knowing smile. I should probably pick up today's paper, but I suspect she was reading about the beneficiaries, how much we own, and guesses about the decision we have to

26

make this week, or the decision I will make, since my vote counts the most. I get about 1⁄8 of the trust, whereas the others get 1⁄24. I'm sure they're just thrilled about that.

'All right,' I say to Esther. 'You can hold out on the nightmares, but keep the rest coming.' I figure I'll work a little on my daughter now while we make lunch, and then I'll get to the King portfolio this afternoon. I'll pick a buyer and be done with it.

'She like handbags and low-rider Seventween jeans.'

She dishes the rice, beans, and chicken onto a steamed tortilla. I arrange the vegetables onto a plate next to a turkey sandwich. I surround the plate with three dipping bowls filled with three different sauces: ranch, mango salsa, and almond butter. Esther eyes the almond butter as though it's a point against her.

'And?' I ask.

'And . . . I don't know. So much more you need to know. She like lots of things, but you need to know what she doesn't like, too. It will take months to explain. Even when your wife come back, she doesn't know a lot.'

We hear Scottie coming down the hall, and Esther lowers her voice. 'She loves for me to read *Mother Goose.*'

'Her baby book?'

'Yes. It brings her so much joy. Sometimes I read the same rhyme over and over again. It makes her so happy. It makes her laugh loud with delight.'

I wonder if Scottie's regressing into an infant stage, if she likes the nursery rhymes because they take her back to a happier and more innocent time.

27

'She should be reading young-adult novels,' I whisper.

'She read whatever she wants,' Esther whispers back.

'No. I think she needs books with moral messages and lessons on how to deal with womanhood, not books about single women who can't stop having kids and who live chaotic lives in a lace-up boot.'

We both see Scottie, and we stop talking. Esther pushes her plate toward the chairs. I push my plate forward as well, and Scottie sits down on a stool, looking at both of us and then at the food in front of her.

Scottie cuts into the enchilada. With her other hand, she types, or texts, a message to one of her friends.

Esther looks at me and smiles. 'She like lard.'

## 4

Just when I'm about to go to my room and get to work, Esther tells me that Mrs. Higgins has called and wants me to return her call immediately. She wipes the stove and uses her fingernail to remove something stubborn, grunting. I swear she does this purposefully to make me feel sorry for her.

'Who's Mrs. Higgins?'

'Lani's mother.'

'Who's Lani?' I ask.

'Scottie's friend, maybe. Call her.' She takes a long sip of her water and exhales loudly.

'Could you call her? You know I have that work

to do.'

'I already talked to her. She wanted to talk to Mrs. King.'

'What did you say?'

'I say Mrs. King's sick. And then she asked to talk to you.'

'Great,' I say. She'll want me to help with a bake sale or a carpool, or I'll have to volunteer at a dance. That's the thing with a crisis. My wife is in a coma, but this doesn't prevent life from happening. There's still Scottie's school that I have to deal with, hours I need to bill, this trust that needs to be tended to.

Esther leaves the kitchen with a bucketful of cleaning products, and I use the kitchen phone to call Mrs. Higgins. All the dishes from lunch are out of sight. The big black pot is upside down on the drying rack. The floor is shiny and slippery. I can see my face in the countertops.

A woman answers the phone, practically singing hello. I like when people answer a phone this way. Or when women answer a phone this way. 'Hello there, is this Mrs. Higgins?'

'Yes?' she says.

Telemarketers must love her. 'Hi, this is Matt King returning your call. Scottie's father. Actually, I don't even know if your daughter is a classmate of my daughter's, I just assumed—'

'Yes, Lani is a classmate of Scottie's,' she says. The sweet cadence of her voice is gone.

'Sorry, my wife's not feeling well and can't return your call, but how can I help you?'

'Well,' she says, 'let's see. Where should I start?'

I assume this is a rhetorical question, but she seems to be waiting for me to tell her where to

29

start. 'I guess you should start at the beginning,' I say.

'Okay,' she says. 'Here's the beginning. Your daughter seems to be text-messaging my daughter some pretty darn awful things, and I'd like her to stop.'

'Oh,' I say. 'What things?'

'She calls her Lani Piggins and Lani Moo.'

Lani Moo is the cartoon cow for a local dairy company. 'Huh,' I say. 'I'm sorry about that. Kids call each other names sometimes, I guess. It's a form of affection.' I look at my watch. I think of Joanie buying it for me.

'She writes *Nice shirt* to my daughter. Or *Nice pants.*'

'That's nice,' I say.

'It's cyber sarcasm!' she yells, and I pull the phone away from my ear not because the yell is high-pitched but because it's low and gravelly and mother-wolf-like.

'But maybe it's not, uh, cyber sarcasm, and it's sincere flattery.'

'She writes *CS* after. That stands for "cyber sarcasm." She also calls my daughter Lanikai, inferring that she's the size of an entire neighborhood.'

I don't say anything. I even sort of smile, because it's clever.

'Also,' she continues, 'your daughter said that she's afraid to be her partner at the rock wall because Scottie doesn't want to fall into my daughter's butt crack. That doesn't even make sense.'

I'm about to say that Scottie may be implying that Lani's butt crack is bigger than most, like a

30

crevasse, because of the blown-up scale of the rest of her body. It's a logical continuation of the fat joke, but I refrain. 'This is terrible,' I say.

'Here,' Mrs. Higgins says. 'Why don't I relay to you her latest work: *We all know you grew pubes over the summer.* That's it. She just sends little messages like that. For no reason at all. My daughter doesn't bother her in any way.'

I think of Scottie eating lunch and wonder if she was text-messaging Lani right there at the kitchen counter.

'Terrible,' I say again. 'And not at all like her. She's very sweet. I'm afraid her mother isn't well, and maybe that's it. Maybe this is how she's dealing with it.'

'I don't give a shit about the backstory, Mr. King.'

'Whoa,' I say.

'I just know that my daughter comes home from school in tears. And yes, she's developing a bit early and is highly sensitive to her growth, and maybe she doesn't shop at Neiman's Kids or wherever you get Scottie's clothes.'

'Sure, sure,' I say. 'I'm sorry. I'm truly sorry.' I haven't read any blogs about name-calling, and Esther hasn't prepared me for this at all. I've been fooled by Scottie. *Who are you, really?* I want to ask.

'Scottie should be the one who's sorry. I want her to come over and apologize, and I want her to be reprimanded.'

'I'll talk to her,' I say. 'I'll get to the bottom of this. I'm afraid we're really busy this week with her, uh, backstory, but I truly am sorry and will talk to Scottie immediately.'

'That's a good start,' she says. 'But then I want

31

an apology to Lani. And I don't ever want Scottie to write to her again.'

'She can in a good way!' I hear a voice say in the background.

'In fact, I'd like her to come by today, or else I'll have to take this up with the dean. You can't buy your way out of this.'

'Excuse me? What are you talking about?'

'It's your choice, Mr. King. Should I tell Lani you're coming by right now, or should you and your daughter handle this matter with the school?'

I get her address. I make promises. Life keeps happening.

# 5

On the way to see the Higginses, who live nearby, in Kailua, I coach Scottie. We need to get in and out quickly.

'You need to say you're sorry, and you need to mean it. I need to get to work, so no dicking around.'

She's quiet. I have taken away her message gadget, and her hands are open in her lap, fingers cupping the air.

'Why would you call her those things? Why would you be so mean to someone? How do you type all those words?'

'I don't know,' she says, her voice full of irritation.

'You made her cry. Why would you want to make someone unhappy?'

'I didn't know she was so sensitive. She writes

back *lol* sometimes, so I thought she wasn't going to be a dork about it.'

'What's "lol"?'

'"Laugh out loud,"' she mumbles.

'Do you just do this texting by yourself?'

She doesn't answer. We pass the antiques shops and the dealership full of gigantic trucks. As we veer toward the strip of newer shops, we both look at the kids who skateboard under the banyan tree. We always look at them; probably everyone does as they turn on Kailua Road.

'You just sit there and write nasty things, then go about your day?'

'No.'

'Well, what then?'

'I write them with Reina. It makes her laugh, and then she shows what I wrote to Rachel and Brooke and them.'

'I knew she had something to do with it. I knew it.'

Reina Burke. Twelve years old. I see her at the club wearing string bikinis and lipstick; she has this collected air about her that no twelve-year-old should have. She reminds me of Alexandra—beautiful and fast, ready to dump her childhood like a bad habit.

'From now on you're not to hang out with her,' I say.

'But Dad, I already have plans with her and her mom on Thursday!'

'You have plans with your own mother.'

'Mom can't even open her eyes!' she says. 'She's never going to.'

'Of course she's going to. Are you crazy?' She stares straight ahead. 'You need to be with your mother, not some other mother.'

'Can Reina come to the hospital? I don't get to see anyone since I'm not in school.'

I'm surprised she would want a friend at the hospital, but I'm thinking that if Reina's there, then maybe Scottie will interact with Joanie. She won't just sit and stare if her friend is present.

'Fine,' I say. 'You apologize to this girl. You be nice to her today and every day after, and Reina can come on Thursday.'

'Well, I need my BlackBerry to tell her and to say nice things to Lani Moo.'

'You can pick up the phone, for Christ's sake, and don't call Lani that.'

We drive through Kailua town, which has been recently remodeled to look like a strip mall in any nice suburb in America. Tourists are everywhere, and they've never come to our town much before. I know that when I sell the land the buyer will develop it into something exactly like this, even though I like the way the strip mall looks, and Joanie does, too. She loves gentrification.

'Can we get smoothies?' Scottie asks.

'No.'

'Can we get burgers?'

That does sound good. 'No.'

'Oh my God, tell me you don't want a Monster Double right now.'

'You just ate, Scottie.'

'Fine. Then a peanut-butter shake.'

My mouth waters. 'Stop it, Scottie. No to everything.'

The traffic slows, and we crawl to the light. A family walks alongside us on the grass, the father carrying a yellow plastic kayak over his head.

Everyone in the family, the two kids and the parents and two other adults, wears purple T-shirts that say FISCHER FAMILY REUNION.

'Dorks,' Scottie says.

We pass them and stop, and then they pass us. The light ahead turns green, and the traffic begins to move once again. As we pass, Scottie leans out the window and yells, 'Dorks!' The father thrusts out his hand to block his wife and kids as though keeping them from flying forward.

'Scottie!' I say. 'What was that?'

'I thought it would make you laugh.'

I look at the Fischer family in the rearview mirror. The father is gesturing wildly at the older son, who is taking off his T-shirt and throwing it to the ground. My head pulses. 'Roll your window up,' I say.

'It doesn't roll. This isn't the twenties.'

'Then press it up, whatever, Christ. And there are still cars that have roll-up windows. They're basic models. Nothing wrong with that.'

'Turn right here,' Scottie says.

'You know where she lives?'

'She invites me to her birthday, like, every year.'

'Stop saying everything to me as if I'm supposed to know.'

'It's that one,' she says.

'Which one?'

'Right here.'

I slam on the brakes and pull over to the rounded curb. I look up at a house that resembles every other house in Enchanted Lakes: a front door that no one uses, the screen door next to the garage, open and with rubber slippers and shoes on a rubber mat. We get out of the car, and as we

35

walk up the driveway, I ask her about Lani: 'So you were friends?'

'Yeah, until last year's party, when she locked me out of the house and I had to sit here all day while everyone laughed inside.' She points to a table in the garage. That's another thing about Enchanted Lakes: No one uses their garages for cars. Instead, a garage is used for outdoor dining and extra refrigerators. 'She thought she was so great, but then I got popular and she got all busted-looking and the world turned.'

'The tables,' I say. 'The tables turned.'

Mrs. Higgins stands behind the screen door. She opens it, and we walk in. I shake her hand and say hello, and because she's still holding the door open, I stand very close to her so that it feels like we're about to kiss or fight.

'Thank you for coming by,' she says pointedly, as though she's giving me a lot by saying this.

'Of course.' I'm so unbelievably tempted to tell her that my wife's in a coma, but I promised from the beginning not to ever use that as an exemption or a victory.

She looks at our shoes, and I look at her feet and realize I'm supposed to take off my shoes, something I hate to do. I remove my shoes and stand there in my black socks. One is a darker shade of black than the other. Scottie runs a few steps, then slides along the floor and snaps her gum. I want to tell her to stop chewing the gum. It looks insolent. Mrs. Higgins leads us to the living room, and I see a girl who must be Lani sitting cross-legged on the couch. She has a white-girl brown 'fro, bushy and soft, and an upturned nose that alludes to her nickname, Lani Piggins. You can

36

tell she loves Scottie because her face brightens and she uncrosses her legs and scoots forward.

I look at her mother, a thin version of what's on the couch, which brings hope, and I see that Lani's eyes are a beautiful blue, her skin white and smooth. In a few years she could be gorgeous, or not.

'Scottie,' I say. 'Do you have something you want to say to Lani?'

'Sorry,' Scottie says.

'It's okay,' Lani says.

'Great,' I say. 'Well, it was nice meeting you both.'

'Scottie,' Mrs. Higgins says. 'The things you said were simply evil.'

I look at my daughter, trying to convey a look that says *Just go with it.*

'I don't know what's going on in your life that has led you to become such a nasty young girl.'

'Hey now,' I say. 'She apologized. Kids are mean. They're mean to show other kids that they shouldn't be messed with, right?'

'She needs to learn to be the same person online as she is in real time,' Mrs. Higgins says.

'I agree.'

'She needs to know not to fight online. It's one of the school's rules.'

'Do you understand that, Scottie?' I say. I get down on my knees so that I'm at eye level with her, something Esther said she learned from a show about militant nannies. 'You have to speak to people to their face.'

Scottie makes exaggerated nods, her chin craning to the sky, then coming down to her chest.

'She doesn't get it.' Mrs. Higgins wears an angry

37

smile that I don't like. 'She's going to keep doing it. I can tell.'

'No,' I say. 'It will be all right. It's like the time Lani locked Scottie out of the house at her birthday party. It was a cruel thing to do, and you probably did it to show off, right?' I say to Lani. Lani nods, then catches herself and remains still.

'Scottie sat out there the entire day,' I say.

'I didn't know about that,' Mrs. Higgins says.

'You brought me cake,' Scottie says.

'You brought her cake,' I repeat. 'Perhaps Lani should be the one to apologize, as it seems this incident was the catalyst for all this . . . "evil" was the word you used.' *You're dealing with an attorney, lady. I can go on and on, even in mismatched socks.*

'I'm sorry,' Lani says.

Mrs. Higgins stands with her arms drawn tightly across her chest, frustrated by how the world has turned, as Scottie says.

I slap my thighs. 'Good! Terrific. Lani, you should come over sometime. Come for a swim or a hike or something. Or scrapbook.'

'Okay,' Lani says. Scottie looks at me and scowls, but I know she'll be appreciative of it later. You need friends who make you feel totally superior. 'Again, Mrs. Higgins and Lani, sorry for the anguish and the tears. I hope to see you both again on better terms.'

Mrs. Higgins turns and walks back to the door.

'SYL,' Scottie says.

'SYL,' Lani says.

See you later. I get it. We walk to the screen door and I look at Scottie, for clues, perhaps. Just when I think I've figured her out, she surprises me with something else. While we've dealt with

38

the technicalities of this problem, the problem is still here. Scottie was cruel and I don't understand it completely. I don't know if it's a symptom of girlhood or a symptom of something much larger.

'I need to work on some things at home,' I say to Scottie as we put on our shoes, 'but Esther says you have some class to go to. Voice class or something.'

'Voice class sucks,' she says. 'She can take me to the beach. You said.'

I look around for Mrs. Higgins so we can say goodbye. I kneel down to tie my laces. I'm down here in a sea of shoes. Mrs. Higgins has a lot of sandals with scuffed soles. All of them have short heels the length of half a thumb. What's the point? For some reason I hold a little heel in my hand. Some of Joanie's heels are the length of a hand.

If Joanie dies before me, I wonder if I'll ever be with another woman. I can't imagine going through all of the preliminary stuff—the talk, the chatter, the dinners. I'd have to take someone places, explain my history, make jokes, dole out compliments, hold back farts. I'd have to tell her I'm a widower. I'm convinced Joanie would never have an affair. It just seems like too much trouble.

Mrs. Higgins stands over me. I let go of her shoe. She stares at me so fiercely, I worry she may kick.

'Good luck with the sale,' she says, and I stand and shake my head. I realize she's not even angry with Scottie for what she did. She's angry with Scottie for who she belongs to.

'So what happens?' she asks. 'Why do you get all this money again?'

'Do you really want to know?' I stand and face her, and she takes a step back.

'Sure,' she says.

'Dad,' Scottie whines. 'I want to go.'

I clear my throat. 'Well,' I say. 'My great-grandfather was Edward King. His parents were missionaries, but he went in a different direction. He became a banker and later the chief financial officer for King Kal‾akaua. He managed the estate of Princess Kekipi, the last direct descendant of King Kamehameha.'

I stop talking. Hopefully, I've lost her interest, but she raises her eyebrows and waits for me to continue.

'Should I get my scrapbook and show her?' Scottie asks. 'No,' I say.

'Yes,' Mrs. Higgins says.

Scottie opens the screen door and walks to the car.

'Okay, then what happened . . . Kekipi was supposed to marry her brother, a weird Hawaiian royalty tradition. Yikes. Just when they were about to tie the knot, she had an affair with her estate planner, Edward, and they married soon after. Annexation happened soon after, too, so marrying a haole businessman was pretty ballsy. Anyway, they had a lot between the two of them, and when another princess died, she left three hundred thousand acres of Kauai land to Kekipi as well as her estate.

'Kekipi died first. Edward got it all. Then Edward set up a trust in 1920, died, and we got it all.'

Scottie comes back and opens to the first page of the album. She ripped out a few pages from three local history books before I caught her, and she's glued these in, making the album smell like cedar trunks. There's Edward, hollow-eyed and serious.

He has on knee-high boots, and his top hat rests on a table behind him. There's Kekipi, which means 'rebel,' her brown and flat, chubby face. Her bushy brows. Whenever I see her picture I think we would have hit it off. I can't help but smile at her.

Mrs. Higgins leans down and looks at the pictures. 'Then?' she asks.

'My father died last year, marking the termination and dissolution of the trust. And now, land-rich and cash-poor, we, the beneficiaries, are selling off our portfolio to . . . someone. I don't know who yet.'

'And your decision will have a major impact on Hawaii's real estate world,' she says in a tone of mock importance. I figure she's quoting something she read in the paper. It bothers me that everything I just said, she probably already knew. I close Scottie's book.

'Lucky.' Mrs. Higgins opens the screen door. I look over at the empty bench and picnic table and imagine Scottie sitting there alone.

'Can Esther take me to the club instead of voice?' Scottie asks. 'You said we'd go to the beach. So can she?'

I look over Scottie's head at Mrs. Higgins. 'It's what I inherited. Like it or not.'

'I'm sorry about your father,' she says.

'Thank you,' I say.

I wait to see if I can be excused, and when she doesn't say anything more, I start to walk with Scottie to the car. I feel exhausted, as though I've just delivered a sermon, but my speech has put me in the right frame of mind. I'll look through the buyers' portfolios with the images of Edward and Kekipi in my head. And then I can stop thinking about it. I feel cold, with my mind preoccupied in business when Joanie's lying there on a kind of long and uncomfortable red-eye flight.

'Can she? Can Esther take me to the club?'

'Sure,' I say. 'Good plan.'

We get in and I start the car. 'Are you going to be good to Lani?' I ask. I think of Tommy Cook, a pale boy with psoriasis; we used to tie him to a chair with bungee cords and put him in the middle of the road, then hide. Few cars would actually come down Rainbow Drive, but when they did, it always surprised me that the drivers would slow their vehicles and swerve around the chair. None of them ever got out of their cars to help Tommy; it was as though they were in on the prank. I don't know how Tommy managed to let us catch him more than once. Maybe he liked the attention.

'I'll try,' Scottie says. 'But it's hard. She has this face that you just want to hit.'

'I know what you mean,' I say, thinking of Tommy, but realize I'm not supposed to empathize. 'What does that mean?' I ask. 'The kind of face that you want to hit. Where did you get that?' Sometimes I wonder if Scottie knows what she's saying or if it's something she recites, like those kids who memorize the Declaration of Independence.

'It's something Mom said about Danielle.'

'I see.' Joanie has carried her juvenile meanness into her adult life. She sends unflattering pictures of her ex-friends to the *Advertiser* to put in their society pages. She always has some sort of drama in her life, some friend I'm not supposed to speak to or invite to our barbecues, and then I hear her on the phone gossiping about the latest scandal in an outraged and thrilled voice. 'You are going to die,'

42

I'll hear her say. 'Oh my God, you will just die.'

Is this where Scottie gets it? By watching her mother use cruelty as a source of entertainment? I feel almost proud that I have made these deductions without the blogs and without Esther, and I'm eager to tell Joanie about all of this, to prove that I was capable without her.

# 6

I study the bids—the plans, offers, histories, credos. I'm on our bed, and the house is quiet without Scottie and Esther. I thought I could just pick a buyer, but it's not as simple as that. I want to make the best decision. I've got those pictures in my head and feel I have to choose on their behalf as well. The plans for the land are virtually the same: condos, shopping centers, golf courses. One wants a Target, the other a Wal-Mart. One wants a Whole Foods, the other a Nordstrom.

Michael Nasser, our attorney, wants us to accept an offer from Holitzer Properties. I know that a few cousins are pissed off because Holitzer didn't make the highest bid, and Michael Nasser's daughter is married to Holitzer's chief financial officer. A few of the cousins balk at what seems to be an insider deal, but I'm thinking it would be good to choose a buyer who has a history here. I remember Joanie thought this as well. She surprised me by bringing it up frequently. She knew a lot about the buyers and the numbers, which shocked me. She was never interested in anything I was working on. When I tried to talk about cases at work, she would cover her ears and shake her head.

Many nights, when she would ask me what was happening with the sale, so uncharacteristically interested, my appreciation would turn into paranoia, and this was before I found the note. I wondered if she was planning to divorce me after I sold my shares. But if that were the case, she probably would urge me to sell to the highest bidder and not Holitzer.

'Just sell to Holitzer and move on,' she said one night. We were on the bed, and she was flipping through a magazine about kitchens. 'The others could back out. And Holitzer is local. His family is from Kauai, comes from a working-class background. Holitzer's your man.'

'Why are you pushing this guy?' I asked.

'He just seems like a good choice. I don't know.'

'I think I'll go with the New Yorkers,' I said, just to see her response.

'Interesting to see how that will turn out.' She flipped a page in her magazine. 'I love that sink,' she said. 'Look.'

I looked at the sink. 'It's just a basin. There's no room to put anything.'

'Exactly. Gets rid of clutter, easy to clean. Sometimes the least practical makes the most sense.'

I saw the edge of her mouth curl up, and I laughed. She had a way of addressing one thing through something unrelated. 'Joanie,' I said. 'You're something else.'

\* \* \*

I look at the highest bidder, a publicly traded firm

44

out of New York that has offered almost half a billion dollars. I'm wary of giving New Yorkers this much land. It just doesn't seem right, and maybe Joanie thought this, too; she wanted our land in the right hands.

I think of my father's funeral, all the people vying for the front pews as though his death were the best ticket in town.

'People are just waiting for me to die,' he told me one day. We were sitting in his back room; he liked to rummage through his books, where he kept newspaper clippings.

'Keep living,' I said.

He flipped through a book about Oliver Wendell Holmes, Jr., and pulled a clipping from the pages to read to me: '"A heavy downpour of rains reached a crescendo just about the time Princess Kekipi died. The Hawaiians said when rain fell at the time of a person's death or funeral, *Kulu ka waimaka, uwe 'opu*, which means 'The tears fall; the clouds weep.' The gods mingle their tears of affection with those who weep in sympathy and aloha."

'It rains in November all the time,' he said, placing the clipping back in the book. 'People were just waiting to get their hands on that land. They couldn't, and now they're waiting for me.'

It must be strange to know that people are waiting for you to die, and now the twenty-one beneficiaries don't have to wait any longer because my father is gone. I want to go with Holitzer since he's local, but choosing a higher bid from an outsider may make for a smoother transaction devoid of lawsuits. I don't want to have to deal with this again further down the road.

I look at everything. I even try to decipher

45

documents and letters from 1920, imagining what two people I've never met would want. The princess, the last in the royal lineage. My great-grandfather, that frisky white boy. What a scandal they must have caused. What fun they must have had. What love and ambition! What do you want, you lovebirds, you rebels? What do you want now?

I look at Holitzer's portfolio and see exclamation points surrounding his name and think of Joanie going through all of my work. Passages are underlined for me with notes in the margins. I press my finger on a smiley face. Then I reach over to her side of the bed and open a koa box she keeps on her nightstand. The only thing in there is a necklace, a silver chain with a charm in the shape of a lopsided heart. I gave this to her years ago. She never wears it. I don't know what I'm looking for, but I get up and continue to look through her things—purses, shoe boxes, drawers, and pockets. Then I go to Alex's room. Something in me needs to be quenched.

I look through my eldest daughter's drawers, for divorce papers, perhaps. I look under the sink of her bathroom, behind the toilet, in between stacks of towels. I rifle through the pages of books and end up getting distracted by Alex's childhood things: old stuffed animals (a monkey, a worm, a Smurf) and old books (*Ping, Ferdinand,* books I remember from my childhood, many about wayward animals with deep psychological problems). I find pictures of Alex with her friends at camp on the San Juans, sailing on Puget Sound, having campfires in front of tepees. I see a stack of yearbooks and read the copious notes telling my daughter to *stay cool.* Some notes take up an entire page and are written in a strange code: *Remember hot pants and dirty Christine! Poison ivy and BYOBucket! Are those ants??? Point, the van, that's my mom's favorite reindeer!*

I imagine Alex reading these words as an old woman and not knowing what any of them mean. Girls take so much time organizing the past. There are various collages documenting Alex's weekends with friends, yet the testimonials to good times seem to stop once she hits her junior year and goes off to boarding school. Joanie came into this room a lot, told me she was rearranging things, maybe turning it into a guest bedroom. I look in the jewelry box where Joanie found the drugs. She showed me a miniature Ziploc bag filled with a clear, hard rock.

'What is this?' I said. I never did drugs, so I had no idea. Heroin? Cocaine? Crack? Ice? 'What is this?' I screamed at Alex, who screamed back, 'It's not like I shoot it!'

A plastic ballerina pops up and slowly twirls to a tinkling song whose sound is discordant and deformed. The pink satin liner is dirty, and other than a black pearl necklace, the box holds only rusty paper clips and rubber bands noosed with Alex's dark hair. I see a note stuck to the mirror and pick up the jewelry box and move the ballerina aside. She twirls against my finger. The note says, *I wouldn't hide them in the same place twice.*

I let out a short breath through my nose. *Good one, Alex.* I close the jewelry box and shake my head, missing her tremendously. I wish she never went back to boarding school, and I don't understand her sudden change of plans. What did they fight about? What could have been so bad?

47

I go back to the bedroom, ashamed to be looking for anything at all. My wife cared about the sale. She appreciated Holitzer. She thought this sale would change our lives. My wife had friends she met at Indigo. Gay men and models adore that restaurant. My wife kept things from the past. My wife had a life outside this home. It's as simple as can be.

# 7

Tuesday. Today is my date with the doctor, and I'm not going to run away. I've let the front desk know that I'm here.

'A slow but gradual recovery,' I imagine him saying. 'When she comes out, she will need you. You will have to help her with the most basic things, everyday actions you take for granted. She will need you. Need you.'

Scottie and I walk down the hall. Her T-shirt says MRS. CLOONEY, and she's wearing wooden clogs that ti-tap-ti-tap-ti-tap on every step. The hospital is so busy, you'd think they were having some kind of going-out-of-business sale. Scottie looks eager; her mouth is moving, and I think she's rehearsing what she's going to say to Joanie. This morning she told me she had a great story for Mom, and I'm excited to hear it. I guess I'll need to talk to Joanie as well. I'll need to relay to her whatever Dr. Johnston says to me.

When we get to the room, I see we have a visitor. A friend of Joanie's whom I don't know well. She's been here before. Tia or Tara. She models with my wife. I remember seeing a picture of her in a newspaper ad. It must have been right before the accident. In the advertisement she was drinking bottled water and holding a straw purse with an expensive-looking diamond bracelet around her wrist. I didn't read the print, so I didn't know if the ad was for the bracelet, the water, the purse, or something else entirely, like a new condo development or life insurance. She was with a man, and they had three children of three different races who were pointing at something in the sky. I remember this because I said to Joanie, 'Are these supposed to be her kids? They don't look alike. What is this an ad for?'

Joanie looked at the paper. 'Hilo Hattie. They like to represent Asians and hapas and Filipinos.'

'But the parents are white. They're not creating a credible family.'

'Maybe they're adopted.'

'That's just stupid,' I said. 'Why not have an Asian mom and a Filipino dad?'

'They never marry that way.'

'A hapa mom and an Asian dad.'

'They like white adult models and ethnic kids.'

'Well, what about the black man? I mean, why not throw in a black kid?'

'The few black people here are military. They're not the target market.'

I closed the paper, annoyed by the entire conversation. 'What the hell are they looking at, anyway?'

'Their glorious future,' Joanie said in a deadpan voice.

I started to laugh and she did, too, and when the girls came into the kitchen and asked what was so funny, we both said, 'Nothing.'

*   *   *

This woman from the newspaper is getting settled on Joanie's bed, and I don't know what to do. I want to leave; I generally don't like being with people here, but it's too late. She sees us and smiles, then turns on a light with a remote control.

'Hi there,' I say.

'Hello,' she says.

I see her looking at Scottie in a sympathetic way that reminds me of how I looked at Lani. 'Mind if we stay and watch?' I ask.

'Sure. I won't be long.' She has a tray on her lap, and she picks up various identical brushes before settling on one and going to work on Joanie's face, working around the tube. She dips the brush into a palette of gloss and dabs at my wife's lips as if she's some kind of French pointillist. Though I find this absurd, I have to admit that Joanie would appreciate it. She enjoys being beautiful. She likes to look luminous and ravishing—her own words. Good luck, I used to tell her. Good luck with your goals.

We don't treat each other very well, I suppose. Even from the start. It was as though we had the seven-year itch the day we met. The day she went into a coma, I heard her telling her friend Shelley that I was useless, that I leave my socks hanging on every doorknob in the house. At weddings we roll our eyes at the burgeoning love around us, the vows that we know will morph into new kinds of promises: I vow not to kiss you when you're trying to read. I will tolerate you in sickness and

50

ignore you in health. I promise to let you watch that stupid news show about celebrities, since you're so disenchanted with your own life.

Joanie and I were urged by her brother, Barry, to subject ourselves to counseling as a decent couple would. Barry is a man of the couch, a believer in weekly therapy, affirmations, and pulse points. Once he tried to show us exercises he'd been doing in session with his girlfriend. We were instructed to trade reasons, abstract or specific, why we stayed with each other. I started off by saying that Joanie would get drunk and pretend I was someone else and do this neat thing with her tongue. Joanie said tax breaks. Barry cried. Openly. His second wife had recently left him for someone who understood that a man didn't do volunteer work.

'Stop it, Barry,' Joanie said. 'Get ahold of yourself. This is just how we work.'

I agreed. When she told Shelley I was useless, I heard the smile in her voice and knew she was pretending to be irritated. Really, she wouldn't know what to do without my uselessness, just as I wouldn't know what to do without her complaints. I take it back. It's not that we don't treat each other well; it's just that we're comfortable enough to know that sarcasm and aloofness keep us afloat, and we never have to watch where we step.

'You are both so cold,' Barry said that night. We were at Hoku's in the Kahala Resort, and Joanie was underdressed in jeans and a white low-cut top. I remember sneaking looks at her breasts. She always overdressed at casual restaurants and underdressed at nice ones. I remember she ordered the onaga and I ordered the kiawe pork chop.

'This is incredible,' she said when she tasted my

51

dish. 'So good.'

I traded plates with her and we continued on, enjoying the food, the view of the ocean, and that feeling of contentment you get when you have picked the perfect restaurant. I raised my glass and she tapped mine, a private moment acknowledging that whatever Barry wanted to call us, we were a team.

\*     \*     \*

Tia or Tara has stopped applying makeup to my wife's face and is looking at Scottie with disapproval. The light is hitting this woman's face, giving me an opportunity to see that she should perhaps be working on her own makeup. Her coloring is similar to a manila envelope. There are specks of white in her eyebrows, and her concealer is not concealing. I can tell my daughter doesn't know what to do with this woman's critical look.

'What?' Scottie asks. 'I don't want any makeup.' She looks at me for protection, and it's heartbreaking. All the women who model with Joanie have this inane urge to make over my daughter with the notion that they're helping her somehow. She's not as pretty as her older sister or her mother, and these other models think that slapping on some rouge will somehow make her feel better about her facial fate. They're like missionaries. Mascara thumpers.

'I was just going to say that I think your mother was enjoying the view,' Tia or Tara says. 'It's so pretty outside. You should let the light in.'

My daughter looks at the curtain. Her little mouth is open. Her hand reaches for a tumbleweed

52

of hair.

'Listen here, T. Her mother was not enjoying the view. Her mother is in a coma. And she's not supposed to be in bright light.'

'My name is not T,' she says. 'My name is Allison.'

'Okay, then, Ali. Don't confuse my daughter, please.'

'I'm turning into a remarkable young lady,' Scottie says.

'Damn straight.' My heart feels like one of Scottie's clogs clomping down the hall. I don't know why I became so angry.

'Sorry,' Allison says. 'I just thought we could use some light.'

'No, I'm sorry. I didn't mean to yell like that.'

She rummages in her bag, pulling out a round jar, and appraises Joanie's face as if she's about to do surgery. She dabs something onto my wife's cheek, frowns, then puts the jar back and extracts a similar-looking jar and repeats the application, this time smiling slightly with satisfaction. I don't see any difference. Makeup is one of the most mysterious things in the world.

'Do you want to talk?' I ask Scottie. I gesture to her mother on the bed.

She looks at Allison. 'I'll wait.' She turns on the television and I feel bad. I'm running out of toys, ideas to entertain her. I can usually find a toy in anything. A spoon, a sugar packet, a quarter. It's my job to distract her. It's my job to make sure she still has the life of a ten-year-old.

I remember that I brought a banana with me so she'd have something healthy to eat. I get her Roxy backpack to retrieve it and am reminded of

53

a game I made up for Joanie, who also needed to be constantly entertained. This was pre-children, and we were having dinner, drinking wine, and she was giving me a look that said, *Look at the boring life we lead. Look how you've squashed my magnetic personality. I used to be positively volcanic; now I'm predictable and four pounds heavier, and I've turned into someone who sits home on a Saturday night munching on bonbons and watching my fiancé shovel food into his mouth and swallow his burps.* That kind of look.

She had just moved into my house, the one we live in now. She was twenty-two and getting a taste of life in Maunawili—the big beautiful home, the huge, lush property, and all of the work that went along with it. We have breadfruit, bananas, and mangoes, but all of these things rot and bring flies. We have a sparkling pool, but at the end of the day, it's filled with leaves. The large circular driveway also gets cluttered with leaves and is cracked from the roots of the big banyan tree. We have tea leaves that yellow and need to be pulled, mondo grass and tiare, plants and pikake that need to be watered. We have gorgeous soft wood floors, but we also have flying cockroaches, cane spiders, termites and centipedes that love these wooden floors and dark rafters as well.

I told her we had a yardman and a cleaning lady who came once a week, but throughout the week we had to take care of things ourselves. If she didn't help me, then I'd do what I could in addition to my full-time job, but I warned her that this wouldn't be enough. She'd have to work, too. She wasn't happy about this, so she was giving me that look. I got up and grabbed a banana and poured her another glass

54

of wine. I concentrated on my task, trying not to let her death stare penetrate me too deeply. I divided the pieces of banana, then put one slice on a linen napkin. The goal was to trampoline the piece up into the air and get it to stick to the ceiling. My mother and I would play this game after she had a few cocktails and we were finished cleaning up the kitchen. I tossed. It stuck. Joanie looked at me, trying to conceal her interest, but I knew I had her hooked. I knew she'd have to one-up me. She finished her bite, took a long sip of wine, then placed one of her pieces on her napkin, locked herself into a good tossing position, and let it fly. It didn't stick.

'Zero to one,' she said, and the game was on. We sat there for hours until the wine and the bananas were gone.

I show Scottie the game I used to play with her mother.

She looks at the TV, looks at me, and decides to come over. I watch her toss a piece of banana, the tip of her tongue pointing out of her mouth. She can't get it to stick, but that doesn't matter. She's laughing and using her entire body to launch the small piece of fruit. When she gets one to stay, she yells 'Score!' and receives a dirty look from Allison. Now she has the peel, which I stop her from throwing, so she takes the biggest chunk of the banana. She's getting a bit too excited for my comfort. It's been happening a lot lately, this spontaneous, deranged elation. She makes a karate sound—'Hi-ya!'—and flings the banana, but her strange energy makes it fly across the room, where it hits the ceiling and then falls. On her mother. Allison quickly moves the makeup brush off of

55

Joanie's face and leans back. The room is silent. I look at the piece of banana on the white sheet in the center of Joanie's body. Allison looks at me, then at the banana, staring as though it's a turd.

Scottie looks like she's done something horribly wrong. I give her another slice. 'Here, Scottie. Try again. A flick of the wrist should do. No need to get . . . crazy.'

She doesn't take the banana. She takes a step back and holds the end of my shirt. I take her hand off of my shirt. 'Here. No big deal.'

'We can't just leave that there on Mom like that,' she says.

I look at the banana. 'Take it off, then.'

She doesn't budge.

'Would you like me to take it off?'

She nods.

I walk over to my wife's bed and pick up the mushy banana.

'There. No problem. Here,' I say, handing it to Scottie. 'Try again.' But she won't look at me. She pushes my hip; I'm in her way. Our game is over. She walks back to her chair and the safety of the TV. I throw the banana at the ceiling, where it sticks, and then I sit down. Allison looks at the ceiling.

'What?' I say. Fuck her. Allison.

'You have an odd way with children,' she says. 'This whole thing you have going.'

'What we have going is working out just fine, thanks.'

She looks at Scottie, zoning out on a show where men are in some kind of competition that involves throwing tires.

'I see,' Allison says. She goes back to making my

56

wife look vibrant.

'Parents shouldn't have to compromise their personalities,' Scottie mumbles.

It's something I've heard Joanie say to Alex after she complained that Joanie dressed too young. Joanie said, 'Parents shouldn't have to compromise their personalities.' Alex asked if her personality was that of a prostitute, and my wife responded, 'Why, yes. Yes, it is.'

'All right, Scottie. Come on. You have something to say. The doctor's going to be here soon, and I'm going to need to talk to him alone, so go on. Let's hear it.'

'No,' she says. 'You talk.'

I look at Joanie and pause, trying to think of something interesting. 'Joanie,' I say. 'I just want to tell you some things.' I try to think of what I should talk about and see that it is pretty hard. 'We miss you. Can't wait until you get home.'

Scottie's unimpressed.

'We'll go to Buzz's when you get out,' I say. Buzz's is one of Joanie's favorite restaurants, and we go there often. Without fail, she ends up at the bar with these spring-break sorts for a drink or ten, and I'm left at the table all alone, but it's sort of peaceful. I like watching her with other people. I like her magnetism. Her courage and ego. But I wonder if I like these things only because she's in a coma and may never resemble her old self. It's hard to say.

The manager of that restaurant once thanked me. She said that she always livened up the place and made people want to drink.

I catch a glimpse of Joanie's face. She looks lovely. Not ravishing, but simply lovely. Her freckles

57

rise through the blush, her closed eyes fastened by dark, dramatic lashes. Her eyelashes are the only strong feature left on her face. Everything else has been softened. She looks pretty, but perhaps too divine, as if she's cased in glass or lying in a coffin.

Still, I'm grateful for what Allison has done. I realize my only job now is to make Joanie happy. To give her everything she wants, and she wants to be beautiful.

'Allison,' I say. 'Thank you. I'm sure Joanie is happy.'

'She's not happy,' Allison says. 'She's in a coma.'

I look at her, shocked and slightly thrilled.

'Oh my God,' Allison says, and she starts to cry. 'I can't believe I said that. I was just trying to sound like you. To get you back. Oh, God.'

She gathers her beauty tools, dropping a few brushes. I go over to her and pick up the fallen brushes, and she snatches them out of my hand and then leaves, sniffling.

'Mercy,' I say. 'I'm an ass.'

'Ass,' Scottie says.

'Yes,' I say. 'That's me.'

'You're a dad-ass. Like a badass but older.'

'Mercy,' I say.

I look at my wife. *I need you,* I think. *I need you here to help our daughters and me. I don't know how to talk to people. I don't know how to live correctly.*

I hear a voice on the intercom: 'Mr. King, the doctor should be in to see you in about twenty minutes.'

Scottie looks at the intercom, then at me. 'It's okay,' I say. 'It's going to be okay.'

58

# 8

I let Scottie continue to watch TV. I try to be quiet and calm, but I'm too anxious. I keep hoping she'll say something to Joanie. I finally speak.

'You said you had something to tell Mom. I want you to do that now. Can you do that? Now that Allison's gone? It will help, you know. It will help Mom.'

She looks over at the bed. 'Let me try it out on you first.'

'Okay. Go for it. I'm listening.'

'Not *here*,' she says, shifting her eyes to Joanie. She tilts her head toward the hall.

I stand up and try not to look disappointed. She was fine the first week Joanie was in here, and I wonder what has changed or what's going through her mind. The doctor says it's normal—it's disturbing to speak to someone who doesn't respond, especially a parent—but in Scottie's case, it's different. It's as if she's embarrassed of her life. She thinks that if she speaks to her mother, she should have something incredible to say. I always urge her to talk about school, but Scottie says this would be boring, and she wouldn't want her mother to think she was a walking yawn.

We step into the hall. 'Okay. Today's the day. You're going to talk to Mom.'

'I think I have an okay story.' She rises up on her toes and lifts her arms in the air so they form an O. She swings one leg back and forth. She takes ballet lessons because that's what her sister used to do, but she doesn't have the same grace or style. Her

59

clog comes down hard on the floor. *Slap!* She looks at the ground then up at me.

'Settle down. Tell me your story.'

'Okay,' she says. 'Pretend you're Mom. Close your eyes and be still.'

I close my eyes.

'Hi, Mom,' she begins.

I almost say hello but catch myself. I keep still.

'Yesterday I explored the reef in front of the public beach by myself. I have tons of friends. My best friend is Reina Burke, but I felt like being alone.'

I open my eyes when I hear 'Reina Burke,' then quickly close them again and tune back in to the story.

'And there's this really cute guy who works the beach stand there. Reina likes him, too. His eyes look like giraffe eyes. So I went to explore the reef in front of his stand. The tide was low. I could see all sorts of things. In one place the coral was a really cool dark color, but then I looked closer and it wasn't coral. It was an eel. A moray. I almost died. There were millions of sea urchins and a few sea cucumbers. I even picked one up and squeezed him like you showed me that one time.'

'This is good, Scottie. Let's go back in. Mom will love this.'

'I'm not done.'

I close my eyes. I wish I could lie down. This is kind of nice.

'So I was squatting on the reef and lost my balance and fell back on my hands. One of my hands landed on an urchin, and it put its spines in me. My hand looked like a pincushion. It hurt really bad, but I lived. I survived. I got up again.'

60

I'm grabbing her hands, holding them up to my face. The roots of urchin spines are locked in and expanded under the skin of her left palm. They look like tiny black starfish that plan on making her hand their home forever. I notice more stars on her fingertips. 'Why didn't you tell me you were hurt? Why didn't you say something? Does Esther know?'

'I'm okay,' she whispers, as if her mom is here and she doesn't want her to hear. 'I handled it. I didn't really fall.'

'What do you mean? Are these pen marks?'

'Yes?'

I look closer. I press on the marks.

'Ow,' she says and pulls her hand back. 'They're not pen marks. They're real.'

'Why did you lie just now?'

'I don't know,' she says. 'I didn't lie that much. I didn't really fall.'

'So the urchin just jumped up and attacked you?'

'No,' she says.

'Well?'

'I slammed my hand into it. But I'm not telling Mom that part.'

'What? What do you mean you slammed your hand into it? Scottie. Answer me. Did Reina have something to do with this?'

She seems surprised and afraid of my anger. 'I wanted to have a good story.' She points her foot out in front of her and tilts her head to the side.

'Don't do that cute thing,' I say. 'That's not working right now.' She brings her foot back.

'Didn't it hurt?' I imagine the spines expanding, the blood, the salt in the wounds. *This is psychotic,* I'm tempted to say. *This is disturbed.*

'It didn't hurt that much.'

61

'Balls, Scottie. It killed. I'm floored right now. Completely floored. Where was Esther?'

'Do you want to hear the rest?' she asks.

I push my short fingernails into my palm just to try to get a taste of the sting she felt. I shake my head. 'I guess.'

'Okay. Pretend you're Mom. You can't interrupt.'

'I can't believe you did this to yourself. What made you—'

'You can't speak! Be quiet or you won't hear the rest.'

Scottie goes on to tell me her tale, and it has all the elements of a good story: visuals, crisis, mystery, violence. She tells me about the needles jutting from her hand and how she climbed back on the rock pier like a crab with a missing claw. Before she returned to shore, Scottie looked out across the ocean and watched the swimmers do laps around the catamarans. She says that the ones with white swimming caps looked like runaway buoys.

I don't believe her. I'm sure she didn't stop to gaze at the sea. She probably ran right to Esther or the club's medic. She's inventing the details, setting the stage, making a better story for her mother. Alexandra had to do the same thing—knock herself out to get some attention from Joanie. Or perhaps to take the attention away from Joanie. I guess Scottie is realizing what needs to be done.

'Because of Dad's boring ocean lectures, I knew these weren't needles in my hand but more like sharp bones—calcitic plates, which vinegar would help dissolve.'

I smile. Good girl.

'Dad, this isn't boring, is it?'

'"Boring" is not the word I'd use. "Boring" is the last thing that comes to mind.'

'Okay. You're Mom again, so shut up. Then, Mom, I thought of going to the club's first aid.'

'Good girl.'

'Sshh,' she says. 'But instead, I went to the cute boy and asked him to pee on my hand.'

'Excuse me?'

'Yes, Mom. That's exactly what I said to him. "Excuse me," I said. I told him I hurt myself. He said, "Uh-oh. You okay?" like I was an eight-year-old.'

'Wait,' I say. 'Time out. I am not your mother.'

'He didn't understand,' Scottie continues, 'so I placed my hand on the counter.'

'Scottie. I said time out. What is going on here? Are you lying right now? Tell me you've made this up. Tell me you're just a very creative, imaginative, and remarkable young lady and that you've made this up.'

I've read about children starting to lie a lot around this age. I'm supposed to tell the child that lying can hurt people. 'Listen,' I say. 'This is a great yarn. We'll tell it to Mom, but between you and me, are you telling the truth?'

'Yes,' she says, and unfortunately, I believe her. I don't say anything. I just shake my head.

Scottie continues, cautiously at first, but then she plunges right back into her disaster. 'He swore like a maniac. I won't repeat what he said, and then he told me to go to the hospital. "Or are you a member of that club?" he asked. He told me he'd take me there, which was totally sweet of him. He went out through the back of his stand, and I walked around to meet him. I told him what he needed to

63

do, what would get the spines out, and he blinked a thousand times and used more curse words in all sorts of combinations. There was a piece of lint or something in his eyelash, and I almost pulled it out. He kept looking around for help, but we were all alone, and I repeated what he needed to do—you know. Pee. But then he said he saw something on *Baywatch* where a lifeguard sucked the poison out of a woman's inner thigh. "But then she had this seizure," he said. "Her body was just bucking on the sand!" '

The way Scottie imitates his voice makes him sound illiterate.

'"I'm not trained for this," he kept saying. "I just sell sunscreen, and there's no way I'm going to piss on your hand," but then I told him what you, Mom, always tell Dad when you want him to do something he doesn't want to do. I said, "Stop being a pussy," and it did the trick. He told me not to look, and he asked me to say something or whistle.'

'I can't listen to this,' I say.

'I'm almost done,' Scottie whines. 'So. To distract him while he peed, I talked about your boat races, but how you weren't all dykey, and I told him that you were a model, but you weren't all prissy, and that every guy at the club was in love with you but you only love Dad.'

'Scottie,' I say. 'I have to use the bathroom.'

'Okay,' she says. 'I'm done anyway. Wasn't that hilarious? Was it too long?'

I feel sick. I need to be alone.

'It's fine. It's great. Go tell Mom what you told me. Go talk to her.' *She can't hear you anyway,* I think. *I hope.*

I walk down the hall, wishing someone could step

64

in and give me some direction. Scottie shouldn't have to create these dramas. She shouldn't have to get hurt. She shouldn't have to be pissed on, and the thing is, Joanie *would* think that story was hilarious. I think of her while we were dating. She loved creating dramas that involved pain, men, sex.

'We're over,' she'd say countless times. 'I can't stay in every night and play house. I think we should see other people.' She never did. She stuck around, and she'd be soaring one moment and critical and miserable the next, but she'd never go. I wonder why she didn't just go.

# 9

Scottie is sitting on the bed when I enter the room. The sight of her so close to her mother almost frightens me. A Polaroid of Joanie rests on the bed. Joanie with makeup. Her twenty-fourth day. I don't like the picture. She looks embalmed.

'I don't like that,' I say, pointing to it.

'I know,' Scottie says. She folds it in half, then crushes it in her hand.

'Did you talk?' I ask.

'I'm going to work on it some more,' Scottie says. 'Because if Mom thinks the story is funny, what will she do? What if the laugh circulates around in her lungs or in her brain somewhere since it can't come out? What if the laugh kills her?'

'It doesn't work that way,' I say, though I have no idea how it works.

'I just thought I'd make it sadder. That way she'll feel the need to come back.'

'It's already sad.'

She looks at me, not understanding.

'It shouldn't be this complicated, Scottie.' I say this sternly.

'Why are you yelling at me?'

'You need to talk.'

'I'll talk when she wakes up,' Scottie says. 'Why are you so mad?'

I can't tell her I'm angry because I feel like I'm losing control. I can't tell Scottie that I want to show her mother how well I handled her, that I'm returning her in better condition. I can't tell her I don't know why I feel this desperate need for her to talk to Joanie, as though time is running out.

I sit on the bed and look at my wife: Sleeping Beauty. Her hair seems slippery. It looks the way it did when she gave birth. I put my ear to where her heart is. I bury my face in her gown. This is the most intimate I've been with her in a long time. What drives you, Joanie? My wife the racer, the model, the drinker. I think of the note, the blue note.

'You love me,' I say. 'We have our way and it works. You're going to come out of this. Right?'

'What are you doing?' Scottie says.

I lift my head and walk to the window. 'Nothing.'

'We need to go,' she says. 'I need a new story.'

I tell her we can't go yet. We have to wait for Dr. Johnston. Just as I say this, he enters the room, looking down at his chart.

'Hey, Scottie,' he says. 'Hey, Matthew.' He looks up but doesn't make eye contact. 'I was calling to you yesterday. Did you see me?'

'No,' I say.

'Hi, Dr. J,' Scottie says. 'I just told my mom the

66

greatest story.'

*Liar.* Why is she lying? 'Scottie, why don't you run down to the little store and get some sunscreen for the beach.'

'I've got some in my backpack,' she says.

That damn backpack has everything in it. It's pretty much stocked to get us through the next ten years.

'They've got some good candy, I bet,' Dr. Johnston says. He takes a plastic hospital card out of his coat. 'Here. Use this.' His mood seems upbeat, positively optimistic.

'I'm full,' she says and sits down. 'I'll stay here. I want to hear about Mom.'

Dr. Johnston makes eye contact with me. He suddenly seems stunned and exhausted. His shoulders are rounded, and his chart hangs by his side—it almost seems as though he's going to drop it.

I look at him and slowly shake my head. Scottie sits on the chair with her legs crossed and her hands in her lap, waiting.

'Well, then.' He straightens his posture. 'As you know, her scores have been okay, but they have gotten lower this week. Some very low-scoring individuals have achieved excellent recoveries, just as higher-scoring patients sometimes show no improvement at all, but in this case, we . . . we—'

'Scottie. I need to talk to Dr. Johnston alone.'

'No, thank you,' she says.

'Well, we should have a greater indication later as to . . . how much longer . . . she'll be in this unit at this point in time,' he says.

'So it's good, then?' Scottie says.

'What's good to know is that if a patient in a

coma survives the first seven to ten days following the injury to the brain, then longterm survival can be expected, but—'

'Mom has been here longer than that! Way longer than seven.'

'No, Scottie,' I say.

'She can survive, but the quality of that survival will be poor,' the doctor says.

'She won't be able to do the things she could once do,' I say. I look at Dr. Johnston to see if I'm right. 'No motorcycles. No boats.'

'Then she won't get hurt,' Scottie says.

'Let's go, sport. Let's go to the beach.'

I look at Dr. Johnston, his unruly eyebrows, his grooved and spotted hands. I remember him at our many gatherings in Hanalei, the families getting together for Christmas break in the old plantation homes with their creaky floors and poor lighting, mosquito nets and ghosts. Dr. J's face was hidden most of the time behind a cowboy hat, and he'd spend the days fishing or playing guitar, something my father couldn't do; it lured us kids in, placated us. My dad would always go fishing out in the deep sea, one time bringing in a marlin, its swordlike nose pointing like an accusation. Most of the time he'd bring in tuna, and in a reversal of roles, the men would clutter the kitchen, fussing over sauces and getting the barbecue to the perfect temperature.

I'm wondering if he's remembering these times as well, me as a young boy watching openmouthed as he strummed his guitar. This must be hard for him and strange. He has known me since I was one hour old, raw and slippery. He writes something down on his chart. I have the urge to put my arms around him and tell him I don't know how to do any of this and to help me. Tell me exactly what's going to happen. Play me a song. Get me out of here.

'So, Mom's okay,' Scottie says. Dr. Johnston doesn't say anything, and I still don't know what's going on except that it's something unfavorable. Scottie gathers her things, and when she is turned away, he puts his hand on my back. His stoic expression frightens me.

'Can you come back later?' he asks. 'We need to talk privately.'

'Of course.'

He walks out of the room, and when he turns to walk down the hall, I can see his profile, which looks determined and almost angry.

'Beach!' Scottie says, walking out of the room, not even glancing at her mother. I silently apologize to my wife for leaving her here, for her low scores, and for not knowing what they mean, for going to the beach and possibly enjoying ourselves. Will she be paralyzed? Will she not know the ABCs? I kiss her on the forehead and tell her I'll take care of her. Whatever happens, I will be there for her. I tell her I love her, because I do.


# 10


At the club the shrubs are covered with surfboards. There has been a south swell, but the waves are blown out from the strong wind. We walk on the sandy walkway alongside the dining room, an open terrace with coral pillars and ceiling fans.

My cousin's grandfather, a lover of water sports, was the founder of this club one hundred years ago. He leased the beach-front property from the estate of the queen for ten dollars a year. In the lobby next to a picture of Duke Kahanamoku, a plaque reads, LET THIS BE A PLACE WHERE MAN MAY COMMUNE WITH SUN AND SAND AND SEA, WHERE GOOD FELLOWSHIP AND ALOHA PREVAIL, AND WHERE THE SPORTS OF OLD HAWAI'I SHALL ALWAYS HAVE A HOME. Today anyone can commune with sun and sand and sea at a starting price of fifteen thousand dollars, monthly dues, and an initiation process that tends to blackball those with unfavorable pedigrees. I tried to explain this to Scottie when her friend's father wasn't accepted. Board members believed he had ties to the Yakuza. She didn't understand.

'Unfavorable pedigrees?' she asked. 'Like a Pekingese?'

We all hate those little dogs.

'Sort of. Well. No. It's not a good process, sweetie.' I liked her friend's dad. He was quiet. So many people I know gab your ear off, but whenever I happened to come across him, we never ventured into the land of small talk, and our brief exchanges always managed to be comfortable. The rumors that he was connected to the Japanese mafia made me like him even more. I mean, everyone wants a friend in the mafia.

I follow Scottie past the big open windows with the wooden jalousies. She walks to the outer terrace and up the steps to the dining room, which is relatively empty. Everyone is outdoors, engaging in the sports of old Hawaii and the sports of new Hawaii—the club is also credited with the invention

70

of beach volleyball, and balls are constantly being lobbed out of the courts and onto the heads of unsuspecting sunbathers.

'We can't leave until something funny, sad, or horrible happens to me,' Scottie says.

'I'm not letting you out of my sight.'

'Nuh-uh!'

'Uh-huh. I'll stay out of your way, but I'm not leaving you alone.'

'That's not fair. That's so embarrassing.' She looks around.

'Just pretend I'm not here,' I say. 'It's nonnegotiable. All your friends are in school anyway.' I should just put her back in. I could work, she could learn. I don't know why I need her in my constant sight all of a sudden.

Scottie points to the tables on the perimeter of the dining room and tells me I can sit over there. There are a few ladies playing cards at one of these tables. I like these ladies. They're around eighty years old, and they wear tennis skirts, even though I can't imagine they still play tennis.

Scottie heads to the bar. The bartender, Jerry, nods at me. I watch Scottie climb onto a bar stool, and Jerry makes her a virgin daiquiri, then lets her try out a few of his own concoctions. 'The guava one is good,' I hear her say, 'but the lime makes me feverish.'

I read the paper that I borrowed from one of the ladies. I've moved to a table that's a little closer to the bar so I can listen and watch.

'How's your mom?' Jerry asks.

'Still sleeping.' Scottie twists atop her stool. Her legs don't reach the metal footrest, so she crosses them on the seat and balances.

71

'Well, you tell her I say hi. You tell her we're all waiting for her.'

I watch Scottie as she considers this. 'I don't talk to her,' she says to Jerry, and her honesty surprises me.

Jerry sprays a swirl of whipped cream into her drink. She takes a gulp of her daiquiri and rubs her head. She does it again. She spins around on the stool. She snaps a picture of Jerry and then begins to sing: 'Everybody loves me, but my husband ignores me, guess I'll have to eat the worm. Give me a shot of Cuervo Gold, Jerry baby.'

Jerry cleans the bottles of liquor, trying to make noise.

I wonder how often Joanie sang this little song. If it's her standard way of asking for tequila.

'Give me two of everything,' Scottie yells, caught in the fantasy of being her mother. I want to relieve Jerry, but I don't. I let him deal with the discomfort because I can't right now.

'What other songs do you like?' he asks. 'Maybe sing another one.'

I watch the ceiling fans shuffle the air. The sun hits the right side of my body and makes me sink a little farther into my chair. I zero in on the paper I have been pretending to read and look at the weekly feature called 'Creighton Koshiro's Kidz.' The column highlights the lives of the island's children—those who embody the aloha spirit and have a good GPA, those who have done something remarkable like run a marathon with no left leg, or something charitable like donate all their Bratz to girls in Zimbabwe. I don't like this feature in the same way that I don't like bumper stickers that boast an honor student is on board. Neither of my

72

girls will ever be one of these Kidz.

I hear Scottie's voice and lower the paper and see her looking over her shoulder at her butt, which she's shaking back and forth. She's singing, 'I like it like that. Keep working that fat.'

That's it. I start to get up, but then I see Troy walking toward the bar. Big, magnanimous, golden Troy. I quickly pick up the paper again and hide behind it. My daughter is suddenly silent. Troy has killed her buzz. I'm sure he hesitated when he saw her, but it's too late to turn around.

'Hey, Scottie,' I hear him say. 'Look at you.'

'Look at you,' she says, and her voice sounds strange. Almost unrecognizable. 'You look awake. Smile.' I hear the sound of the camera.

'Uh, thanks, Scottie.'

Uh, thanks, Scottie. Troy is so slow. His great-grandfather invented the shopping cart, and this has left little for Troy to do except sleep with lots of women and put my wife in a coma. It's not his fault, but he wasn't hurt. It was an annual race Joanie competed in with Troy. They raced a forty-foot Skater catamaran and Joanie was the only woman on the circuit. Troy told me that on turn #8, they were right on the tail of another boat, and he tried to make a pass. He ran out of room and had to quickly move left to maintain course.

'What do you mean *you* tried to pass?' I asked Troy.

'I was driving,' he said. 'Joanie was the throttle man this time. I just really wanted to drive.'

Rounding a mile marker while Troy tried again to pass the other boat, they launched off a wave, spun out, and Joanie was ejected. She wasn't breathing when rescue divers got her out of the

73

water. When Troy came in from the race, he kept saying, 'Lots of chop and holes. Lots of chop and holes.' It was his first time driving. Joanie always drives.

'Have you visited her?' Scottie asks.

'Yes. Your dad was there.'

'What did you say to her?'

'I told her the boat was in good shape. I said it was ready for her. I told her she's brave.'

What a Neanderthal. I hate when people say how brave someone is when really they're just surviving. Joanie would hate it, too.

'Her hand moved, Scottie. I really think she heard me.'

Troy isn't wearing a shirt. He never wears shirts. The man has muscles I didn't even know existed. He's athletic, rich, and dumb, with eyes the color of a hotel swimming pool. The exact kind of person Joanie befriends.

I'm about to lower the paper until I hear my daughter say, 'The body has natural reactions. When you cut off a chicken's head, its body runs around, but it's still a dead chicken.'

I hear Jerry coughing and then Troy saying something about life and lemons and bootstraps.

When I come out of hiding, Troy is walking away and Scottie is running out of the dining room. I get up to follow her. She runs toward the beach wall; I catch up to her before she jumps off it. Tears are brewing in her eyes. She looks up to keep them from falling, but they fall anyway. I want to join her. I want to kneel down and sob.

'I didn't mean to say dead chicken,' she cries. 'It's just that Mom always twitches. It doesn't mean anything!'

74

'Let's go home,' I say.

'Why is everyone so into sports here? You and Mom and Troy think you're so cool. Everyone here does. Why don't you join a book club? Why can't Mom just relax at home?'

I hold her and she lets me.

'I don't want Mom to die,' Scottie says.

'Of course you don't.' I push her away from me and bend down to look in her brown eyes. 'Of course.'

'I don't want her to die like this,' Scottie says. 'Racing or competing. I've heard her say, "I'm going out with a bang." I hope she goes out choking on a kernel of corn or slipping on a piece of toilet paper when she's really old.'

'Christ, Scottie. Where do you get this? Let's go home. You don't mean any of this. I don't like you talking this way. And Mom's not going to die.'

Her face is puffy. Her hair is greasy. She has this look of disgust on her face. It's a very adult look.

'Look. Your mother thinks you're great. She thinks you're the prettiest, smartest, silliest girl in town.'

'She thinks I'm a coward.'

'No, she doesn't. Why would she think that?'

'I didn't want to go on the boat with her, and she said I was a scaredy-cat.'

'She was just joking. She thinks you're the bravest girl in town. She told me it scared her how brave you were.'

'Really?'

'Damn straight.' Joanie often said that we're raising two little scaredy-cats, but of all the lies I tell, this one is necessary. I don't want Scottie to hate her mother, as Alexandra once did or maybe

75

still does.

'I'm going swimming,' Scottie says.

'No,' I say. 'We've had enough.'

'Dad, please.' She pulls me down by my neck and whispers, 'I don't want people to see that I've been crying. Just let me get in the water.'

'Fine. I'll be here.' She puts her camera in her backpack and strips off her clothes and throws them at me, hands me two pictures, then jumps off the wall to the beach below and charges toward the water. She dives in and breaks the surface after what seems like a minute. I sit on the coral wall and watch her and the other kids and their mothers. The mothers have so much gear: snacks, toys, umbrellas, towels. I don't have anything, not even a towel Scottie can run into when she's done. To my left is a small reef. I can see black urchins settled in the fractures. I still can't believe Scottie slammed her hand into one of them.

I look at the picture of Jerry and then the one of Troy. His smile is so genuine, his muscles so shiny, it's like he greases them. The outside dining terrace is filling up with people and their pink and red and white icy drinks. An old man is walking out of the ocean with a one-man canoe on his shoulder, a tired smile quivering on his face as if he's just returned from some kind of battle in the deep sea.

The torches are being lit on the terrace and on the rock pier. I can still see the booze cruises floating past the wind sock and heading back to shore. The soaring sun has turned into a wavy blob above the horizon. It's almost green flash time. Not quite yet but soon. When the sun disappears behind the horizon, sometimes there's a green flash of light that seems to sparkle out of the sea.

76

It's a communal activity around here, waiting for this green flash, hoping to catch it. I realize I still need to get Scottie home and then go back to the hospital.

Children are coming out of the water, running into the towels their mothers are holding out for them. I hear a mother's voice drifting off the ocean. It's far away yet clear. 'Get in here, little girl. They're everywhere.'

Scottie is the only child still swimming. I grab her things and jump off the wall. 'Scottie!' I yell. 'Scottie, get in here right now!'

'There are Portuguese man-of-wars out there,' the woman says to me. A toddler clings to her leg; she's trying to shake him off. 'The swell must have pushed them in. Is she yours?' The woman points to Scottie, who is swimming in from the catamarans.

'Yes,' I say. She's mine, but I don't know what to do with her, where to put her.

Scottie finally comes out of the water. She's holding a tiny man-of-war—the clot of its body and the clear blue bubble on her hand, its dark blue string tail wrapped around her wrist.

I grab a stick and take it off of her. 'What have you done? Why are you doing this?' I pop its bubble so that it won't hurt anybody else's child.

The other kids are looking at her arm, which is marked with a red line. They take a few steps back. The toddler walks toward the man-of-war. 'Bubbles?' He reaches for it, and his mom grabs his hand. He throws himself to the sand and wails.

'Should I get the lifeguard?' the woman asks.

'I'll handle it,' I say. 'Scottie. Go rinse your arm off.' She heads for the terrace. 'No. In the salt water.'

77

'It's not just my arm,' she mumbles. 'I was swimming with, like, a herd of them.'

'Are you okay?' the woman asks. The other kids head back to the water, and she yells, 'Stay out!' so loudly she sounds like an umpire.

'She's fine,' I say, wanting the woman to leave. Her child is still crying, and it's annoying. Can't she give him a bottle or some candy?

I turn my back to her and walk toward the ocean. 'Why would you stay out there, Scottie? How could you tolerate that?'

I've been stung by them hundreds of times; it's not so bad, but kids are supposed to cry when they get stung. It's something you can always count on.

'I thought it would be funny to tell Mom I was attacked by a herd of minor wars.'

'They're not minor wars. You know that, don't you?' When she was little, I would drink a few beers on the beach in front of the reef and watch the sun set while Joanie worked out. She'd point out sea creatures to me, and I'd give them the wrong names. I called them minor wars because they were like tiny soldiers with impressive weapons—the gaseous bubble, the whiplike tail, the toxic tentacles—advancing in swarms. I called a blowfish a Blow Pop; an urchin, an ocean porcupine; and sea turtles, saltwater hard hats. I thought it was funny, but now I'm worried that Scottie doesn't know the truth about things. I'm worried my lessons are getting us all in trouble.

'Of course I know, duh,' Scottie says. 'They're manowars, but it's our joke. Mom will like it.'

'It's not manowar, either,' I say.

She dunks her body in the water.

'It's man-of-war,' I say. 'Portuguese man-of-war.

That's the proper name.'

'Oh.' She walks out of the water and begins to scratch herself. More lines are forming on her chest and legs.

'I'm not happy,' I say. 'You need to just tell Mom that you miss her. She doesn't need a story.'

'Fine. Then let's go back. I'll tell her what just happened.'

'We need to get home and put some ointments and ice on the stings. Vinegar will make it worse, so if you thought Giraffe Boy could pee on you, you're shit out of luck.'

She agrees as if prepared for this—the punishment, the medication, the swelling, the pain that hurts her now and the pain that will hurt her later. She seems okay with my disapproval. She's gotten her story, after all, and she's beginning to see how much easier physical pain is to tolerate than emotional pain. I'm unhappy that she's learning this at such a young age.

'The hospital will have ointments and ice,' she says.

We walk up the sandy slope toward the dining terrace. I see Troy sitting at a table with some people I know. I look at Scottie to see if she sees him, and she is giving him the middle finger. The dining terrace gasps, but I realize it's because of the sunset and the green flash. We missed it. The flash flashed. The sun is gone, and the sky is pink. I reach to grab the offending hand, but instead, I correct her gesture.

'Here, Scottie. Don't let that finger stand by itself like that. Bring up the other fingers just a little bit. There you go. That's the cool way to do it.'

Troy stares at us and smiles a bit. He's

completely confused.

'All right, that's enough.' I suddenly feel sorry for Troy. He must feel awful.

I place my hand on Scottie's back to guide her. She flinches, and I remove my hand, remembering that she's hurt all over.

'Can we go to the hospital?' she asks. We make our way past the locker rooms to the parking garage.

'I'm going to take you home,' I say.

'I have a story, and I want to tell Mom.'

Her voice is loud in the garage. She stops walking.

I stop and look back. 'Come on.'

She shakes her head. I walk to her and grab her hand, but she pulls away from me. 'I want to see Mom! I'll forget what I need to say to her.'

I grab her wrist, more forcefully this time, and she screams. I look around and walk away and she keeps screaming and then I scream and we're both screaming in the garage, our angry shouts bouncing off the walls.

*     *     *

Scottie is sulking in the car. I decide to call Dr. Johnston. I don't want to go back to the hospital. There is too much to do. I ask a nurse to page him, and he calls moments later. Scottie presses the horn. I ignore her.

'Matthew,' he says.

'Can you tell me now?' I ask. 'Just tell me everything.' I stand in the garage and watch Scottie in the car.

'There's been an increase in pressure to her

brain,' he says. 'We've drained fluid, and we could do surgical intervention, but with her GCS, I'm afraid it wouldn't help. You may have noticed that lately, she's had no eye movement or any movement whatsoever. The damage to her brain is very severe. I'm sorry,' he says. 'We've spoken of this, the possibility of this . . .'

I want to help him. I don't want him to have to say every word he has to say to a boy he has known his entire life.

'Plan B?' I say. This was the term I used.

'Yes, I'm afraid. Plan B.'

'Okay,' I say. 'Okay. I'll see you then. I'll see you tomorrow. Is it all starting now? Are you going to take everything away right now?'

'I'll wait until I see you tomorrow, Matthew.'

'Okay, Sam.' I close the phone, afraid to go to the car. There's a girl in there waiting for me to make things better, a girl who thinks her mother is going to be okay so her father can retreat once more, appearing at night to entertain and dine, and in the morning to eat breakfast around the kitchen island, stepping over schoolbooks, bags, gadgets, and clothes, then heading out the door. I stand still in the parking garage and think about Plan B. This plan means that my wife is in a persistent vegetative state. She has severe neurological disabilities. I will be approached for organ donation. Plan B means we'll stop feeding her, caring for her, helping her breathe. IV fluids will be removed, medications will stop. It means we will let her die.

I hear a car's tires turning the corners. I see the car driving down to our basement level. The tears come, and I wipe them away. The driver stops when she sees me. She's an old woman who can barely see over the steering wheel of her Cadillac. I can see her fingers gripped around the wheel, and I think, *Why do you get to live so long?* I see her window going down and I stand there, curious to see how she'll get me to move.

'May I get by?' she asks.

'I'm sorry,' I say and move out of the way.

# 11

We drive on H1 and sit in traffic behind a lifted truck, its back window airbrushed with an image of a woman with breasts as round as dinner plates. I can't see around the vehicle to understand the reason for the holdup, but there probably isn't one. Traffic is as mysterious as the brain or makeup or ten-year-old girls. Scottie's stings are now raised red lesions, and I take her hand when she tries to scratch herself. There are dusty white patches on her skin, since I wouldn't let her rinse off. The salt water should stay on her wounds.

'Are you dizzy?' I ask. 'Nauseated?'

She sniffles. 'I think I have a cold.' She won't admit it's from swimming with poisonous invertebrates. She's miserable, and I think she's not insisting we go to the hospital anymore because she realizes this isn't a good story after all.

To cheer her up, I say, 'Tomorrow, when we're home, you'll have to shave your legs to get rid of any remaining nematocyst.'

She looks at her legs, covered with faint brown hair, and she smiles. 'Reina will freak. And then I'll have to start doing it all the time. It will be such a hassle.'

'No,' I say. 'You'll do it just this one time.'

'Do you think I hurt the urchin as much as it hurt me?' Scottie asks.

'I don't know.' I can hear the music from the truck, or not music but a throb that makes our windows vibrate. I think about the urchin. I never thought about it getting hurt.

'Why does everyone else call them manowars?'

'Words get abbreviated, and we forget the origins of things.'

'Or dads lie,' she says, 'about the real names.'

'That, too.'

The traffic clears magically, and I pass the exit we always take home. Scottie doesn't notice.

Last week, when Dr. Johnston and I discussed the unimaginable alternative, he said typical protocol for a person like Joanie, whose living will prohibited tube feeding and mechanical ventilation, was to gather friends and family and let them say their goodbyes.

'Let them handle all of the arrangements and say what they need to say. By the time the last day comes, they feel ready. Or as ready as they can be for something like this.'

I listened in the same way I listen to a flight attendant telling me what to do in case of a water landing.

*Plan B.*

A sea of red lights, and I slow down. My job now is to gather everyone together and tell them we have to let her go. I won't tell anyone over the phone, because I didn't like hearing the news from the doctor that way. I have maybe a week to handle the arrangements, as the doctor said, but

83

the arrangements are overwhelming. How do I learn how to run a family? How do I say goodbye to someone I love so much that I've forgotten just how much I love her?

'Why is it called a jellyfish?' Scottie asks. 'It's not a fish and it's not jelly.'

'A man-of-war isn't a jellyfish,' I say, not really answering the question. 'You ask good questions. You're getting too smart for me, Scottie.'

I'm not sure it's the right choice to bring her with me, but I figure I can't depend on Esther anymore. I can't depend on anyone. I need to take control of my daughters, and I've decided they will both sleep at home tonight.

I see the airport exit and look at the clock on the dash.

'What are we doing?' Scottie finally asks. A jet roars over our heads. I look up because it's so loud and see its big gray belly, heavy in the sky.

I take the exit. 'We're going to get your sister.'

# PART II

# The King's Trail

# 12

Whenever I land on the Big Island, I feel as though I've gone back in time. There's an abandoned look to Hawaii, like it's just been hit by a tsunami.

I drive the familiar road, moving past the prickly kiawe trees and black sand beaches, the coconut palms with their wild parrots. The air gets colder, and there's a slight vog hanging over everything—a cross between fog and volcanic ash, the smell of it like gunpowder—that adds to the mood of abandonment and destruction. I drive through the black lava fields that glow with the white rock chalk that teenagers use to declare themselves. It's our island graffiti: *Keoni loves Kayla, Hawaiian Pride,* and the lengthiest pronouncement, *If U R Reading This U R Gay.* In the fields of sharp rocks, I see heiaus and stones stacked on tea leaves, offerings to the gods.

'What's that?' Scottie says. She's curled against the seat so I can't see her face.

'What's what?' I look out at the emptiness.

'It's a running path,' she says.

I look again and see the corridor of water-tumbled stones through the lava beds. 'It's the King's Trail.'

'Is it named after us?'

'No. Haven't you learned about the King's Trail in school?'

'Probably,' she says.

'What kind of Hawaiian are you?'

'Your kind,' she says.

We look at the wide and endless path, which

87

wraps all the way around the island.

'King Kal¯akaua had it made. He had it revamped. It's how your ancestors got around.' We drive alongside it as though it's an old highway, which it is, I suppose, built by criminal labor, then smoothed by cattle and human traffic. I've always remembered that about the trail—those who didn't pay their taxes were the ones who built it.

'How old is it?' she asks.

'Old,' I say. 'Eighteen hundreds.'

'That's old.' She stares out at the trail and its long rock curb, and when we get to the hills and ranches of Waimea, I notice she's asleep. In the daytime the green hills are spotted with cows and horses, but I don't see any animals now. I drive past crooked gray wooden fences and let my window down to smell the cold, the pastures, the manure and leather saddles, the fragrance of Kamuela. My grandparents had a ranch here, and I'd visit as a child, picking strawberries, riding horses, driving tractors. It was a strange world of sun, cold, cowboys, beaches, volcanoes, and snow. Mauna Kea was always visible, and I would wave to it, thinking that the scientists were watching me instead of the silent planets.

I turn onto the dirt road and drive past the lower stable, the school buildings, then up to the dormitories.

I'm eager to see my daughter. And a bit nervous. Last week I talked to her and she sounded strange. When I asked her what was wrong, she said, 'The price of cocaine.'

I asked, 'Seriously, what else?'

'Is there anything else?' she said.

She claimed she was joking. It was a horrible

joke, considering.

I don't know what I did wrong. It seems there's something about me that makes a person want to destroy herself. Joanie and her speedboat, motorcycles, alcoholism. Scottie and her sea urchin, Alex and her drugs, her modeling. Alex told me she first did drugs to terrify her mother, but maybe she did them to see what it felt like to be her mother. Alexandra seems to love and despise her mother with equal intensity, but these problems surely must be gone now, or at least they will be. You can't be angry with someone who's dying.

I think about Buzz's, where the manager told me Joanie livened up the place. I'm sure if she died—when she dies—she'll put her picture up, because it's that kind of restaurant: pictures of local legends and dead patrons haunting the walls. I feel sad that she has to die for her picture to go up on the wall, or for me to really love everything about her, or for Alex to forgive her for whatever she did wrong.

I drive slowly because there are dips and bumps in the road. I look over at Scottie, who's still asleep. I like that the school still hasn't paved the road.

I stop the car in the lot and turn off the engine, and Scottie opens her eyes.

'We're here,' I say.

# 13

It's ten p.m. The dorm mother looks at me as if I'm the most irresponsible person in the world. It's cold outside, and Scottie's wearing shorts, her legs pocked with stings. I'm in a dorm, fetching my daughter, when I could have done it during regular hours. We stand in the dorm mother's doorway, and I see a television on in the background. She's wearing a hideous flannel nightgown, and from what I can see, she was watching *American Idol*. I'm terribly embarrassed for all of us.

She leads us to a stairwell, and Scottie runs ahead of us, taking two steps at a time. I can hear the dorm mother breathing and slow down.

It's good to know that everyone is asleep and that it isn't like a college dorm, where ten p.m. is the time things are just getting started. I tell the woman that I'm impressed. I know this is one of the best private schools in Hawaii, but still, it's good to see children away from home behaving.

'We try to emulate the home,' she says. 'Most kids who live at home are in bed or quietly reading. On weekends it's a little different, but the curriculum is so difficult that studying and sports keep them busy during the week, and they're pretty worn out by now. Alexandra's at the end.' She stands at the top of the stairs, holding the railing, and points to the end of the hall.

Scottie runs. 'Which door?' she yells.

'Keep it down,' I yell back, and the woman frowns at our yelling.

She tells me she'll knock and go in first just in case Alex or her roommate isn't decent. We wait

90

for her to catch her breath and walk down the hall.
I look at my watch. When she finally nears the end,
Scottie knocks on the door, and I swear the woman
almost hits her.

'That's the wrong door!' she says.

A girl's head appears and I look away, just in
case she's indecent.

'Sorry to bother you, Yuki,' the dorm mother
says. 'We knocked on the wrong door.'

'May I go, then? I was asleep.'

'Yes. Go back to sleep.'

'Good night,' I say, amazed by how smoothly this
residence runs. I imagine rows of girls, tucked in
and dreaming.

The dorm mother knocks on the correct door.
No one answers. My girl is tucked in and dreaming.
'I'll wake her,' she says, ducking into the darkness.

Scottie cranes her head, trying to get a glimpse of
her older sister's room. I think of what I will say to
Alex. How will I tell her she is losing her mother?
The words are strange: losing a mother. We are
losing a mother. My wife will soon be dead.

The dorm mother comes out and closes the door
behind her.

'Is she asleep?'

'No,' she says.

I wait for her to continue. 'Is she getting decent?'

'No,' she says. Her hand is still on the doorknob.
'Alexandra isn't here.'

*       *       *

We search the the bathroom, the study, the TV
room. We look into the rooms of her friends.

The dorm mother is panicked, worrying not so

much about the safety of my daughter but about how Alexandra's absence reflects on her. She has been talking endlessly. I feel I'm being sold something.

'The girls are in the dorms by seven,' she says. We are walking to the lower level to wake another friend. 'Then they have study hall until nine. No games, movies, heavy chatting.'

Scottie looks thrilled by the situation. Her red sores are bright in the hall's fluorescent light. Her T-shirt says VOTE FOR PEDRO, whatever that means, and her hair is sticking up in places and matted down in others. In one section near her ear, the hair is held together by some unknown substance. She had fruit punch on the plane, and her lips and chin are stained the color of raw meat. She looks a bit like roadkill, which makes me try and sell myself back to the dorm mother so that we seem to be in a competition at a marketplace over our abilities to care for our young.

'I'm sure she's just with a friend,' I say, 'doing what girls do.'

'They're talking about boys,' Scottie says.

'Well, we have a strict lights-out policy, so that would be unacceptable.'

'What will happen to her?' Scottie asks. 'Will she lose privileges? That's what happens to me. I lose TV privileges, but I TiVo my shows anyway. Esther doesn't know what TiVo is.'

'I use TiVo, too,' the dorm mother says.

'Esther used to help us out,' I explain.

'She still does,' Scottie says. 'She cooks, cleans, rubs my back.'

I laugh. 'Scottie, don't be silly.'

'I'm not being silly.'

'Where is this friend of hers?' I ask. We seem to be walking down an endless hall. The dorm mother finally stops in front of a room. She knocks and enters, then shuts the door behind her. We're left looking at two names, HANNAH and EMILY, which are drawn with purple markers on lavender construction paper and encircled with yellow cutout flowers. I recognize the smell of purple Crayola pen. Someone must have put a lot of time into these name tags, and it makes me happy that Alexandra has this camaraderie of girls. Girls who draw on poster board and make intricate cardboard cutouts of flowers.

The dorm mother comes out, and her expression tells me she doesn't have good news. 'Emily isn't here, either. We'll go back to Alexandra's room. Maybe she's returned.'

'Or maybe that roommate of hers will let us know what's going on,' I say.

*     *     *

The roommate caves. It takes awhile. She claims that Alex will kick her ass for telling, and I assure her that my daughter will do no such thing. Her poor roommate. I can't think of a more ill-suited match. She's a mouth breather with scraggly hair and hay allergies. On her side of the room, there are stuffed animals on her navy blue comforter and no posters or pictures or anything, really, illustrating her taste, popularity, or parents' income. Her side is a testament to her loneliness, whereas Alexandra's side is beset with tributes to herself and her identity. I can see the gloss of photographs and posters of boys jumping motorbikes over mounds of dirt. I see

93

CDs, makeup, clothes, shoes, and more bags than one girl could possibly need.

The three of us walk to the soccer field. I don't know what we'll find, and I think the dorm mother and I are both afraid. She has put a down coat over her nightgown, and I rub my arms to stir up some warmth. Scottie holds my hand in the darkness. Parts of the ground are hollowed out with holes, and Scottie stumbles every now and then. The grass is wet. The cuffs of my pants are wet. I look at Scottie's bare ankles. She exhales loudly because the air is so cold and she's enthralled by the look of her breath.

At last, in the distance, I see two people with what look like golf clubs in their hands. Then I see a white ball shoot through the sky, followed by shouts of enthusiasm. My daughter is playing golf in the moonlight on a soccer field with her friend. I become nostalgic for a life I've never had: boarding school, girlhood.

'Girls!' the dorm mother yells.

I see the girls' faces turn toward us.

'Alex,' I call. Her hair has grown past her shoulders, and even from here I can see the beauty in her face, the way her features seem to build off one another, collaborating.

'Dad?'

'Alex,' Scottie yells. 'It's me.'

The other girl takes off running but doesn't make it very far before falling with her golf club in hand. I go over to see if she's okay and find her facedown in mud, her body splayed out as if she's sunbathing. I bend down and put my hand on her back. She rolls over, her mouth agape, her eyes closed. I realize she's laughing, and then I realize she's

94

completely smashed. When she is able to speak, she says, 'Par me, bitches!'

Now Alexandra is by my side, leaning on me and convulsing with laughter. 'What are you doing here, Dad?'

'Mrs. Murphy,' the other girl slurs. 'You come out to play a round with us? Eighteen holes?'

The cycle begins again. The girls hold in their laughter for a second until it all detonates. Alexandra falls to her knees. 'Oh, God,' she says. 'Oh my God.'

Scottie starts to laugh, too, copying her older sister's inebriated joy.

'Eighteen holes,' Alex's friend breathes between laughs. 'Eight. Eeen. Holes.'

'Girls!' Mrs. Murphy keeps yelling. I don't know what I could possibly do to make this all stop and get us back to the airport to catch the last flight so I can be back on Oahu to gather all the loved ones and tell them this is it. Joanie, our fighter, has lost.

It's Scottie who gets them to quiet down. 'Alex,' she says. 'Mom's going to come home.'

Alex looks at me to see if this is true, and I look up. It's a beautiful night. Without the city lights of Oahu, the stars invade the sky. 'No,' I say. 'That's not true.'

'What's happening, then? She's gotten better or something?' Alex leans against the golf club and smirks.

'I'm going to bring you home,' I say. 'She's not all right.'

'Fuck Mom,' Alex says. She takes a few purposeful strides, then launches her golf club into the night. We all look up and around, but no one sees where it goes.

95

When we get home, Scottie walks from the garage to her room without saying a word. I carry Alex. She is so heavy, her limbs seemingly drenched. I strain to get her to her room. I could stop and let her sleep on the sofa in the den, but I want her to sleep in her old bed, which used to be my bed, and part of me enjoys carrying her, the way she's curled into my chest like a baby.

I slip off her shoes and pull the covers over her. She looks like Joanie. I watch her sleep for a while. *What has happened?* This sentence seems to be on rotation in my head. I leave her room without closing the shutters. Tomorrow the sun will rise over the Ko'olaus, and the light will smack her in the face.

# 14

I try to give Alex space and time to apologize for her behavior of her own accord. We're in the kitchen, and she's drinking a Coke and eating cereal that looks like large rabbit pellets.

'How are you feeling?' I ask.

She shrugs and chews and then lifts the bowl to her mouth.

'Does Mom let you have soda at breakfast?'

'She never saw me eat breakfast.'

'Where's Scottie?' I ask.

She shrugs again.

'Well, nice to see you, Alex. Welcome home.'

She lifts her spoon and circles it in the air, then gets up and puts her dish in the sink.

'Put it in the dishwasher,' I say.

She walks out of the room, and I go to the sink to rinse her bowl and load it in the dishwasher. She reappears, talking to someone on her cell phone. She carries sunglasses, a book, a towel, and another Coke.

'Alex,' I say. 'I'd like to talk to you.'

'I'm going swimming,' she says.

'Fine, then I'll go swimming, too.'

'Fine,' she says.

In the pool, she bobs from foot to foot. She tilts her head back, then wrings her hair out. I dive in, aiming for a big splash, and when I surface, she looks at the water with disgust. The water is cold, and clouds block the sun. On the way to the other side, I swim through fallen leaves from the mango tree and the cinnamon-colored bodies of termites.

'Sid's coming over,' she says.

'Who's Sid?'

'My friend. You'll meet him. I just called him and he's coming over.'

'What friend? From HPA?'

'No, he's from here. My class at Punahou. I've known him for ages.'

'Oh,' I say. 'Okay.'

'He's got some issues. He'll probably stay over, and he'll be around a lot for me, since all this shit is happening.'

'Well,' I say. 'You have it all figured out. Where does he live?'

'Kailua,' she says.

'And would I know his parents?'

'No.' She locks eyes with me.

'Looking forward to meeting him,' I say.

We hear banging on the sliding door that leads

97

out to the pool. Scottie runs out on the brick patio wearing a black negligee. She has dabs of white cream all over her skinny body. She takes a picture of Alex.

'What the fuck,' Alex yells. 'Get out of my underwear!'

'Don't yell at her like that,' I say.

'Well, she's wearing my fucking underwear.'

'So what, Alex? In the scheme of things, is it really that big a deal?' I look at Scottie. It sort of is a big deal. The negligee sags off her chest and between her legs. 'Scottie, get back inside and change into a real swimsuit.'

'Why?'

'Now, Scottie.'

She gives me the finger, the proper way I taught her, and runs back inside.

'Real good job you're doing,' Alex says.

'I think the bigger deal isn't Scottie wearing your underwear, or my parenting skills, but finding you inebriated at boarding school, where you're supposed to be getting your act together.'

'I was just drinking, Dad! I have gotten my act together. I've been doing really well, but you guys never even noticed that part. No one has said balls about how I'm doing better and how I was in that stupid play you guys didn't bother to see. So what if I got drunk on the night you happened to drop in. So what!'

'Calm down,' I say. 'Just get ahold of yourself and calm down.'

'Get a clue, Dad,' she says.

'About what?'

'You have no idea about anything. I want to go back to school.'

She lifts her head to the sky to submerge her long brown hair in the water. When she brings her chin back down, her hair is slick and shiny. She sits on the step in the pool and picks termites out of the water and lines them up on the edge. 'What's with the cream all over Scottie?' she asks.

I tell her the story: the urchin, the man-of-wars, Lani Moo.

'That's insane,' she says.

'You need to help me with her.' I rest my arms on the warm brick patio and let my legs kick out behind me.

She moves off the step and ducks under the water, surfacing with a small diamond-shaped leaf stuck to the side of her hair. I pick it off and place it on the water.

'Maybe I'll talk to her,' Alex says. She tilts her head to the sun and closes her eyes. 'I guess. Whatever. Someone has to.'

'I'd like that. You can't yell at her anymore, you know. You're her idol, and you have no reason to yell, even if she's in your underwear. And what are you doing with that kind of underwear, anyway?'

'Mom gave it to me,' she says. 'I don't even wear it.'

'That's good,' I say. 'Anyway. Be good to her.'

'Maybe I will. Maybe I won't. No one was good to me, and I've turned out fine. Strong as an ox.' She lifts her arm out of the water and flexes her biceps.

This gesture warms me, then saddens me, because we can't joke around. Life isn't funny right now. It may never be. I need to tell her.

Alex turns around and props herself on the edge of the pool, floating her lower body. I think of her

99

postcards. Why did Joanie ever let her model for those?

'Your mother isn't well, Alex.'

'Obviously,' she says.

'Watch what you say. I don't want you to say things you might regret, like last night. She isn't going to wake up. The doctors are going to stop caring for her. Do you understand what I'm saying? We're giving up.'

She stands still.

'Did you hear what I said? Come here.'

'What? What do you want?'

'Nothing. I was just comforting you.'

'Oh yeah. Yeah, right.'

'Why are you yelling?'

'I need to get out of here!' She brings her hands down onto the water and flinches as it splashes into her face. 'Stop it!' she yells. Her face is red and wet.

'Stop what?' I say. 'I haven't even said anything.'

She covers her face with her hands.

'Alex.' I try to bring her toward me, but she pushes me away.

'I don't get what's happening,' she says.

'We're saying goodbye. That's what's happening.'

'I can't.' She takes two quick and loud inhalations, and then her shoulders shake.

'I know,' I say. 'We're going to help each other through this somehow. I don't know what else to do.'

'What if she comes through?'

'I'm going to ask Dr. Johnston to talk to you. You'll understand. Mom wanted it this way. She has a will, see, that says we have to do this.'

'This is so weird.' Tears stream down her face, and her breath is choppy. 'Why'd you have to tell

100

me in the goddamn pool?'

'I know. I know. It just happened, okay?'

'I can't even deal right now,' she yells.

'I know. We'll go see her. How about right now? We can go see her now.'

'No,' Alex says. 'I need a little time.'

'That's fine,' I say. 'I was thinking of our friends last night. People who should know what's going on. And I thought I should tell our friends, but I thought I should do it in person. You know, out of respect for them. For your mother. Maybe you can come with me?'

We've moved out to the center of the pool for some reason and are keeping ourselves afloat, kicking our legs and pushing the water away with our arms. I can tell she's getting tired.

'We can talk about your mother with our friends. Console one another and honor her.'

Alex laughs.

'I know, it sounds hokey. We'd just do it for her close friends, and Barry and your grandparents. Even if we just say what's happening. We don't have to stay, but I'd like to tell them in person.'

'That's not what I was laughing at,' she says.

'So will you come with me? We can go to Racer's first and then to your grandparents'.' I've put a lot of thought into this—who should be told—and I've narrowed it down to our family and the people who love and know her the best.

Last night I went over the list of names and looked at the other side of the bed, Joanie's two pillows stacked on each other just the way she likes them. I'm not used to sleeping alone, and even though I have much more room, I keep to my side and never veer to hers. This is where we'd watch

101

TV and talk about our day, and it was also the time of night when we'd realize how well we knew each other, how it seemed that no one could join us and understand us. 'What if someone were recording this conversation?' She'd laugh. 'They'd think we're nuts.'

But I also remembered all the nights she was out late with the girls. She'd eventually sway into bed smelling like tequila or wine. She would come home so late, and sometimes she wouldn't be drunk. She'd sneak into bed quietly and gracefully, her gardenia perfume on her skin. I wonder if part of me was satisfied that she was keeping busy, allowing me to focus on my work, so caught up with creating my own legacy instead of borrowing the legacies of those who came before me. Yes. Part of me must have enjoyed being left alone.

Alex is pale and out of breath. She looks at me with such pain in her eyes, as though pleading with me for something. *I can't help you,* I want to say. *I don't know how to help you.*

'Hold on,' I say.

She hesitates, then holds on to my shoulders like she used to do. I swim toward the shallow end, tugging her back with me. We go to the edge, and I place my hand on her back. The sun appears, then quickly hides again. The pool water is dark, like deep-sea water.

'Let's all go to Racer's, since it's right here, then your grandparents', and then the hospital? That's a good route.'

'I don't see the point,' Alex says. 'Just call them or something. I don't want to talk about Mom with everyone. It's stupid.'

'Alex, whatever you fought about at Christmas,

102

you need to drop it. It's nothing. You love your mother. Your mother loves you. Move on.'

'I can't drop it,' she says.

'Why not? What could possibly be so bad?'

'You,' she says. 'You're the reason I fought with her.'

The sun appears again. It feels good on my shoulders. 'You were fighting about me?'

'No,' Alex says. 'I was just angry at her for something she was doing to you. And you're still so devoted to her.' She looks at me then down at the water. 'She was cheating on you, Dad.'

I watch her face. It remains still and blank except for her nose. It flares a little in anger. Then I hear a noise, like someone at a typewriter rapidly punching the same key, and I look up and see a helicopter rising over Olomana. It hovers over the incline before the peak.

It seems that I should feel something right now, like a deep chill, or a red heat, or a sensation like ice water surging through my veins, but the only thing I feel is that I've been told something I already know. It's as though a panic has settled within me. I think of the blue note and let out a loud breath.

'Did she tell you?' I ask. 'Did you catch them?'

'No. Well, sort of. I sort of caught them.'

'Tell me,' I say. 'Just tell me. This is fantastic.'

I pull myself out of the water and sit on the edge of the pool.

She does the same, and we let our legs dangle in the water.

'I was home for Christmas, obviously,' she says, 'and I was driving to Brandy's, and I saw her with him.'

103

'Driving where? Where were you driving?'

'Kahala Avenue. To Brandy's.'

'And what, you just saw her walking with another man and assumed something was going on?'

'No, I was going into Black Point, and I saw them in the driveway of a house. His house.'

'He lives on Black Point?'

'I guess,' she says.

'So then what?'

'He had his hand on her back and led her into his house. Or into a gate where the yard is.'

'Then what?'

'Then nothing. She went into the house. His hand was on her back.'

'What did you do?'

'I kept driving to Brandy's and told her what happened, and we basically talked about it all day.'

'Did you say anything to your mom? Why didn't you tell me?'

'I don't know. I just wanted to get away. It made me sick to see her near you. I was so pissed at her and so sorry for you. I actually went back to school thinking that this was it. I was done with her. She knew I knew. That's why she sent me away again. She didn't want me back.' Alex draws her knees to her chest. 'Then I was going to call and tell you everything, but the accident happened and I didn't want to tell you anymore. I was going to wait until she came back, I guess.'

'I'm sorry, Alex. You shouldn't be dealing with these kinds of problems.'

'No shit,' she says.

'I can't . . . we can't be angry with her right now.'

Alex doesn't say anything. We watch the helicopter circle around the same spot.

104

'What did he look like?' I ask.

Alex shrugs. 'I don't know.'

'How did she know you knew?'

'I told her I couldn't stand seeing her and I knew what she was doing. I never came out and said it, though. We got into a fight. And then I left. And everyone cheered that I was gone again.'

'Alex,' I say. 'We need to get along.'

She looks away, which usually means she's agreeing to something.

'I need to know who he is,' I say.

Alex slips back into the water. I follow her, letting myself sink to the bottom. We both push the surface away from us, our legs and arms making tiny circles. Her hair moves slowly over her head. The pool water glints along her body. My toe brushes the bottom of the pool. We look at each other until a line of bubbles shoots out from her mouth. She pushes off, and I follow her to the surface to breathe.

'I'm going to the Mitchells",' I say. 'Do you want to come with me?'

'To do what?' she asks.

'To tell them about Mom and ask them who he is.'

'I need to wait for Sid,' she says.

We get out of the pool, and I must look bad, because my daughter keeps asking if I'm okay. We walk back into the kitchen and I stand at the counter, water dripping off my shorts onto the floor. Scottie is spooning ice cream onto a bagel, and I look at the tip of her little tongue sticking out of the corner of her mouth as she digs into the carton. I want to weep. Alex touches my wrist, and I flinch, then look at her and smile, but my lips tremble.

'I'm going to the Mitchells',' I say again.

Esther walks in with a stack of dish towels. She looks at the girls, then looks at me. I must be pale. I must look utterly lost, because she shakes her head and clucks her tongue. She puts the towels in a drawer. She whispers something into Alex's ear and then walks pointedly toward me. I take a step back, but she grabs my head and pulls me to her breast. I stare at her chest, horrified, but then I give in, and for the first time, I actually cry, as though I've just now realized what's happening to my wife and to me and to this family. My wife's not coming back, my wife didn't love me, and I'm in charge now.

# 15

I pull into the Mitchells' circular drive. Their yard is lush with ferns and teas. Even the pillars of the carport are fertile, the white posts bound with ropy vines. Alex told me to bring pastries from the bakery, but I think she just wants the leftovers. She can eat a box of malasadas in one sitting.

I walk up the steps with my box of pastries, which seem to dampen my authority. I haven't called them to say I'm coming, so they couldn't rehearse their answers.

'Hello?' I look into the screen door. I let myself in and call up the stairs. 'It's me, Matt.'

They come down at the same time, their faces flushed. Mark and Kai Mitchell are our friends, but they're both closer to Joanie than they are to me. Mark has on pajama bottoms and seems embarrassed about it. It looks like they've just had sex, but I doubt this is the case. Married people don't have morning sex—I'm pretty sure about that.

'Were you still sleeping? I'm sorry.'

Kai dismisses this with a wave of her hand. 'No, we were just fighting. Come. Sit down. Want some coffee?'

'Sure,' I say. 'I have pastries.'

I lay out my offering on the kitchen table, but Mark shakes a box of cereal.

'Whole grain,' he says.

'Ah.'

They both sit down with their coffee, whole grain, and a box of vitamins. A porcelain cow is filled with half-and-half and I pour some into my cup.

'What were you fighting about?' I ask.

'Stupid,' Mark says.

'It is not stupid. He wants to throw parties and have people over, and who does all the work? Me.'

'But my point is you don't have to do anything. You don't need to clean and go shopping and get a new outfit and think of some kind of theme cocktail. I'd invite people over and we'd drink and have a laugh.'

'It isn't that simple.'

'It is! That's my point.'

'Oh my God,' Kai says. 'Is Joanie . . . Is everything all right with Joanie? Here we've been rambling on—'

'Yes,' I say. 'I mean, she's okay right now.' I stop myself from continuing, envisioning their faces when I break the news. I want them to be able to keep eating their cereal. I don't want to deal with condolences, giving or receiving, and I realize I'll never be able to do this for everyone on my list.

107

'I'm trying to come to terms with a few things,' I say. I look at Kai. 'Closure,' I add.

'Sure,' she says.

Mark is quiet. He can go hours without saying a word. He looks permanently stunned by life.

'Who is he?' I ask.

They hold their mugs to their lips for an unreasonable amount of time. Mark reaches for a custard pastry and stuffs a large chunk of it into his mouth.

'Does she love him? Who is he?'

Kai slides her hand across the table so that it almost touches my own. 'Matt,' she says.

'I know this is uncomfortable for both of you, and I'm sorry to put you in this position, but I need to know. I would very much like to know who's been screwing my wife.' And just like that, I see that where once I was warm, now I'm very cold.

Kai's hand slides back across the table. 'You're angry,' she says.

'No shit.' I put some pastry into my mouth to keep myself from talking, but I still add, 'No shit I'm angry.'

'This is why,' Kai says softly.

Mark's eyes widen.

I chew the creamy dough. It's so good that I almost say something. 'This is why what? What's why?'

No one says a word. I smile because Kai's in trouble now. 'This is why she cheated on me? Because I talk with my mouth full? Or because I use curse words? Because I'm a cusser with shitty etiquette?'

'Wow,' Kai says, shaking her head. 'I think we

108

should talk another time. I think you need to cool it.'

I look at Mark. 'I'm not leaving.'

'You don't know him,' Mark says.

'Oh, don't you even, Mark,' Kai says. 'You're her friend. Shame on you.'

'I'm Matt's friend, too,' he says. 'And this is a particular situation.'

Kai stands. 'This is betrayal.'

'Hey, excuse me,' I say. 'Betrayal? What about me? She's cheated on me, remember?'

'Listen,' Kai says. She rests an elbow on the table and points a finger at me. 'It's not her fault. She has needs. She was lonely.'

'Was it still going on up until the accident?'

Mark nods.

'Who is he?' I ask again.

'I stayed out of it,' Mark says. 'Anytime Kai talked about it, I walked away.'

'And you just ate it up, I bet,' I say to Kai. It's my turn to point my finger. 'You probably encouraged her to have an affair, adding some drama to your life without having to take any risks.'

'You are being awful.' Kai adds a whimper to her accusation, but I'm not buying it.

'Who exactly are you guys protecting?' I say. 'Joanie doesn't need your protection.' A pain lodges in my throat. 'She's going to die.'

'Don't say that,' Kai says.

'She's not recovering. She's gotten worse. We're withdrawing care.'

Kai starts to cry, and I'm relieved. I redirect myself into comforting her, and so does Mark.

'I'm sorry,' I say. 'I'm obviously upset. I don't mean to take it out on you guys.'

Kai nods her head, agreeing with me, I guess.

'Does she love him?' I ask.

Mark looks at me blankly. I can tell he has no idea. This is women's territory.

'How can you ask about him when she's going to die?' Kai says. 'Who cares? Yes, she loves him. She was crazy about him. She was going to ask you for a divorce.'

'Stop, Kai,' Mark says. 'Goddammit. You just stop talking.'

'She was going to ask me for a divorce? Are you serious?' I look at both of them.

Kai cries into her hands. 'I shouldn't have said anything. Especially now. What does it matter now?'

'But it's true?'

'I'm sorry, Matt,' she says. 'I'm sorry. I don't know what I was thinking.'

Mark closes his eyes and takes a deep breath and moves just slightly away from his wife.

'So, Joanie had an affair,' I say. 'She had an affair, and she loves this other man and not me. My wife is now dying, I'm a wreck, and you still haven't told me who this guy is.'

'Brian,' Mark says. 'Brian Speer.'

I stand up. 'Thank you.'

Kai continues to cry. Her tearful face reminds me of their son, Luke, how he looked when he would cry. I remember when he was a little younger than Scottie is now, he would answer only to Spider-Man. Even teachers succumbed to this whim, and when he raised his hand in class, they would say, 'Yes, Spider-Man?' I'm the one who finally got him to drop the phase and answer to his real name. My method was, and remains, our secret. I'm not sure if even Luke remembers.

I walk out of the kitchen, taking my pastries with me, and I think about how many times I've seen the Mitchells in the past year and how they never even hinted at a problem between Joanie and me. It's embarrassing. Mark walks me to the front door. He opens it and ducks his head, and I walk out without saying anything to him. I don't think I'll say anything to both of them for a long time.

I walk to the car and think about the night I broke Luke's bad habit. Joanie and I were over for dinner, and I was standing outside, overlooking the Mitchells' yard. Luke was trying to catch toads. He had the pool net in one hand, his Spider-Man action figure in the other, and was becoming discouraged.

'Look, Luke,' I said. 'Here's one right here.'

Luke turned to look but caught himself and stared straight ahead.

'Luke,' I said again. His parents and Joanie were chatting near the bar. They had just smoked a joint, the three of them, and they were being loud and stupid. I knelt next to Luke. 'Let me tell you something,' I said. 'Spider-Man has a vagina.'

Luke looked at me and then at the figurine in his hand. 'Look,' I said, pointing to Spider-Man's crotch. 'No bulge. Nothing there, see?'

He ran his hand along the plastic crotch.

'Spider-Man is a loser. The other superheroes call him a douche bag. They say, "Get out of here, you sticky red douche bag."' I didn't know why I was telling him this, but then I heard his parents' stoned, exclusive laughter, and I knew why.

Luke looked at his doll.

'Do you still want me to call you Spider-Man?'

111

He shook his head.

*    *    *

I pull out of the Nu'uanu neighborhood, and as I drive back over the Pali Highway, there are only two thoughts going through my head: *My wife is going to die, and her lover's name is Brian Speer.*

# 16

Sid is here. He's lanky and tall. When Alex introduced us, he said, ''Sup,' and took my hand, pulled me in to him, thumped my back, and cast me back out.

'Don't ever do that to me again,' I said, and he hiccuped out a small laugh. For some reason we're all standing on the lawn, and when he got here, I offered him a drink, out of habit from when guests come by. I poured his 7-Up into a glass, and seeing him with a glass and a cocktail napkin feels ridiculously formal, like I'm meeting my future son-in-law, which I hope I'm not.

Alex is quiet around him, cool, and I'm embarrassed for her. 'Alex, do you still want to go with me to Racer's, then Grandpa's? I'm leaving soon, so . . .'

'You know a person named Racer?' Sid asks.

'I said I'll go,' she says. 'We'll both go with you.' She leans in to Sid, and he scopes out our home then picks something off her shoulder.

I look at Sid's shoes. They're surprisingly clean and white. 'He doesn't have to come,' I say. 'This isn't something he should do.'

'I want to do whatever Alex wants me to do,' he says. 'I'm just drifting.'

'Does he know what we're doing?'

'Yes,' Alex says. 'He knows everything.'

An unexpected surge of jealousy runs through me.

'I think this is a family matter,' I say. 'This next week, or however long or short, is a family matter.'

'Dad. I told you he was going to be here. Just let it go, okay? I'll be more civil with him here, believe me.'

Sid opens his arms out wide and shrugs. 'What can I say?'

I look at Alex, hoping she senses my disappointment.

'Don't you have school?' I ask Sid.

'I have it when I want it,' he says.

'All right. Get Scottie. Let's just go.'

*     *     *

Scottie sits in the front seat, Alex and Sid in back. Scottie has never been so quiet. I notice she has left her camera and scrapbook at home.

'You know E.T.?' Sid says. 'Remember E.T.?'

I look in the rearview mirror because I have no idea whom he's talking to. His cheeks are stubbled, and his eyes are dark blue. He's looking out the window, addressing no one.

'What did they want?' he asks. 'Why did the E.T.'s come to Earth in the first place?'

'Ignore him,' Alex says. 'He gets like this in cars. Stoner Seinfeld.'

'Who's E.T.?' Scottie asks.

'I don't know,' I say. I don't want to have to

113

explain. I pull into Lanikai and see Racer's house. Racer is a good friend of ours, especially mine, although not so much anymore. I have to drive around the loop of the neighborhood, since it's a one-way road. I'm tempted to drive the wrong way on the empty road, but I don't. I enjoy the quiet street, the white sand blown onto the pavement. The look of desertion makes me feel as though I've survived something.

'What if E.T. was the dork of the planet?' Sid says. 'What if all Earthlings went to a planet and, say, Screech or Don Johnson were the ones left behind? They'd get a totally wrong impression of us.'

'This is fascinating.' I pull into the driveway. 'You philosophers stay in the car. I'll be right back.'

I walk around to the back door and am startled to see Racer sitting on the small cement terrace. He's in a bathrobe, has his hands around a mug of steaming coffee, and is staring out at the beach, at the low tide and little curls of waves.

When he sees me, he gives me a tired smile, not at all surprised by my visit.

'Racer,' I say. I head to the table and pull out a chair, but the seat is wet.

'Hey, Matt,' he says. He looks at the wet chair. 'We can go inside.' He stands, and I see that the back of his robe is soaked from the chair.

We go to the kitchen, where he pours me a cup of coffee. 'Thanks,' I say. 'Got any half-and-half?'

'No,' he says.

'That's okay,' I say.

He begins to search the cupboards. 'We might have that powdered stuff. I don't know where anything is. Noe. She arranged everything. I'm out of milk.'

'How is Noe?'

He sits down at the kitchen table. 'I canceled the wedding. She moved out.'

'What? Are you serious? Why?'

He drums his fingers on the table. Brown-spotted mangoes rest on a piece of newspaper. 'It just didn't feel right.' He holds his head in his hands. 'My parents didn't like her. They never said anything, but I just knew they didn't like her, and I couldn't get past it. She's a nanny, you know? And a dancer. She's just from a different place, you know?'

I think of his family, another plantation family, sugar heirs. Still, his parents are so warm, it seems unlikely they wouldn't take to Noe. That's the thing about Hawaii society. There aren't many snobs.

'It shouldn't matter, but it matters, you know?'

'Sure, sure,' I say.

'I felt I was making the wrong choice.' He sits up. 'But it's fine. It will be fine. It wasn't meant to be.' His eyes glaze over and then come back into focus on me. 'Did you just come over to say hello?'

I look at the mangoes and take a sip of my black coffee. 'Yeah, haven't seen you in a while. Thought I'd stop in on my way to . . .' I wave my hand toward Kailua. His house, I realize, isn't on the way to anything. It's a dead end.

'How is she?' he asks.

'She's okay,' I say. I have never seen Racer feel much of anything, and it's as though I don't want to intrude; losing his fiancée is a moment of sorts. I don't want to interrupt his pain with more pain. I think of his parents not approving of Noe, me not approving of Sid, Joanie's father not approving of me.

115

'Princess Kekipi,' I say. 'You know she married against her parents' wishes. I think we all do. You should do what you want to do.'

Racer nods. 'It's not too late,' he says.

'It's not,' I say.

He drops his shoulders. I wonder what he will do.

'Anyway, my kids are waiting in the car.' I stand up to leave, even though I've had only a few sips of my coffee. He doesn't seem to notice how absurdly quick this visit is, the purposelessness of it. He walks me to the front door. There's a comforter on the couch, a bottle of wine on the coffee table, and an open *TV Guide* with listings circled in red ink. He holds the door open and shields his eyes from the sun. He waves at my family. 'It will be okay,' I say, and he agrees and shuts the door. I walk to my car a little stunned, hoping to God he marries that girl. I don't know why it matters to me, but it does.

'I couldn't do it,' I say when I sit down.

'Do what?' Scottie asks.

'Well, the next one you'll have to do,' Alex says.

Racer was my warm-up. The next house is the main event. Now I'm prepared to face people who don't approve of me. I start the car, back out of the driveway, and take us to our next stop.


# 17

We sit on the wraparound deck because that's where Scott was when we drove up, sitting in a wicker chair with a drink balancing on his knees. I can see Scottie in the lower yard with her grandmother, pointing to the various things they see. 'Rock,' I imagine her saying. 'Pond.' Joanie's mother has Alzheimer's, and Scott has been carrying on with his altered wife and her nurse, doing yard work, swimming laps in the pool. I've seen him swimming before, and when he comes up for air, the sight of him in his goggles and swimmer's cap is heartbreaking, his face slick with water, his mouth drawn out like that of the creature in Munch's *The Scream*. Drinking is another one of his hobbies. It runs in the family. I could smell the Scotch on his breath when he saw Scottie and said, 'Bingo!,' something he always says when he sees her.

I have told him the news and given him her living will, which he is now looking over. Sid has been quiet, for which I'm grateful, but then I really look at him in the lounge chair, his black sunglasses on, his black cap pulled down, his stillness, and I realize he's asleep. Alex sits on the end of the lounger by his legs. It's irritating seeing her so close to him all the time.

'This is like some other language,' Scott says, flipping through the pages.

'I know,' I say.

'What is this?'

'It's a living will. You have one, too.'

'Yes, but it's not a bunch of gibber-gabber. This is like reading Korean.' He shakes the pages at Alex and me.

'I'm sure yours is the same. Do you want me to explain the gist of it?'

He ignores me and focuses on the pages, probably not wanting to have me explain anything to him. He has never liked me. Early on in Joanie's and my marriage, he'd try to get me to back these business ideas he had, but I always told him I don't do business with friends or family. This was just an excuse to get myself out of his grand plans, most of them being theme restaurants. I have endured countless pitches from my father-in-law, many of them purporting that such-and-such town had the potential to become the new Waikiki. I almost bit once just to get him off my back, but I never did, thank God.

'Gibber-gabber,' he mumbles.

'I'll explain it to you, Scott. I know it's a difficult language. It's complicated, but this is what I do. I can help you.' I think of the statements, almost like vows from your healthy self to your dying self: *If I am in a permanent coma, I do not want my life to be artificially prolonged and I do not want life-sustaining procedures used. I authorize the withholding or withdrawal of life-sustaining procedures, of artificial nutrition and hydration, of comfort care.* The way the comfort-care section is phrased always gets to me. *I do not want comfort care that would prolong my life.* This makes it sound like Joanie doesn't want to be soothed or held. This is the part of the will that Scott can understand, the part that clearly states she doesn't want to live.

'Do you want me to go over it with you?' I say again. 'It's an advanced directive—basically her instructions telling us what medical procedures she wants or, in this case, doesn't want. No mechanical ventilation, no—'

'I don't want to hear it. I know exactly what it says. It says that she doesn't want everyone waiting around while she spoils like milk. It says the doctors can't do squat, and she'd prefer to go on to another place.'

118

'Gramps,' Alex says. 'Are you okay?'

'I'm fine. I prepared myself for this, and I'm glad Joanie had the good sense to write this thing here and wasn't a selfish person. She's a brave girl,' he yells, his voice shaking. 'She was always stronger than her brother. Barry whines his way through life. He looked thirty when he was sixteen. He may even be a homosexual, for all I know.'

'Barry's not a homosexual,' I say. 'He likes women very much.' I think of Barry. He used to be so chubby and warm. Now he does hot yoga and something called Budokon and he's nimble and tough, like wild game.

'She's stronger than you, Matt,' Scott continues. 'She lived more in a year than you did in a decade, sitting in your office hoarding your cash. Maybe if you let her have her own boat and bought her some safe equipment or let her go on one of those shopping sprees that women like, then maybe she wouldn't have engaged in these reckless sports. Maybe if you provided more thrills at home.'

'Gramps,' Alex says.

'And you, Alexandra. You fought with your mother when all she was trying to do was instill some drive in you. Joanie had passion! She's a good girl,' he says as though arguing with someone. 'I never told her all this. But I'm saying it now!'

Scott stands up and walks to the porch rail so his back is to us. His shoulders shudder. He looks up with his hands on his hips, as though gauging the weather to come. He lifts his flannel shirt to wipe his face and coughs, spits, then faces us. 'You guys want some rolls? I made rolls. You want a drink?'

His eyes are glassy and his hands drum in his pockets. I like the way men cry. They're efficient.

119

'Sure, Scott. We'd love some rolls and a drink.'

When he goes into the house, I look at Alex. 'You okay? He's just upset.'

'I know. It's fine.'

She doesn't look fine. Her brow is furrowed, her jaw flexed.

'So what happens when you do that?' she asks.

'Do what?'

'Remove everything? I mean, how long does it take?'

I talked to the doctor this morning, listened as he told me that Joanie could breathe quite well on her own and could live up to a week without help. 'About a week, I guess.'

'When do they do this?'

'They're waiting for us to come in,' I say.

'Oh,' Alex says. She touches Sid's leg, but he doesn't move. Scottie and her grandmother walk toward us with stalks of white ginger in their hands.

'It must be hard for Grandpa to handle this without Grandma,' I say.

Scottie holds her grandmother's hand and leads her up the stairs. I never know what to say to Alice. Our encounters are similar to when someone shows me an infant and I feel like I'm the one on display, everyone watching to see how I interact with it.

'Hi, Grandma,' Alex and I sing.

She glares at both of us. Scott comes out with his rolls and a tray of drinks. Scotch on the rocks. I don't even bother to take the drink meant for Alex. I know she won't drink in front of me. Sid suddenly sits up and looks around like a dog that smells bacon. He reaches for a drink, and I stare at his hand around the glass. He lets go and leans back in the chair. Scott glares at him and Sid salutes.

'Who are you?' Scott asks. 'Why are you here?'

'He's my friend,' Alex says. 'He's here for me.'

Scott still stares at Sid, then turns to Alice and hands her the Scotch. 'We're going to go see Joanie today,' he says.

Alice grins. 'And Chachi?' she asks.

Sid bursts out laughing and Scott turns back to him, then places a hand on his shoulder, which makes me fear for his life. 'You be quiet, son,' Scott says. 'I could kill you with this hand. This hand has been places.'

I shake my head and look at both Sid and Alex.

Scott lifts his hand off Sid's shoulder and turns again to his wife. 'No, Alice. Our Joanie. Our daughter. We're going to give her anything she wants.' He glares at me. 'Think about what she would want, Alice. We're going to get it for her and bring it to her. Bring it right to her bed.'

'Joanie and Chachi,' Alice chants. 'Joanie and Chachi!'

'Shut up, Alice!' Scott yells.

Alice looks at Scott as though he just said 'Cheese.' She clasps her hands together and smiles, staying in the pose for a few seconds. He looks at her face and squints. 'Sorry, old gal,' he says. 'You go ahead and say whatever you want.'

'It was funny,' Sid says. 'All I was doing was laughing. She has a good sense of humor. That's all. Maybe she knows she's being funny. I think she does.'

'I'm going to hit you,' Scott says. His arms hang alongside him, the muscles flexed, veins big like milk-shake straws. I know he's going to hit Sid because that's what he does. I've seen him hit Barry. I, too, have been hit by Scott after I beat him

121

and his buddies at a game of poker. His hands are in fists, and I can see his knobby old-man knuckles, the many liver spots almost joining to become one big discoloration, like a burn. Then he pops his fist up toward Sid, a movement like a snake rearing its head and lunging forth. I see Sid start to bring his arm up to block his face, but then he brings it down and clutches his thigh. It's almost as if he decided not to protect himself. The end result is a punch in his right eye, a screaming older daughter, a frightened younger daughter, a father trying to calm many people at once, and a mother-in-law cheering wildly as though we have all done something truly amazing.

# 18

I'm driving along Kahala Avenue, headed for Shelley and Lloyd's house. I don't want to tell Shelley that my wife is going to die soon, not because I don't like relaying that kind of news but because Shelley is a pit bull and a senator's wife and thinks she can do anything by calling the right person.

Sid sits in the back, stunned.

'My father always made me warn the person before I hit them.' This was all Scott had to say to Sid after punching him in the face.

'Right.' This was all Sid had to say to Scott after getting punched in the face.

They looked at each other, and then Sid walked to my car and Scott walked inside the house. He called to Alice, telling her they needed to gather things for their daughter. He wouldn't say Joanie's name, most likely to avoid hearing about Chachi.

'How's your eye?' I ask. 'Christ, Alex, could you come to the front, please? I feel like a chauffeur with the two of you in back like that.'

'That would be nice,' Sid says. 'If we had a chauffeur. My eye's fine.' He pulls the block of frozen spinach we picked up at 7-Eleven away from his face. 'What do you think?'

I look in the mirror. My daughter's leg is strewn over his, and I wonder, *How did I inherit this guy? Where can I return him?* The color of his lid is a light blue. The skin below the eye is puffy, and instead of looking like a man with a good story, he looks like a kid with a bad allergy.

'Looks good,' I say.

'I can't believe that just happened to me,' Sid says. 'I mean, how often do old people hit someone in the face? That was unreal.' He squeezes Alex's thigh.

'Alex,' I say. 'Come up here.'

She moves over the console to slide into the front seat, and I hear the sound of a hand smacking an ass.

I exhale loudly.

'Why'd you make Scottie go to the hospital with Gramps?' Alex asks.

'What do you mean, why? She needs to see Mom. You need to see her.'

'But maybe it's not good for her to see Mom all the time. Especially now. Isn't she going to start looking different?'

'I don't know,' I say.

'What if she's in pain and we can see it?'

'Then be there for her,' Sid says. 'And get it all out so it doesn't build up and make you fucking

123

crazy. I can't believe your grandfather just punched me in the eye.' He looks at the block of spinach.

'He does that,' I say. 'Actually, it's been a while. That was pretty incredible.'

'You need to go see your mom,' Sid says.

Alex doesn't argue with him. If I had said the same thing, she would have resisted, and I'm not sure if I'm grateful to Sid or the opposite of that.

I turn on Pueo and slow my speed. I feel like I'm on the King's Trail, traveling over rough and crooked ground to sell my goods to people who may not want them. I think about the other reason people used the trail—to flee. When they broke the rules, they used the path to run for their lives.

'How come in *AFV*, they always pick the least funny video?' Sid asks.

'What are you talking about?' Alex says.

'*America's Funniest Home Videos*. They always pick the lamest video.'

'*AFV*? You call it *AFV*?' I ask.

'They're all lame videos, Sid,' Alex says. 'Get a grip.'

'Actually, no,' he says. 'You're mistaken. I laugh really hard.'

'Shut up, both of you, okay?' I turn down the radio and pull up

to the curb. The house is obscured by a web of bougainvillea and

a high stone wall.

I see a girl in the second-story window looking down at us. Then she disappears.

'That was K,' Alex says.

'K? Why K?'

'People do that. David Chang is making everyone call him Alika, his Hawaiian name. She's, I don't

124

know, getting a reduction. She won't use her last name, either. Just her middle name. I think she gets sick of hearing about Lloyd.'

'She's in my creative writing class,' Sid says. 'Remember that party she had where she hired those pole dancers? That was so tight.'

'Do you guys want to go in, go say hi, while I talk to Shelley?'

Alex looks back at Sid. 'Sure.'

We get out of the car and open the wooden outer door, then walk the path to the main door. I ring the bell and hear footsteps.

Their daughter opens the door, and I wave and let Alex handle the talking. She gives K a hug.

'Are you back?' K asks. She looks at Sid. 'What's up?'

She leans forward and he leans forward and they kiss on the lips. Teenage boys have it so good. They don't realize that this casual affection will soon be over.

'Hi, Mr. King,' K says. 'Lloyd's not here.'

'In the office?' I say. 'Improving our society?'

'Surfing,' she says. 'South swell.'

'Didn't he just have surgery?'

'Yeah, he kept the hip. Want to see it?'

'And didn't he lose some toes? He can surf like that?'

'He's determined.' A flash of pride, and then she moves away from the door to let us in.

'Your dad rules,' Sid says, and those are my thoughts exactly. He rules. I think of Alex's friends, and their parents are huge, their pasts, goals, and endeavors looming and ruling. I wonder if our offspring have all decided to give up. They'll never be senators or owners of a football team;

125

they'll never be the West Coast president of NBC, the founder of Weight Watchers, the inventor of shopping carts, a prisoner of war, the number one supplier of the world's macadamia nuts. No, they'll do coke and smoke pot and take creative writing classes and laugh at us. Perhaps they'll document our drive, but they'll never endorse it. I look at both of these girls and see it in their eyes, their pity for us and yet their determination to beat us in their own way, a way they haven't found yet. I never found a way to beat my rulers.

'Is your mom around?' I ask K.

'She's on the back porch,' she says.

'I think everyone on this island is on their porch. I'm going to go say hello.'

The kids all stand close together. I take a few steps, then look back at them. They're huddled by the stairs. I hear K say, 'Want to see my prom dress? It's so slutty,' and then I hear Alex begin to tell K about her mother and I wonder if she—if all the children— know about my wife's affair.

I see Shelley under a beige canvas umbrella. She has her ashtray and her crossword on the table, and she wears a black bathing suit under a black translucent caftan. When she sees me, she slaps her hand to her chest. 'Scared me to death,' she says and swats me with her paper. Her face is a rich brown. She smokes and doesn't wear sunscreen or exercise, which makes her sort of revered in our circle.

'K looks well,' I say. 'Why does she go by K now?'

'Who knows,' Shelley says. 'She's trying to annul her Hawaiian blood or something. And now she's writing these poems that are just awful. Sit down.' She takes her newspaper off the chair and I sit. I

126

look at her pool, glistening and turquoise, the way a pool should be.

'I have news about Joanie,' I say. 'Things have taken a turn for the worst, as they say. We're going to let her rest. We're going to let her go. Christ, I need to find a better way to say this.'

Shelley pushes her sunglasses onto her head. 'Who's her doctor?'

'Sam Johnston.'

'He's good,' she says and seems disappointed. She leans forward, clasping her hands together— she's in her action pose, ready to cure the incurable—and for a moment I believe there's someone she can call, a letter she can write. She can fund-raise her way out of this.

'It's what it is,' I say. 'I just wanted to let you know so you can see her.'

'Oh, fuck, Matt. I don't know what to say.'

'You just said it.'

She leans back and I pat her warm leg.

'You doing this for everyone? Making house calls?'

'I'm trying to. Just our close friends.'

She looks at her pack of cigarettes and lowers her sunglasses. 'You don't need to do that. I can do that. I can call or I can go by in person, just like you. God, I can't believe this is happening.' She whimpers, and I see tears falling from under the sunglasses.

'I don't mind telling people. I need to do something.' I think of my route from house to house; I'm like lava, slowly approaching and altering foundations forever. 'Is there anything about Joanie you want to tell me?' I ask. 'Did you know anything?'

'What?' She wipes her fingers across her face. 'What do you mean? Are you asking me to say something at her . . .'

Shelley doesn't want to say the word, and I don't want to hear it. 'No,' I say. 'You know how it is. It's nice to hear what other people know about her, but never mind. Not now.' I stand up. 'I'm keeping my visits short. Sorry about that. I feel like I'm wrecking the place and not cleaning up.'

She doesn't stand to hug me. She's not a hugger or a person who walks you to the door, and I'm glad to do away with those things right now. I didn't mean to ask about Joanie, her affair; I shouldn't be thinking about that.

'I'll tell Lloyd,' she says. 'We'll go see her today. Please let us know if we can do anything. Please.'

'Thanks, Shelley.'

'Actually, forget it. Don't ask. I'll be in touch with you whether you like it or not. I'll get the ladies together. We'll take care of everything, the details. You just tell me what you want.'

'Thank you,' I say, remembering the death arrangements, food and flowers, ceremony. She lifts her caftan to her face and then reaches for her cigarettes.

'Shelley?' I ask. 'Could you call Racer? Could you tell him for me? I was going to tell him, but I didn't.'

'Of course!' she says, and I realize how happy it makes people to have a specific chore.

The kids are standing in the kitchen eating chicken lo mein out of an aluminum pan.

'Want some?' K asks. Her expression is full of sorrow and sympathy. 'It's from Lloyd's fund-raiser. We have sushi, too, if you want.'

I take a pair of chopsticks and eat a few bites,

and then I tell Alex and Sid we need to get back on the road.

The kids all kiss and hug and make promises to call. K walks us to the door, then heads up the stairs. We get into the car and I drive away slowly.

'She's going to write about this,' Alex says. 'I know it.'

'She better make me look good,' Sid says.

'What's there to write?' I ask. A woman lives. A woman dies.

I drive and think of who should be next, whose house we should flatten. Russell Clove is just down the block, but I don't want to deal with him right now, so I choose Bobbie and Art instead.

I look over at Alex but pretend to be looking at the street signs beyond her. Her face looks so tired. She looks ruined, like something that was grand a long time ago.

As we near Bobbie's house, she says, 'I know where he lives, you know, if you want to see him.'


# 19


Alex tells me to stop. 'This is it,' she says.

I try to look at the house, but a coral wall surrounds it. I can see the crests of waves beyond the roofs of homes. His house isn't far back, which means he's rich, relatively, but not filthy. At first I like this, but then it seems worse. If we had pulled up to a home with stone lions guarding the entrance, then I would get it, but this home is average, which makes their love seem more real. I pull in closer to the curb and park in front of my wife's lover's home.

'I like his wall,' Alex says.

I look at the coral wall. 'It's okay.'

'Are we just going to sit here until he comes out?' Sid asks.

'No,' I say. 'We came, we saw.' I make to start the car, but I don't.

'I wonder if he's home?' Alex asks. 'Should we ring the bell?'

'You should,' Sid says.

'You should,' she says back. He kicks the back of her seat, and she turns and reaches for his leg. He grabs her arm and she laughs.

'Stop it,' I yell. 'Stop touching each other.'

'Whoa,' Sid says. 'Maybe that's why your wife cheated on you, if you're so against touching.'

I snap my head around to face him. 'Do you get hit a lot?'

He shrugs. 'I've had my share.'

I face my daughter. 'You know you're dating a complete retard. You know that, don't you?'

'My brother's retarded, man,' Sid says. 'Don't use it in a derogatory way.'

'Oh.' I don't say anything more, hoping he'll interpret my silence as an apology.

'Psych,' he says, and now he kicks the back of my seat. 'I don't have a retarded brother!' His little trick is giving him a great amount of amusement. 'Speaking of the retarded,' he says, 'do you ever feel bad for wishing a retarded person or an old person or a disabled person would hurry up? Sometimes I wait for them to cross the street and I'm like, "Come on already!" but then I feel bad.'

'Shut up, Sid,' Alex says. 'Remember what we talked about. And we're not dating, Dad.'

This seems to work. He's quiet. I watch him

130

remembering whatever it is they talked about.

'This is completely bizarre,' I say. 'Just sitting here. Stalking him.'

'We're not stalking him,' Alex says. 'He's at work, I'm sure. Man's got to work to get a wall like this.' She reaches to turn on the ignition and then puts the radio on. 'Why do you need to see him? Are you going to say anything to him?' She turns on the air conditioner, and it blows into my face.

'That wastes gas,' I say.

'Oh, please,' she says.

'You think this car just runs on God's own methane?' Sid yells. Alex and I both turn our heads.

Sid's sitting in the middle of the backseat now, his legs spread out, staking claim on every part of the car. 'What? It's from a movie.'

'I just want to see him,' I say. I listen to the music, but Alex changes the station, waits, and changes it again and again and again.

'Just find something.'

'It's all R&B crap.' She continues to run through the stations.

'Turn it to 101.7,' Sid says. He leans forward, his face right next to mine. I smell cigarettes and a mixture of cheap cologne and Twizzlers.

'101.7.' Alex keeps pressing the changer, and with each touch, a hollow beep emits from the stereo.

'Just put it on 101.7,' I say.

A growling voice invades the car. It's soothing, in a way, to be reminded that other people around the world are angry. It isn't just me. A breeze comes through my open window, carrying the scent of sea salt and a slight tinge of coconut husk. The radio station muffles the singer's every other word, which

131

makes me think of the dirty words even more. *Fuck,* I think. What a beautiful word. If I could say only one thing for the rest of my life, that would be it. Sid bobs his head to the right then the left over and over again. He looks like a pigeon.

'Do you know what he does?' Alex asks. 'Is he married?'

'I don't know. I don't know anything about him.' I say this more to myself than to her. I never even thought about the fact that he might be married, though I doubt he is. His house seems like a bachelor's, and even his name, Brian Speer, sounds independent and unattached, a solo-flying weapon. It's such a familiar name. Maybe that's why I want to see him. Because I feel that I know him. Everyone knows everyone here. I must know him.

'You mean you didn't ask Kai and Mark?'

'I didn't get into it with them.'

'Why not?'

'I just didn't.'

A car drives up the road and we all crouch lower in our seats, which makes me feel silly. The car continues on, then disappears behind the hill that leads to the estates by the ocean. I look at Alex hunkered down, and a feeling of utter incompetence washes over me. I'm soaked in bad parenting. Drenched. I imagine how all of this looks through her eyes. Her mother, who has cheated on her father, is in a coma, and she's accompanying her father to get a look at her mother's lover. Her sister prances around in her lingerie and stabs herself with sea creatures. Why have I let her bring me here? Why have I exposed my needs?

'This is stupid.' I start the car, forgetting that it's already running, and I hear the engine grind.

'If someone messed with my girl, all hell would break loose,' Sid says.

'Whatever, Sid,' Alex says. 'A girl doesn't need a knight.'

It's as though Joanie is sitting beside me. It's exactly something she would say. I want to ask my daughter, *Why not? It would be so easy. I'd love to have a knight. What's wrong with being rescued?*

I drive back toward the avenue.

'He has dark hair,' Alex says. 'If you just want to know what he looks like.'

We move away from the houses and drive up the wide road to the lookouts below Diamond Head. I slow to let the boys with surfboards tucked under their arms cross in front of us. One boy with long rusty-colored curls does a sort of waddle across the street. His long board is in one hand, and he's trying to keep his trunks up with the other.

'I used to drop you off here, remember?' I say this quietly, so we can have our own conversation.

'Yup,' she says. She releases a short, almost angry laugh.

'Why'd you stop surfing?'

'Just happened. Why'd you stop playing with LEGOs? Just happens.'

'It's a little different. You were good at it.'

'You never even saw me.'

'But I heard you were good.'

She looks at me and I give her a wide, supportive, good-parenting smile.

'You were a surfer?' Sid asks. 'A cute little surfer chick?'

'Why'd you stop?' I ask again.

'At first I stopped because I got my period and didn't know how to use a tampon, so I wouldn't go for, you know, five days or so, and then I just got out of the habit.'

'How do you not know how to use a tampon?' Sid asks.

'Couldn't your mother . . . show you how . . . or teach you, or whatever?' I ask.

'I didn't tell Mom I got my period for an entire year.'

'Even I know how to use a tampon,' Sid says.

I turn up the volume on the radio.

'The first time I thought I shit my pants,' Alex says. I can feel her staring at me, waiting for a reaction.

'Ew, Alex,' Sid says. 'Maybe you did.'

'Well,' I say. 'It's your private personal business.'

'I hid my used pads under the mattress because I didn't know where to throw them away. Mom would have seen them in the trash. The blood soaked into the mattress. She found out that way. When she flipped the mattress.'

Alex looks at me expectantly, but I don't face her. I feel a good response is crucial, as though this is some kind of exam.

'Why did you keep it a secret from her? Sounds like a lot of work.' And shame, I want to add. And shame.

'I don't know,' Alex says. 'Maybe it's because she was always pushing me to look older and act older, and this would have confirmed it. Me being a woman and all. Maybe I didn't want to be one yet. I was thirteen.'

It sounds as though she has put thought into this. I wonder what else she thinks about, what troubles her. We round the bottom of the dormant volcano.

'Hey, Alex?' Sid asks. 'Did you ever get that

134

not-so-fresh feeling?'

'Sid, shut it.'

'Are you sure he knows what's going on?' I ask. 'Because he sure doesn't act like he knows our family is having a difficult time.'

'Dad,' Alex says, and she says this so abruptly and loudly that I brake and pay attention to the road.

'Go back,' she says.

'Back where?' We're alongside Kapiolani Park. Joggers are everywhere. One crosses the street in front of me. His shorts are slit up the sides of his legs. I can see his dark leg hair matted down with sweat. An iPod is strapped around his biceps.

I hear the back window go down. 'Watch it, dick spank,' Sid yells.

'Just turn at the fountain and go back,' Alex says.

'Why?'

'I thought I saw something. I'm not sure. Just drive around.'

I turn toward the coast, then loop around at the fountain onto Kalakaua and backtrack. 'Is this far enough?'

'I think so,' she says. 'Don't pull out.'

'That's what she said,' Sid says.

'Shut up!' Alex yells. 'Just pull up to the stop sign.'

I do as she says.

'Look.' She points to the house across the street.

It's a light blue cottagelike home with white plantation shutters. The home is for sale. Joanie always used to push us to move to town, to this side of the island, where her friends live, away from Maunawili, where it rains. I never wanted to live on this side, with the joggers and gaudy mansions on

135

Kahala Avenue. Alex likes this side, too, or at least she used to. The cottage is across the street from the ocean side of the road, but it's prime Diamond Head real estate and remodeled to look old.

'It's really nice,' I say. 'But the avenue.' I point to the cars speeding by. 'It would be hard to get out of the driveway.'

'No,' she says. 'Look at the sign.'

I squint to read the for-sale sign and see his name and understand why it sounds so familiar. I pass his name every day, embossed in white and blue: BRIAN SPEER. REAL ESTATE BROKER. 978-7878.

In the photo, I can see his dark hair. I can see his confidence. He looks like an advertisement for teeth whitening. He looks like he's in love.

'No way,' Sid says.

'Now you know what he looks like,' Alex says.

I stay at the stop sign and we look at his picture, not speaking for a while.

'Are you satisfied?' she asks.

'No,' I say.

# 20

I memorized his number but haven't called. I don't know what to say. The number keeps running through my head. I know I'll have to dial it eventually.

I'm sitting alone at the dining room table, looking at our yard and the mountain. I'm drinking whiskey and feeling old. I couldn't go to any more houses after I saw his picture. I just wanted to come home. The phone is in my hand. If I dial the number, I'll just get his work voice mail, since it's nine at night. I'll call and listen to his voice and then hang up. I guess I'm stalling, because once I dial his number, it's as though I'm committing myself to something, locked in to a contract.

I dial to hear his voice. On the third ring, I get the recording: 'Hi, this is Brian. Sorry I missed your call. If you leave me a message, I'll get back to you as soon as I can.'

What kind of businessman says, 'hi'? I remember being reprimanded by my mother whenever I said 'hi' instead of 'hello.' His voice is strong, almost impatient, which is good. You want to make clients feel you're doing them a favor by taking their money. At the beep, I hang up and walk down the hall toward Scottie's room. I hear Esther reading and walk past, but when I get near my room, I hear both of my girls laughing hysterically. I remember Esther saying that the nursery rhymes make Scottie laugh with pure delight. I backtrack down the hall to listen to her read.

'"Little Jack Jingle, he used to live single."'

'Read the one about the rooster again,' I hear Alex say.

'I already read that three times.'

'One more time,' Scottie says.

I hear pages turning and then: '"Oh, my pretty cock. Oh, my handsome cock, I pray you do not crow before day. And your comb . . ."'

I can't hear the rest because of the laughter. I shake my head and continue to my empty room. I'm surprisingly pleased that Scottie knows 'cock' has another meaning and that she isn't genuinely enthralled by nursery rhymes. I'm also pleased that my girls are having a laugh together—I haven't

137

heard this in some time. Or perhaps ever. Alex would hardly come out of her room when she lived at home. Still, their laughter excludes and saddens me. I feel I'm stepping in too late for this father thing to really work. And why can't they laugh at other things, normal things?

'Hey, boss.'

I turn to see Sid coming out of Alex's bedroom in his boxers and no shirt.

'Did you call him?' he asks.

'It's none of your business,' I say. 'And you're not sleeping in that room. And put some clothes on, please.'

'Why?' he asks.

'I think you should go home,' I say.

'Alex wouldn't like that,' he says.

This is true, and I know if I forced the issue, I'd have to deal with her rage.

'You can sleep in the extra room,' I say. 'Take it or leave it. And I think you're going to want me to trust you.'

He rubs his stomach. It's got too many muscles. It looks unnatural. I sense my own stomach and suck it in.

'We're going to do what we're going to do,' he says.

'Yeah, but I'm not going to make it easy,' I say. I remember my boyhood. Yes, kids will find a way to do whatever it is they're going to do, but I remember that finding a place to have sex was one of the hardest things in the world. A girl won't have sex just anywhere. A woman might, but not a girl.

My room is right next to Alex's. I move from side to side. 'Creaky floors,' I say.

He laughs. 'Don't worry. I was just joking. We're

138

not like that. It's not about that. I wouldn't sleep in her room anyway.'

The light blue on his face has become black, with a hint of deep red like a berry stain around his eye.

'He's nobody,' Sid says. 'Just call him. Raise hell.'

I turn around and walk back toward my room. I think of Sid's hand beginning to block the hit and then coming back down and clutching his thigh. He must have decided to take the punch. I could ask, but I don't want a reason to like him.

When I get to my room, I call Brian again and listen to his voice mail, but this time I find that his voice and words and tone relax me. I realize that he doesn't intimidate me, as a true competitor should. I imagine him sitting in one of those homes, wiping down the counters, baking bread to make the staged rooms cozy. I imagine him dusting. He's nobody. In fact, he could work for me.

After the beep, I say, 'Hello, Brian.' I pause. 'I'm interested in the house on Kalakaua. The blue one with the plantation shutters.'

I hear the girls laugh again. I leave my number, hang up, and remain still, as if movement would ruin everything. What do I want? Just to see him? To humiliate him? To measure myself against him? Maybe I just want to ask him if she ever loved me.

# 21

The next day we go to the hospital. It's Alexandra's second time seeing her mother since the accident. She came when Joanie was first admitted and hasn't been here since. She stands near the end of the bed, her hand on Joanie's leg, which is covered with a blanket. She's looking at her mother as if she's about to say something, but I wait and she doesn't.

I notice all the cans of macadamia nuts in the room and see that Scott was being literal. He was going to give Joanie the things she always wanted and craved.

'Say something,' Scottie whispers.

Alex looks at Scottie, then looks back at her mother, who is still hooked up to the machines.

'Hi, Mom,' she says.

'Tell her you were drunk,' Scottie says. 'Tell her you're an alcoholic.'

'I guess it's in the genes,' Alex says.

'Girls,' I say, but I can't think of what I should reprimand them for. 'Be serious.'

Joanie looks as though she has just been washed. She has no makeup on, and her dark hair seems damp. Suddenly, I want to get the girls out of here. I know they don't know what to say, and it's making them feel guilty. Maybe they shouldn't have to see this. Maybe they shouldn't be serious. Maybe I'm wrong and shouldn't want them to spend every last moment in this room.

'Where's Sid?' I ask. It feels strange, asking about him.

'He's smoking a cigarette,' Alex says.

'Tell her you're sorry,' Scottie says.

'For what?' Alex says.

'For being drunk. For not being a boy. Mom wanted boys. That's what Grandma told me. We're girls.'

'Sorry for being bad,' Alex says. 'For wasting Dad's money on coke and liquor. Money you could have used for face lotion. I'm sorry.'

'Alex,' I say.

140

'Dad lets me have Diet Coke,' Scottie says.

'Sorry for everything,' Alex says, and then she looks up at me and says, 'Sorry, Mom, that Dad wasn't good enough for you.'

'Alex, you're out of line. Stop talking that way now.'

'Or what? Are you going to ground me? Or ship me to some other school? Are you going to give me a time-out?'

I don't know what to say or do—I don't want to yell 'Your mother is dying' in front of Scottie—so I resort to what I used to do: I grab Alex's shoulder, pull my hand back, and spank her.

'You got served!' Scottie says.

'Scottie, step into the hall.'

'But she's the one out of line.'

I raise my hand. 'Now.'

Scottie runs into the hall.

'Did you just spank me?' Alex asks.

'You have no right to talk to your mother that way. She's going to die, Alex. These are your last words. She's your mother. She loves you.'

'I have every right to speak this way, and so do you.'

'Yesterday you were in tears. I know you love her and have more to say.'

'I'm sorry. I don't. I do, but not right now. I'm mad right now. I can't help it.'

Alex has lowered her voice and seems sincere. I believe her, or at least I understand her. 'It's not going to get us anywhere,' I say. 'Being angry. Fine—so your mom wasn't satisfied with us. Let's try and satisfy her now. Think about the good things. The good parts. And I don't want you to say this stuff in front of Scottie. Don't ruin her

141

for Scottie.'

'How can you be so calm and forgiving?' Alex asks. I don't know the answer to that right now. I don't want to tell her that I'm furious and humiliated and ashamed of my anger toward Joanie. How do I forgive my wife for loving someone else? I think of Brian. I never considered how he must be dealing with this. He can't see her. He can't talk to her. He can't grieve, really. I wonder if Joanie misses him from her coma, if she wishes he could be with her instead of us.

'I can be angry later,' I say. 'I just want to understand her, I guess.'

We face Joanie once more.

'Say something nice,' I say.

'I always wanted to be like you,' Alex says to her mother, and then she shakes her head. 'I am like you. I'm exactly like you.' She says this as though it has just occurred to her. 'That felt so dramatic. That came out wrong.'

'No,' I say. 'It's fine. You are like her, and that's good.'

'She knows all the other stuff,' she says. 'She knows I love her. I just want to say the things she doesn't know.'

'She knows those things, too,' I say. 'You don't need to say them.'

'I heard you got spanked.' Sid walks into the room with Scottie at his heels. She's enamored with him. All morning she would take his hat off and run away shrieking as he chased after her. She doesn't copy me anymore. She copies Sid.

'Hi, Joanie,' he says. He walks to her bed. 'I'm Sid, Alex's friend. I've heard all about you. Tough chick like you, I'm thinking you're going to make

142

it out okay. I'm not a doctor, but that's just what I think.'

I see Alex and Scottie smiling at him and almost yell, *He's wrong! She's not going to make it.*

'I'm staying at your house to help Alex. She talks to me. I'm helping her out.'

Alex seems mollified. She walks toward the head of the bed and touches Joanie's cheek. Scottie presses into me and stares at Alex's hand on their mother's cheek.

'Don't worry,' Sid says. 'Your husband's got me on lockdown at night. He's holding down the fort. And your pops can pack a mean punch, boy. Look at this.' He moves the right side of his face toward Joanie. 'Wow,' he says. 'You're beautiful.'

Scottie walks toward the bed and stands beside Sid. The room is quiet for a while as Sid stands over my wife and looks at her face. I clear my throat, and he walks to the window and lifts the curtain. 'Nice day,' he says. 'No clouds. Not too hot.'

I look at my wife, almost expecting her to respond. She would like Sid, I'm pretty sure about that.

'Reina just texted me!' Scottie yells. 'She's here. She's here in the hospital.'

'Dammit, Scottie, I said no. No Reina.'

'You said Thursday she could come, and it's Thursday. I need her. And I really want her to meet Mom, okay? And Sid—Reina will totally appreciate his personality. And I want her to meet Alex.'

'What about me?'

'You, too,' she says.

'I don't think it's right.' When I told her Reina could come, I didn't know my wife was dying.

'But Dad. Alex gets Sid.'

143

'Fine,' I say, not wanting to argue or even talk. 'If that's what you need. Then fine.' And of course it's fine. Whatever helps. Scottie runs out into the hall.

'Great,' I say. 'You guys ready for this?'

*       *       *

Moments later, REINA appears in the doorway with Scottie standing behind her, presenting her to us. Reina looks around as though the room is dirty.

'Dad, this is Reina. Reina, that's my sister and Sid, and that's my mom on the bed.'

Reina puts her hand in front of her and wiggles her fingers. She's wearing a terry-cloth tennis skirt and a hooded terry-cloth sweatshirt. Both are emblazoned with a logo that says SILVER SPOON.

'So this is your mother.' She walks to the foot of Joanie's bed. 'I guess it's true. That's one down.'

I look at Alex, but she seems just as bewildered as I am. Scottie stands next to her friend and touches her mother's shoulder. 'Should I shake her hand?' Reina asks.

'If you want,' Scottie says.

'No, thanks,' Reina says.

'This is ridiculous,' Alex mumbles.

I didn't even know little girls were made this way. Reina doesn't give us notice. I feel like her servant. Sid looks at her with his brow furrowed as if she's the most difficult equation he has ever seen.

Reina carries a bag the size of a missile. Scottie walks away from the bed and goes to stand beside Sid. He puts his hand on her head and ruffles her hair. Scottie leans against him, and when Reina turns around, she looks at them and nods. Then she looks at her watch.

144

'Where's your mom?' I ask.

'At the salon,' she says.

'She didn't come here with you? Who's with you?'

'No one's with me,' she says. 'I mean, my mom's helper is in the car waiting for me, but no one's, like, *with me* with me.'

There's something about Reina's voice that makes me want to shoot her with a BB gun. If she were to hurt herself and scream in pain at this very moment, I would smile before I sought help.

'Look, girls. Why don't you talk outside, get an ice cream or something—'

'Too many carbs,' Reina says.

'What?'

'Carbs,' she says.

'Get a piece of lettuce, then, and after that, Reina, you should probably meet your helper—don't want to keep her waiting—'

'Him waiting. He's a Samoan with a heart of gold.'

'Okay, him waiting, and Scottie, you'll come back so we can have our family time together.'

'That's okay,' Reina says. 'I'm done.' She looks at Scottie and waves. 'You aren't a liar after all.'

Scottie darts her eyes among Sid, her sister, and me. I wonder what Reina is talking about.

'Don't you want to hang out?' Scottie says, pushing herself off of Sid.

'No, I have to choreograph this dance sequence.' Reina reaches into her purse and looks at her text-messaging gadget and rolls her eyes. 'Justin is so ree,' she says. 'Okay, I'll see you at the club. Hope your mom gets better. Smooches.'

We all stare after her with our mouths open.

145

After she's gone, I ask Scottie, 'What did she mean by "You aren't a liar after all"? And what's "ree"? What does that mean, "Justin is so ree"? Why'd she call you a liar? What is wrong with that girl?'

'She didn't believe that mom was sleeping and . . .' Scottie pauses and looks at Sid. Her face takes on a cherry tomato–like hue. 'And "ree" is short for retarded.'

'And . . .' Alex says.

'And that's all,' Scottie says.

'So you just had to prove to that twat that Mom was in a coma?' Alex asks. 'What the fuck is in your skull? A bunch of stupid pills?'

'Shut up, you motherless whore,' Scottie says.

'Whoa,' Sid says. 'Easy there.'

'What else did she think you were lying about?' Alex asks.

I think of Scottie cozying up to Sid and the way Reina looked them over.

'Was it about Sid? Did you say something about Sid?'

'No!' she says.

'You don't need to make things up for that girl,' I say. 'She may do things with boys, but that doesn't mean you do things, too.' I now feel it's my only duty in life to make sure Scottie doesn't resemble Reina in any way, because I know the potential is latent within her, quickly surfacing.

'I just told her he was my boyfriend so she'd get off my back,' Scottie says.

'You're such an idiot,' Alex says.

'Whatever. He told me he's not your boyfriend. He probably finger-fucks thousands of girls.'

'Scottie!' I yell.

Alex has a wounded look in her eyes. 'I don't

146

care,' she says. 'It's not like we're together.'

Sid opens his mouth to say something, but then he just shakes his head. I look at Joanie, lying there silent.

'Your phone's vibrating,' Scottie says. She takes my cell phone out of her pocket, the phone she has stolen from me to text her friend. She doesn't even care that she has disobeyed. She doesn't care that she said 'finger-fucked' in front of me. It's as though I'm not a father.

I don't recognize the number, so I don't answer. I like to let people leave messages, and then I'll call back after I rehearse what to say.

'You never answer your phone,' Scottie says. 'What if someone needs help?'

'Then they can leave a message and I'll call right back.'

Alex takes the phone out of my hands. 'Hello?' she says.

'What the—? Do I not exist, girls? Do you realize I'm in charge here?'

Scottie whispers, 'Who is it?'

'Oh, no,' Alex says. 'This is the right number. This is his assistant . . . Sharon.'

Scottie opens her mouth, delighted. I've always been impressed by Alex's effortless ability to lie.

'That sounds nice,' Alex says, then punches me lightly on the arm. 'Where? Great. And for how long? Okay. Well, thanks. Maybe we'll peek in on Sunday. Thanks so much. Okay.'

She closes the phone.

'Well?'

'That was a *Realtor,* Dad, from *Brian's* office. She says she'd be happy to show you the house you called about. Well done, Dad. Very clever.'

147

'Good one, King,' Sid says.

'What about Brian?' I ask. I feel strange talking about this with Joanie in the room. I position myself so that I face away from her.

'He's on Kauai,' she says.

'For how long?'

'Until the eighteenth.'

'Did you get a number where I can reach him?'

'No. What do you want to say to him?' Alex asks, and again I'm stumped.

'What are you guys talking about?' Scottie weaves in between us.

'Do you think he knows about Mom?' Alex asks.

'Of course,' I say. It occurs to me that he most likely knows she's in the hospital, but he couldn't possibly know that these are Joanie's last weeks or even days to live. I wonder what they did together. My wife and Brian. I think about what Kai said or insinuated: that I drove Joanie to have an affair. That my chilliness or aloofness led her into his arms. I thought we had something special, that she didn't need as much tending to as other women do.

I look at the macadamia nuts and the pictures of motorcycles and boats Scott taped to the walls. I see gardenias, her favorite flower, and I see a bottle of wine.

'Are we still going to people's houses to tell them about the party?' Scottie asks.

Alex shrugs, and I feel bad that I've made her make up these lies, even though she probably likes doing it.

'No,' I say. 'We're done with that.'

'When is the party?' Scottie asks.

I dust some sand off Scottie's T-shirt. Where does she get these shirts? I'm going to have to get her some new clothes. The shirt has a picture of an elephant on its back, legs in the air, tongue hanging out of its mouth like a playground slide. WASTED, it says, and I notice the beer cans scattered around the desert in the background.

*When is the party?* I wonder, and I realize that this would be a good way to tell the rest of the people on my list. I can't continue on my trail. I'll make them come to me. Again I'll have to talk to Dr. Johnston and tell him to hold on. Wait. I want to make sure everyone has the chance to say goodbye. I want to make sure all the right people are here.

# 22

Almost everyone is here except for Kent Halford, who's in Sun Valley, and Bobbie and Art, who often don't show up to anything and never bother to make excuses. I had Alex and Sid take Scottie to a movie.

The sun is going down. I have platters of sushi and fruit and lavosh on the dining room table, and everyone stands around the table with cocktail glasses and chopsticks in their hands. It's like a party, and I'm beginning to feel terrible because they don't know why they're here. They don't realize that they're the remnants of people I still need to inform.

I've let my guests chat and mingle for a while, and now it's time. I'm ready. I walk to the head of the table so I can see everyone. I clear my throat. I need to just say it, get it out, and then I can back up.

'Everyone,' I say. 'I know you have all asked

about Joanie tonight, and I've given some ambiguous answers, but I want to tell you that Joanie's coma is permanent. Soon she will not be receiving any artificial help. She's not going to make it through this.'

Buzz laughs at something Connie says, and Lara whispers something. Buzz's smile fades.

'I'm sorry to do it this way. I just wanted to tell you in person. You're all our dear friends, our best friends. I appreciate everything you've done for us. Goddammit.' My throat burns and my eyes water, which isn't how I planned it. I had a good speech. I practiced it, and this didn't happen when I practiced. Everyone is looking at me, and then the women begin their approach. I hug every one of them, Lara, Kelly, Connie, and Meg, inhaling their perfume, hiding tears in their hair.

'Are you sure?' Connie asks. 'You're sure?'

'Yes,' I say.

'Can we see her?' Lara asks.

'Yes,' I say. 'Please see her. Now, or tomorrow morning, or when you get a chance. That's what I wanted to tell you. That's why you're here.'

'What about Kai?' Lara asks.

'I've already told her.'

Russell and Tom walk up to me. I feel bad for Russell, who has a sheepish grin on his face as he reaches to hug me. It's the same look I get when someone tells me bad news. I can't help it—I just grin, stupidly. Russell pats my back roughly, and my chin presses into his shoulder.

'Did two doctors make this determination?' Orson asks. He's a plaintiff's attorney with an abundance of female clientele he calls his Suing Circle. 'Because you need the diagnosis of two

150

doctors.'

I stare at him.

'Of course,' he says. 'You know what you're doing.'

'How long?' Kelly asks. 'What happens now?'

'Not long,' I say. 'That's all I know. And it would be great if you all went in the next few days so the girls can have their time alone. I mean, if you want to go in. You don't have to.'

Kelly's new boyfriend seems relieved. I see him trying to hide the fact that he's chewing something. Kent Halford's son, Kent, Jr., doesn't even try to hide his appetite. He spreads the Brie onto the cracker and pushes it into his mouth. I like that he's eating, that he's doing what he wants to be doing, though I suppose he always has. I remember when he used to live next to us; he stole our tractor in the middle of the night and rode it to the H3 lookout to meet his friends. He rode it back inebriated, and I found him on the tractor doing doughnuts on our front lawn. I walk over to him and spread some cheese on a cracker. I know his grandfather just died, and Kent was extremely close to him. I'm assuming his grandfather's death will give Kent license to either really screw off or try to get his act together.

'This sucks,' he says.

'I know,' I say.

'I really like Mrs. King. She's always so nice to me.'

'She likes you,' I say.

He's deep in thought. He's such a better guy than his father. I like the way he seems to be working his hardest with the hand he's been dealt.

'I've stolen beer from your outdoor fridge,' he

says. 'I've done it a lot.'

'I know,' I say.

Buzz walks up to us and shakes his head. 'I can't believe this is happening. That motherfucker Troy.'

'Don't say that.' I look around at the guests, Connie and Kelly huddling together to talk about Joanie, about me. Kelly's boyfriend and Meg's new husband, Kula, standing together on the lawn with their cocktails, looking at the mountain, not knowing what else to do. Russell sits on the arm of a chair, close to the bar. Meg: Who knows what she's thinking as she gathers empty cups and plates. She and Joanie always seem to be annoyed at each other; they bicker often and openly, a testament to their closeness. Orson seems to be lecturing Lara, perhaps listing all of the things to blame: Queen's Hospital, the cigarette boat, Howard Aaron, the owner of the boat, Troy Cook, the engine, the wheel, the rough offshore waters, the love of competition and speed.

Lara walks over to me. 'What about Shelley?' she asks.

'I've told her. I've told everyone who I think needs to be told. I've called Troy.'

'We're missing someone,' Meg says. She goes over to Kent and takes the pieces of sushi out of his hand and glares at him.

'Mom? What the hell? I love sushi.'

'He can eat the sushi, Meg.'

The guests stare at me, expecting more, as they should.

'I need to get out of here,' I say so that just Buzz and Kent can hear.

'You go,' Buzz says. 'I'll take care of it. We all understand. Don't even say another word.'

152

I stare at the cheese, the crackers, the tiny red eggs in the sushi.

'I'm sorry, you guys,' I say. 'I know you want me to say more, to explain. She has a living will, you see. That's why.'

'Stop,' Lara says so everyone can hear. 'You don't need to say another word. It's been a while, Matt. We were prepared, we understand. We are here for you and stand by your side.'

Lara and Joanie have this hula group. The last time I saw Lara was in my living room, practicing with the other women, their bare feet patting the carpet, their arms drawing a large circle in the air, their gazes following their hands as if to say, *Look at this abundance. What a beautiful place.* I feel myself beginning to cry and take a drink of Kent's Coke, which tastes strongly of rum. He looks at me with alarm in his eyes and I pat his back. 'Boy,' I say. 'That's something.'

The rum is wonderful on my throat. Buzz is standing so close to me, it's like he's the Secret Service. 'You guys should go,' I say. 'If you could get everyone going . . .'

Buzz claps his hands together. 'Okay, everyone. We should let the family have their time alone now.'

I feel my face reddening. 'Please take your time,' I say, but they get the hint and understand that they're being ushered out. The men come first, shaking my hand so that I feel like the godfather, with Buzz next to me overseeing the farewells. The women come next, giving me fierce hugs that hurt a little. 'Is there anyone else we can tell?' Meg says. 'We're not missing anyone? I'd be mortified if we missed somebody.'

153

Kent finishes his drink. 'Mom, if we think of anyone, we'll let him know.' He hugs me, then takes his mother's hand and leads her out. 'We love you, Matt,' I hear her say. I thank Buzz, who momentarily forgets that he, too, needs to leave. 'I'm going to lie down,' I say. 'Be in touch.' I turn and walk away, concentrating on the smooth stone walkway, trying to make it to a couch or a bed where I can take a moment to rest. I am satisfied that I did it this way, even though it was hard. It's something Joanie would have wanted. I remember the things her father brought for her—the wine, the pictures, the chocolates, symbols of her desire—and when I get to the den, I find myself thinking of the things I can bring, the symbols and mementos she would like from me, and a thought comes to me that I wish had never occurred. I think of the trail I blazed from house to house, the people I rounded up to say goodbye.

What about him? I never considered that he could be the one who knows and loves her best. I never considered that this is what she wants most of all. He doesn't know what's happening, and this is unfair. If I put my emotions aside, I can see the pain his unawareness could bring—to him, to her, and possibly, eventually, to me. Now I know who's missing and what I need to do. I need to tell him to return from Kauai to say goodbye to Joanie. I need to write him onto my map. I need to bring him home to her.

# 23

The kids saw a movie about two boys who are stoned and crave hamburgers. I try to listen to Alex explaining that it was about much more than their yearning for hamburgers. I tell her I'm sure it was.

'Do you think he deserves a chance to say goodbye?' I ask Alex.

She's standing in the door of my room, which means she's in a good mood. When she'd get home sometimes after an evening out with friends, she'd stand in our doorway and tell us about her night while Joanie and I lay in bed. She'd make me and her mother laugh, and this would make her stand there longer, trying to prolong our amusement. I love when she stands in my doorway.

'You mean *him*? Tell *him* to say goodbye?'

'Yes,' I say. 'Brian.'

'No,' Alex says. 'That's crazy.'

'Is it?'

She looks at the Dictaphone in my hand.

'Are you recording this?'

'No, Alex, I was summarizing a deposition.'

'How can you work?'

'How can you see a movie? How can you have a friend over?'

She looks away. Half of the room is bright from my lamp. The other side is dark, the sharp silhouette of the mountain framed by the window running across the room. The image always reminds me of a panoramic picture.

'You're going to tell him to come back to say goodbye?' she asks.

155

'Yes.' Although I feel I should at least say 'fuck you' before all the Good Samaritan stuff.

'You're a better person than I am,' Alex says.

'No, I'm not.'

She shakes her head and I feel I'm appealing to someone much older.

'I'd like you to come to Kauai with me,' I say. 'And Scottie. I think it would be good to get her away from the hospital for a day. We can leave in the morning, find him, and be home tomorrow night. If it takes us a day longer, that's fine, but we won't stay more than two nights. That's our deadline. If we don't find him, then at least we know we tried.'

'And this will make you feel better somehow?'

'It's for her,' I say. 'Not for him or me.'

'What if he's a wreck? What if he loses his shit?'

'Then I'll take care of him.' I imagine Brian Speer wailing on my shoulder. I imagine him and my daughters by Joanie's bed, her lover and his loud sobs shaming us. 'Just so you know, I am angry. I'm not this pure and noble guy. I want to do this for her, but I also want to see who he is. I want to ask him a few things.'

'Just call him. Tell his office it's an emergency. They'll have him call you.'

'I want to tell him in person. I haven't told anyone over the phone, and I don't want to start now.'

'You told Troy.'

'Troy doesn't count. I just need to do this. On the phone he can escape. If I see him in person, he'll have nowhere to go.'

We both look away when our eyes meet. She hasn't crossed the border into my room. She never

156

does during her nighttime doorway chats.

'Were you guys having trouble?' Alex asks. 'Is that why she cheated?'

'I didn't think we were having trouble,' I say. 'I mean, it was the same as always.'

This was the problem, that our marriage was the same as always. Joanie needed bumps. She needed rough terrain. It's funny that I can get lost in thoughts about her, but when she was right in front of me, I didn't think much about her at all.

'I wasn't the best husband,' I say.

Alex looks out the window to avoid my confession. 'If we go on this trip, what will we tell Scottie?'

'She'll think we're going on a trip of some sort. I want to get her away from here.'

'You've already said that,' Alex says. 'Why should I go?'

'You're the only person I have,' I say. 'And I want us all to be together. It will be good for us.'

'Oh, so now I'm back in the picture again.'

'Alex. Something bigger than you is occurring right now. I'm sorry about your unhappy childhood.'

She glares at me in that special way of hers and Joanie's that makes me feel worthless and foul-smelling.

'So we'll tell Scottie we're going on a vacation while Mom is in the hospital?'

'It's for a day or two,' I say. 'Scottie's been in the hospital every day for almost a month now. She needs a break. It's not good for her. I'd like you to be in charge of answering any questions she may have. She looks up to you. She'll hang on whatever you say.'

157

I'm hoping a leadership role, a specific chore, will make Alex act like an adult and treat Scottie well.

'Can you do that?'

She shrugs.

'If you can't handle things, let me know. I'll help. I'm here for you.'

Alex laughs. I wonder if there are parents who can say things to their kids like 'I love you' or 'I'm here for you' without being laughed at. I have to admit it's a bit uncomfortable. Affection, in general, is unpleasant to me.

'What if Mom doesn't make it for two days?'

'She will,' I say. 'I'll tell her what we're doing.'

Alex looks uncomfortable with this idea, that what I'll say will make her mother want to live. 'I'm bringing Sid,' she says. 'If he doesn't come, then I'm not going.'

I'm about to protest, but I see the look in her eyes and know this is yet another battle that I'm bound to lose. Something about this guy is helping her. And Scottie seems to like him. He can keep her distracted. He can work for me.

'Okay,' I say. 'Deal.'

\*　　　\*　　　\*

I call the Realtor who spoke to Alex, and she doesn't know, or won't tell me, where Brian's staying, but she does tell me he's in Hanalei. I print out a list of Hanalei hotels and call them all with no success. I make a reservation for two rooms at Princeville; I'm surprised he's not staying there. Either he's staying in an unlisted B and B, he's rented a house, or he hasn't checked in. I don't know what to do.

He needs to be found, but I'm sure I can go and run into him somehow. It's what happens on islands, especially in the miniature town of Hanalei.

I think about what else I need to take care of before I go. I need to finish that motion, ask someone to cover a deposition. I need to get my daughters to join forces with me. I need to get Sid to go home. I need to be with my wife, to forgive my wife. I need to be able to look at her without thinking of him.

I need to talk to Joanie's doctor. I call Sam at the hospital, and when he isn't there, I call him at home.

'No,' he says. 'I can't put it off any longer.'

'I just need a few more days,' I say. 'One more day. I need to go to Kauai to get someone.'

He tells me he needs to abide by the will now that the permanent coma assessment has been made. Tomorrow it has to be done. 'But it's okay,' he says. 'You can go. You have time.'

I pack my bags and hope he's right.

159

# PART III

# The Offering

# 24

It's a beautiful morning.

I look at Joanie's side of the closet and touch her clothes. Then I close my eyes and walk into the clothes, letting her blouses and dresses fall over me. Today her ventilator will be removed, her room will be stripped of the things that sustain her, and our family will leave her on her own. I don't feel good about this, yet it needs to be done, and as the doctor says, it can be done. He says it will be good for the girls, so I let myself look forward to the trip. Maybe we can use this time away to create something special, something that acknowledges it will be the three of us now. I want the experience to be successful.

I leave the closet and see the girls slowly entering the bedroom.

'We're packed,' Scottie says.

'Then let's go,' I say, walking toward the hall.

The girls don't move.

I realize they're eyeing my room, their mother's room. They're looking at the place where their mother used to sleep.

I go to the dresser, pretending to gather more things so the girls can stay a bit longer. The birds are making a racket. I look out the window at the banyan tree and see the birds vying for position. One keeps getting pushed off, then flying back to the same spot.

The sun is glaring over the Ko'olaus, and a few clouds are floating in from Waimanalo, trapping the heat in our valley.

'When you sell our land, can we buy Doris Duke's estate and can I hire my own Samoan?' Scottie asks.

'No,' I say.

'Can I have Mom's diamonds?' she asks.

I turn to see Scottie on the bed, looking through the drawers of Joanie's nightstand. She takes a photo of the contents, which makes me feel like I'm at a crime scene.

'No, you can't have her diamonds,' Alex says.

'Why?' Scottie asks.

'Because you're a selfish little worm, and diamonds would implode as soon as they touched your ugly skin.'

'Alex!'

'Well, what a goddamn awful question. And I don't care that she's ten. I had my first beer when I was ten. She needs to grow up. And stop taking pictures. Why are you documenting this? Is this something you want to remember?'

'Yes,' Scottie says. 'When Mom comes back, I'll just ask her myself.' She puts her camera and the photograph on the dresser, then closes her mother's drawer. Fake pearls and real pearls. Fake diamonds and real diamonds. Intertwined necklaces glint in the photo. 'Let's go,' I say. 'We're racing the clock these next few days. We have no time for any of this.'

'Why are we racing the clock?' Scottie asks.

I ignore the question and walk briskly down the hall to the garage. The girls follow, bickering. 'On Xbox, I shoot pro sluts, so watch what you say,' Scottie says.

'Seriously,' Alex says. 'You're a spaz. Get some Ritalin.'

'Get some acne medication,' Scottie says. 'You have a volcano on your chin that's about to spurt like Mauna Kea.'

'Mauna Kea's dormant, asshole.'

'Your asshole's dormant.'

'You don't even know what that means, Scottie.'

'How do you know?'

'Shut up!' I yell, which makes me feel like my father-in-law. I put our bags into the trunk, furious yet at the same time thinking about what to do with Joanie's diamonds, jewelry, clothes. Of course Scottie can have her diamonds. I see that it's a practical question, yet I can't admit to Scottie that it's okay she asked.

'Where's Sid?' I ask. 'Why do I always have to ask where that idiot is?'

'Don't call him that,' Scottie says.

Sid comes out the back door.

'Did you lock it?' I say.

He goes back and I look to make sure he presses the lock in.

'Shotgun,' Scottie yells, but Alex opens the passenger-side door and sits down. Scottie has a virtual seizure until I force Alex to climb into the backseat. Before Scottie gets in, I say to Alex, 'Didn't we just talk about you helping me with her? You're acting like a complete dick. Come on. Get with it.'

I sit at the steering wheel, glowering at the stuff in our garage. There will be so much to clear out, to claim, to fight over.

Sid gets in the back. With him comes the scent of cigarettes and a fresh dose of marijuana, so strong I feel a contact high. Scottie plants herself in the front seat and buckles her seat belt. 'Go,' she says,

165

and even though I'm having second thoughts about all of this and am on the verge of either snapping or bawling, I go. I take this strange detour and hope for the best.

# 25

The security line is longer than it should be. Still, most of the people in line seem content, which is irritating. There's nothing worse than being angry and seeing tranquil faces all around you. Security is checking everyone's bags, even though we're just going inter-island.

'I swear they do this just to feel like real security, which isn't really something to aspire to,' Alex says.

Thank God my daughter isn't a happy person. We watch a man rifle through the bag of the woman ahead of us. Her hair is crispy and white, and her back is rounded with a bump the size of a hard hat. The man shakes a package, then puts it back in her bag. *It could have been a grenade,* I want to say. *If you're going to check, then check.*

Four boys right in front of us are being asked where their shoes are.

'We knew we had to take 'em off,' one says. 'So we never went wear any.'

'Never wore any,' Scottie says. The boys look back at her. They all have shark's-tooth necklaces around their necks, and their stomachs are stout and hard. One carries a ukulele and has a tribal tattoo entwined around his right leg. Another wears a tank top that reveals the entire side of his torso, a black nipple, and a wild bushel of armpit hair. I look back at Scottie, pretending I don't know who she is.

'You need shoes,' the security woman says.

'Why?' the shortest boy of the group says. Security pulls a fish out of his cooler. It's black and its fat lips are parted, a gelatinous eye wide open. It looks appalled. The woman picks up the fish by its tail, and the three boys look on proudly.

'Gross,' Scottie says.

Alex takes Scottie by the sleeve and pulls her back and says something to her. 'Nice catch,' Sid says and all the boys nod. Another security officer comes to the table and waves me forward. I don't have much in my carry-on, just my wallet and some work in a binder. He looks at what's on top, then moves on to the girls, and I do all I can to keep myself quiet. *If I had a bomb,* I want to say, *wouldn't I do a better job of hiding it?* He skips Scottie's bag and checks Alex's with more thoroughness than he used with mine. He pulls out a pack of Marlboro Reds.

Scottie gasps and looks at me, her eyes wide open like the fish's. 'Are you going to spank her?'

The security guard looks at me and hesitates, then hands me the cigarettes.

I hand them back to him. 'She's an adult,' I say to him, but for Scottie to hear. 'She makes her own choices.'

With a sort of reverence, Scottie looks at the cigarettes being placed back in her sister's bag, and as we walk out to the gate, I sense something has shifted. Alex walks beside me and Scottie walks behind her, not saying a word. 'Were those your cigarettes?' Scottie asks Sid.

'No,' he says. He pats his pocket. 'Mine are here.'

167

She looks at me, almost angry that I'm not reprimanding her sister.

'Get over it, Scottie,' Alex says.

\*     \*     \*

During the flight, Scottie is quiet and Alex reads magazines about dangerously thin actresses. Scottie writes in a notebook. They sit on either side of me like wings. Sid is across the aisle. I look over and see him studying the laminated safety card with great concentration. The flight attendant passes out cartons of guava juice. The barefoot boys miraculously made it onto the plane; I can hear one of them playing the ukulele. My mind is blank. I feel I need a game plan, but I can't seem to think of one other than: *Find him.*

Scottie is writing down something with purpose.

Alex looks out the window, seeming defeated. I nudge her. 'What if the doctor's wrong?' she asks. 'What if she's okay and she'll wake up?'

'Even if,' I say, 'she'd be—' I try to think of a good word. 'She'd be broken.'

'I know,' Alex says. 'I get it.'

I look out the window at Kauai, its steep cliffs and sharp coast. I usually look forward to coming here. There are two-lane roads and one-lane bridges and long, deserted beaches. Everything moves at a slow, slack pace, and I hope to mimic the island's ease. I wonder what he's doing right now. If he's waiting to cross a bridge, if he's in a hotel boardroom or having a business lunch, if he's relaxing on the beach. I wonder if he knows what I look like, if he's been in my bedroom and has seen pictures of me on the dresser. I'm going to change

168

this man's life.

As we descend, I glance over at Scottie's paper to see what she's working on that has consumed her so. I read: *I will not make fun of big Hawaiians. I will not make fun of big Hawaiians.* This promise fills the page. I look over at Alex and gesture to Scottie.

'What?' Alex says. 'I handled it.'

*     *     *

Scottie watches for our bags with Sid, and I ask Alex what Scottie thinks we're doing on Kauai.

'I told her we're looking for a friend of Mom's.'

I look around the airport. I keep thinking I'll see Brian or at least someone I know. It's hard to go anywhere here without running into someone you know; you can't get lost on an island. I wonder if we should move, head for the hills of Arkansas or some ridiculous place.

Sure enough, I hear, 'Yo, Matt King!' and cringe, recognizing the voice of one of my cousins. I don't know which one. I don't even know all of their names—they all look the same, like chestnut horses. I turn to see Ralph, aka Boom—God knows what that's supposed to mean. All of the cousins have nicknames with mysterious origins that imply something rowdy or nautical. Ralph is wearing an outfit almost identical to mine: khakis and a Reyn's Spooner, rubber slippers and a briefcase, the briefcase proving he has some responsibilities in the world. I don't know what he does. I don't know what any of them do. To their credit, the cousins are not greedy or gaudy or ostentatious. Their sole purpose in life is to have fun. They Jet Ski, motocross, surf, paddle, run triathlons, rent islands in Tahiti. Indeed, some of the most powerful people in Hawaii look like bums or stuntmen. I think of our bloodline's progression. Our missionary ancestors came to the islands and told the Hawaiians to put on some clothes, work hard, and stop hula dancing. They make some business deals on the way, buying an island for ten grand, or marrying a princess and inheriting her land, and now their descendants don't work. They have stripped down to running shorts or bikinis and play beach volleyball and take up hula dancing.

Ralph slaps my back. He grins and nods repeatedly. He looks at Alex and I know he has forgotten her name. She walks away from us to Sid. I almost tug her back so I won't be alone with Ralph.

'You're looking tan,' I say.

He keeps grinning and says, 'All right.' I know that the tan has been sprayed on. 'Are you here to talk to some of the cousins?' he asks. 'Make sure they're happy with your choice?'

'No,' I say. 'Tell you the truth, I want to make a decision without being influenced by the majority.'

'Right,' he says and looks confused. 'How's Joanie?'

'She's the same,' I say.

'She's a strong lady,' Ralph says.

'Yes,' I say. 'She's strong.'

We both feign interest in the circling luggage.

'I saw her a few months ago,' he says. 'Right before . . . She looked good, too.' He stares into the distance. He slaps my back. 'She'll be fine.'

'I know,' I say, wanting to escape from this conversation, but then I see an opportunity. 'Hey, is your car here?'

'Yeah,' he says. 'You need a ride? Princeville?'

'That would be great.'

I see Sid carrying all of our bags. His eyes are bloodshot. The pot has made him mute. Am I supposed to confront him about smoking pot in my house? Is Alex doing it? Or do I just let it go? Sail away out of my care. Let it all go. Easy.

'You okay?' I ask Sid.

'What?'

'Are you all right, I said.'

'Yeah,' Sid says. 'Just thinking about some things.'

We follow Ralph to the parking lot. I force my shoulders down and take a deep breath. I watch my family walking ahead of me. They look normal from the back. They look good.

*     *     *

Ralph has a Jeep Wrangler, which thrills Scottie and even Alex to a barely perceptible extent. Sid's hair flies up, making him look as though he's being electrocuted. It's the most uncomfortable car I have ever been in. Even as we drive down smooth and flat roads, I feel as though we're out of control.

'I'm starving,' Scottie yells from the back, and then I hear, 'Ow,' and I wonder if Alex has hit her. I don't want to know.

'I notice you have a Ducati shirt on.' Ralph looks in the rearview mirror at Alex. 'Do you know how to ride?'

'Yes,' Alex says. 'My mom taught me.'

'What?' he yells over the wind.

'Yes!' Alex yells.

'Did your mom teach you? Or this guy?' He

171

punches my arm, and I look at the spot where his fist touched me.

'My mom,' Alex says.

Joanie rode a Ducati. It surprises me that Alex is wearing the shirt. 'Where did you see Joanie?' I ask Ralph. It would be so embarrassing if everyone knew about her lover but me. Her lover. Jesus.

'I saw her at the last shareholders' meeting,' Ralph says.

'Joanie?'

'Yeah. Remember?'

'Oh, sure,' I say, having no idea what he's talking about. 'I remember.' I imagine her jumping on a flight, going to a shareholders' meeting, then coming right back in time to pick up Scottie. That makes no sense.

'You're lucky you have someone that fired up speaking on your behalf.'

'Right,' I say.

'I'm hungry!' Scottie yells again.

Ralph careens off the main road and into Kapaa, then drives into the parking lot of the fish market. The gravel crunches loudly under his tires, and when he stops, we all fall forward then back. I give Alex money to get some poke to tide us over. Sid gets out of the car and Scottie follows. He raises his arms over his head and bends to the right and Scottie looks at his stomach.

When they walk toward the store, I ask, 'So, what did she say? At the meeting?'

'Oh, she was saying how it was ridiculous not to accept Holitzer's offer. He had a solid plan and he was going to open up so many opportunities for Kauai and so on. And as the largest shareholder and last direct descendant, you'd appreciate

172

everyone's support because it was going to happen with or without our consent. That's what she said. It kind of pissed people off. I don't know about Holitzer, though. He isn't the highest bidder. Don't we want to go with highest bid? Doesn't that make sense?'

'She liked his plan.' I look at Ralph, hoping for more clues. 'She liked that he'd lease some land to the conservancy. And with the rest, he's just selling off and subdividing, right?'

'And redeveloping when leases expire.'

'Sure,' I say. Her actions don't make sense. All the buyers' plans are pretty much the same. Everyone's going to bring in new businesses, develop the land, develop homes, then sell the land and the homes. Why would she sneak off to a meeting behind my back? Why would she bully my cousins?

'I want to work with you guys, Ralph. You know that, don't you? I know I have a big vote, but I'm not here to make people angry.'

'I'm heading to Princeville!' Ralph says.

'That's right,' I say. He's like a child.

'No way!'

I nod, not really knowing how to respond, but then I see that he's talking into one of those little headpiece phones, and I feel immensely foolish. The girls come out of the shop with cartons of poke and plastic forks. Sid carries a few candy bars and about five small bags of chips. We continue on, driving past a few of my ancestors' homes that have been turned into museums. I point them out to the girls. They've seen them before but look anyway. Ralph slows as we pass the estate, the tropical gardens, the tourists riding in carriages pulled by

Clydesdale horses.

'It used to be a sugar plantation,' Scottie says.

'That's right,' I say. I look at the house, thinking it strange that the ancient inhabitants have somehow shaped the lives of people they never met or even considered. Am I shaping the life of a bunch of people who haven't been born?

'I wish we lived in the old days,' Scottie says.

'We do,' Alex says. 'We will.'

This makes Scottie quiet. I wonder what's going through her head. Sid is going through all of the chips. Each bag is open on his lap. He hasn't said a word the entire trip. I keep waiting for one of his idiotic musings, but it doesn't come.

We begin to descend into Hanalei. 'Look,' I say to the girls. 'Look at that.'

I see the taro plantation below, warming in the sun. I imagine the valley doesn't look much different than it did a hundred years ago. The ocean beyond is dark blue, and as we approach the bottom of the hill, the stretch of beach unfolds before us. *Look*, I almost say again, because I have this urge to make sure they're seeing what will no longer be in our name. Why did Joanie go to that meeting? Why did she want Holitzer?

I try to think of more questions I could ask Ralph. I look back at the kids. 'Sid,' I say. 'You all right?'

'Doing good,' he says. 'Thanks.'

# 26

The girls and Sid stand next to the marble pillars in the lobby. I'm asking to exchange the two rooms for a deluxe suite. We will all stay together. The girls are impressed. They look at each other and grin. They don't realize I'm getting a suite because I don't trust them. I check again to see if Brian Speer is a guest, but he's not.

As we walk to the elevator, three girls walk toward us so quickly I'm afraid they might run us down.

'Alex!' they all scream. I notice my daughter wince before she yells back, 'Oh my God! What's up?'

'What are you doing here?' one asks. She has sunglasses straddling her head. A handbag swings on her elbow. She looks at Scottie and me as though what she fears is true: Alex is here with us, her family. Then she sees Sid. 'Oh my God, what's up?' She gives Sid a hug and then gives Alex a hug.

'What are *you* doing here?' Alex asks.

'Spring break,' says another girl, breaking from her cell phone, then going back to it: 'Just bring your suit and a few going-out clothes. Not dressy. Just cute clothes.' She eyes me as she talks.

I take Scottie to sit on a nearby bench.

'You guys should totally meet up with us,' I hear the blonde say.

Alex nods. 'For sure.'

I've never heard her speak this way. She's usually so quiet and grumpy. This chirpiness is unsettling.

The girls' voices get quiet and then escalate

175

in volume and I hear: 'I'm all, shut up!' from the blonde.

'Boo-ya,' the other girl says and laughs.

I look at Scottie, but she's just as lost.

'There are, like, choke people down there, but you should go. We just went. You should fully go.'

'It's so good to see you, doll. We miss you. You never come out. We'll call your room tonight, then? Or, Siddy, do you have your cell?'

'Yeah,' he says. 'But we're probably just going to chill.'

'Oh, I'm sad,' one of the mascot girls says. She makes a sad face. 'I'll call anyway.'

Alex grins ecstatically, but her enthusiasm doesn't seem real. I think it has less to do with her mother than with these girls. I wonder if mothers or involved parents do this all the time: watch their children interact with their peers, seeing things no one else does.

The girls strut past, waving their fingers at Scottie and me.

'Such bitches,' Alex says as we head to the elevator.

'Ho bags,' Scottie says.

'What does that mean, Scottie?' I ask.

She shrugs.

'Who taught you that?' I ask.

She points at her sister.

'They only asked me because Sid was with me,' Alex says.

'Can we go to the beach?' Scottie asks.

'Sure,' I say. 'We'll cruise the beach.' I look at Alex, but she stares ahead.

'You could have gone with them,' I say. 'Your friends.'

'They didn't ask,' she says.

I always thought Alex was one of the girls conducting the social scene. She has all the right equipment.

'The last time I hung out with those girls was at our house,' Alex says. 'You must have been working in your room or whatever. Mom was wasted. She wanted to go dancing. I wouldn't go, but my friends were all enthralled with her. So she took them. She just took them with her. Out dancing. And I stayed home.'

We stop on floors five, six, seven, eight, nine. I look to see all of the elevator buttons lit up. 'Jesus, Scottie. Is this fun for you?'

'Sid's the one who did it.'

'Are you serious?'

Sid laughs. 'It's funny.'

'Why didn't you ever stop Mom?' Alex asks me.

We finally get off on the right floor. Alex walks out first and Scottie follows, saying, 'Boo-ya, boo-ya, boo-ya,' down the hotel hall.

'I didn't know how,' I say.

'You didn't notice,' Alex says.

'But you're talking about your mom. Why don't you like those girls?'

'I like them,' she says. 'They just don't like me for some reason. They don't think of me.' She seems deep in thought, and when she looks at me, her eyes are watery. 'I've never understood it, really. They've just always made me feel bad. I don't think I like girls.'

'Your mom didn't, either.' I'm about to ask Alex what she sees in Sid. He's walking ahead of us and holding something over Scottie's head, making her jump up and down. He's suddenly alive. I don't

177

ask what Alex sees in him because I'm afraid my disapproval will make her latch on to him even more. That's how it works. I'll have to pretend he doesn't bother me and that I don't want to drown him in the bay. Something about him isn't right. Actually, a whole lot about him isn't right, but not until today in the car did I feel unnerved by him. His silence was so strange.

*     *     *

Alex is on the balcony of our hotel room. I slide the glass door and step out of our air-conditioned room and into the warm air.

She's smoking a cigarette and I sit down and stare at it with longing, not for smoking, necessarily, but for the memory of smoking. At eighteen I never would have fathomed that I'd be dealing with these sorts of problems someday. It would be so much easier to be a bad father. I'd love to smoke with my daughter, to sit here with an assortment of alcohol from the hotel mini-fridge, drinking from the bottles, then tossing them into the pool below. When I was young and on the verge of procreating, I thought kids would be like having my old college buddies back. We'd hang out and do stupid shit together.

'Put that out,' I say.

Alex takes a drag, then rubs the cigarette out on the bottom of her sandal, something I would have admired highly as a boy. A gesture like that almost assures me that she'll be fine in this world.

'You could at least smoke Lights,' I say. 'Like Sid.'

'I could,' she says. She puts her feet up on the

178

railing and leans back in the chair so that she's balancing on two posts. It reminds me of her mother. Joanie could never sit with all four posts on the floor.

'Mom's okay,' I say. 'I checked in, and she's breathing well, doing well.'

'That's good,' Alex says.

'You're doing better with Scottie,' I say. 'Thanks.'

'She's still all messed up.'

'She's just a kid. She's okay. She's not that bad.'

'It's Reina,' Alex says. 'She talks about her constantly. She told me Reina let a boy tongue her hole. That's what she said: "tongue her hole." '

'What's happening to you children?'

'She told me Reina's parents are letting her get a boob job when she turns sixteen because that's when puberty ends.'

'That girl was too much,' I say. 'I mean, did you get a look at her?'

I like talking about all the things that are wrong with another girl. I put my feet against the rail and slowly ease my chair off its front posts. The hotel is built into a cliff, and I look at the bay below, the dots of people, the whitecaps like stars in a dark blue sky. To the left, the Napali coast winds up into another horizon. Alex looks out at the dark sheet of ocean angrily, as though the sea is to blame.

'What about you, Alex? Are you okay? You're not . . . using, are you?'

'Am I using? God, you sound like such a tool.'

I don't answer.

'No,' she finally says. 'I'm not doing anything.'

'At all?' I ask. 'I smell pot. On Sid.'

'That's Sid,' she says. 'Not me.'

179

'You just stopped? Isn't it hard? It's an epidemic and whatnot.'

I realize we never even put her into rehab to make sure she stopped. She convinced us that she didn't have a problem, and it must have been easier for me to forget how well she lies.

'It's not an epidemic,' she says. 'I mean, it is, but not for someone like me. I'm not all ghetto.'

'So you just stopped?'

'Yes, Dad. It's not a big deal. Kids do drugs, then they stop. Besides, you sent me to boarding school, remember? I couldn't get it anymore. I guess Mom knew what she was doing.'

I don't know the proper way to respond to all of this. My mother would have burst into tears and wallowed in her room. My father would have sent me to the marines or shot me. Joanie sent her away, which seems just as bad, but what about me? I did nothing. No rehab, therapy, family discussions. Sending her off couldn't have been the right thing for us, for me, to do, yet it was certainly the easiest. I looked into the conflict from a distance, excusing myself, as though Alex and Joanie were discussing prom dresses.

'I don't do drugs anymore,' Alex says. 'But I still think they were fun.'

'Why are you being so honest with me?' I ask.

She shrugs and puts her chair down. 'Mom's dying.'

A part of me knows Alex will be fine, better than fine. I believe her, even, that drugs were a phase, a passing trend. Perhaps I did nothing because I don't have enough fear to be a good parent. I remember what it was like being a kid and being the son of my mother and father. When I was doing bad things,

I knew, as Alex knows, that no matter how hard I tried, I'd never get into trouble. Maybe kids with money resent this exemption, and it makes them aspire to destruction at an early age. Someone will catch us. We can get out of it somehow. What we do won't lead to the streets. I remember palling around with the boys and how our antics quickly turned into dinner-party anecdotes. This always made me feel like a failure, as if I didn't have it in me to sink as low as others. I wonder if Alex feels this as well: like an unsuccessful loser.

'I'm proud of you,' I say, because dads on TV always say this after candid conversations.

She rolls her eyes. 'Not much to be proud of.'

'Yes, there is,' I say. 'You've figured it out. We shipped you off. Let the dorm mother handle it. And now you're here. Helping me with Scottie. I'm sorry, Alex. I'm really sorry. Thank you for helping me.' She's the new mother, I realize. She assumed the role in an instant. I imagine her in a cup, hot water pouring over her. Instant Mom.

'Yeah, yeah,' she says.

And that's that, I guess. The King family drug talk.

We look out at the beautiful ocean, a view that must accompany thousands of awkward, sad, and beautiful moments.

'Is everything okay with Sid?' I ask. 'He was so quiet earlier.'

'He gets tired,' she says. 'He didn't have a nap, and he needs his nap.'

She looks over at me, obviously to see if I'm buying her story. She sees that I'm not. 'He's having a hard time right now,' she says.

'Oh, really? Well, so are we.'

181

'Just forget it,' she says. 'How are we going to find this guy?'

I think about this for a while. For a moment I forgot about him, that he's the reason we're here.

'You two are going to take Scottie to the beach. I'm going to make more calls. We're on an island, for Christ's sake. There's only about three degrees of separation here.'

She's silent, thinking it over. She stands and holds out her hand to help me up. I realize I'm fascinated with her. She's a person I want to know.

'We'll find him,' Alex says, and the determination in her voice makes me think that she may have a few things to say to him as well.


# 27

He's below me. He's on a working vacation, staying in one of the houses on the bay that I can probably see from this balcony. That's all his office would tell me. Shouldn't he be at my wife's bedside? Shouldn't I?

I stand on the balcony and look down at the coastline, then decide to put on my suit and head to the bay. I'll look for the girls. I'll look for Joanie's lover, and maybe I'll take a dip in the ocean and ride the waves on my stomach, as I did when I was a boy.

\*           \*           \*

The girls and Sid are sunbathing near the pier. I look at Scottie on her towel, her legs pressed

182

together, her head tilted toward the sun. I want her to be playing in the ocean. It seems critical that sunbathing should be put off as long as possible.

I stand over her to block the sun. 'Get up, Scottie. Throw a ball or something.'

She sticks her arm into the air. 'I need some color.'

'What happened to your scrapbook? Why aren't you doing that anymore?'

'It's stupid,' she says.

'No,' I say. 'It's really great. I liked what you were doing.' There's something different about her. I realize it's her breasts—they're huge. I see that she's stuffed her bikini top with wet balls of sand.

'What is that?' I say. 'Scottie. Your suit.'

She shields her eyes with her hand and looks down at her chest. 'Beach boobs,' she says.

'Take that out of there,' I say. 'Alex. Why'd you let her do that?'

Alex is on her stomach, with the straps of her top untied. She lifts her head toward Scottie. 'I didn't know. Take them out, stupid.'

Sid lifts his head. 'Honestly,' he says, 'big boobs look kind of fatty.'

'As Bebe says, boobs suck,' Alex says, 'and Sid's full of shit. He loves big boobs.'

'Who's Bebe?' Scottie lets the sand fall out of her top.

'Character from *South Park*,' Sid says. 'And I love small boobs, too, Alex. I'm an equal-opportunity employer.'

'You should scrapbook, Scottie,' I say. 'I want you to finish it. You need to keep up with school.'

She doesn't believe my concern, I can tell. Scrapbook equals babyhood—she can see that now, and I'm sure it was Alex who made her realize it.

'Any luck?' Alex asks.

'Yes,' I say. 'He's here in Hanalei. Right here.' I look up at the green yards that stretch to the houses.

'Who's here?' Scottie asks.

'The friend of Mom's I told you about,' Alex says.

'The comedian?'

Alex looks at me. 'Yeah,' she says. 'The comedian.'

'Interesting, Alex,' I say. 'Girls, want to take a dip?'

'No,' they both say.

'How about a walk? Maybe we'll see the comedian.'

'No,' Scottie says.

Alex ties her straps while lying on her stomach, then flips over and sits up. 'I'll walk.'

'I was just going to say I changed my mind and that I want to go for a walk,' Scottie says. More sand spills out of her top as she stands. Sid gets up and jumps, butting his head at the air in front of him.

'What are you doing?' I ask.

'Just shaking off.' He thumps my back, then puts me in a neck hold and ruffles my hair. 'Good work finding the guy,' he says. 'That's awesome.'

I dust him off me and shake my head. 'You're such a strange boy.' I start to walk away from the pier and the three of them follow me. I feel like a mother duck.

\*　　　\*　　　\*

We walk until there aren't any more houses, all the way to the part of the beach where the current makes the waves come in then rush back out so that two waves clash, water casting up like a geyser. We watch that for a while and then Scottie says, 'I wish Mom was here.' I'm thinking the exact same thought. That's how you know you love someone, I guess, when you can't experience anything without wishing the other person were there to see it, too. Every day I kept track of anecdotes, occurrences, and gossip, bullet-pointing the news in my head and even rehearsing my stories before telling them to Joanie in bed at night.

It's getting darker, and I'm worried that we won't find him, that I won't be able to ever do anything right for her. Even now, shouldn't we be crying, paralyzed with grief? How are the three of us walking? I can't help but think we don't believe it yet; we're used to being saved, to never falling into the depths. I feel guilty that Scottie doesn't even know what's truly happening.

'Can we swim with the sharks?' Scottie asks. 'I read in our hotel magazine that they put you in a cage in the ocean and throw feed in the water and sharks swim right up to you. Can we?'

'Your mom got chased by a shark once,' I say.

'When?' Alex asks.

We turn around and walk back down the beach. Sid trails behind us, smoking a cigarette.

'She was surfing on Molokai and saw a shark beneath her when she was on a wave. She got down on her stomach so she wouldn't fall and rode the wave closer to the shore.'

'How did she know it was a shark and not a dolphin?' Scottie asks.

185

'She just knew,' I say. 'She said it was wide and dark under the water. The wave eventually flattened out. She kept paddling toward shore. She looked in the water and looked behind her and didn't see anything. Then she looked back again and saw the fin.'

My girls are so quiet, I look to make sure they're still there. Both of them are slightly behind me, their heads down, their feet shuffling through the wet sand.

'She kept going as fast as she could, not looking back. Instead of paddling all the way to shore, she headed to a sharp peninsula, and when she got close enough, she paddled right up onto the rocks.'

'And the shark bit the board!'

'No, Scottie. She never saw the shark again. She climbed up the rocks and walked back to the camp. That night we had fish and your mom sank her teeth into the flesh of the tuna and said to me and the Mitchells, "I could have been dinner today," and then she told us what had happened.'

At least this is the ending of the story she told her friends. In the real version of the story, she ran back to camp. The Mitchells were hiking to the waterfall and I was cooking the tuna. I was sitting beside the fire circle. I saw her from a distance, maneuvering over the slick black rocks. I knew something was wrong and stood up and walked toward her. Her posture was collapsed, her body shaking and her steps unsure. I saw her lean over and knew she was throwing up. When I finally got to her, I saw that she had the chills, her face was white and her bathing suit filthy, and there were scratches on her knees and thighs. I thought she had been attacked by someone and I started to yell.

186

I don't remember what I yelled. But she shook her head and then did something she had never done before. She sank down to the rocks, pulling me down with her, and then she lunged into my chest and wept. We were in the most awkward position on those rocks, but I remember not being able to move, as though the slightest movement might upset either her or the moment. Even though she was sobbing in my arms, it was a nice moment for me, to be stronger than her, to be needed by her, and to see her so fragile. At last she told me what had happened, and I smiled slightly because the way she delivered the story in between hurried breaths and sniffles made her seem like a child in my arms, waking from a nightmare, and only I had the wherewithal to show her that nothing was going to hurt her. I was there. Nothing was in the closet or under the bed.

'I thought that this was it,' she said. 'I thought it was all over. I was so angry that it was time.'

'It's not time,' I said. 'You beat it. Here you are.'

Around the fire circle that night, she was back to her old self, posturing, acting, entertaining. She wouldn't look at me. I wanted to ask her, *What's wrong with saying you were afraid?*

'I could have been dinner,' she said again at the end of the telling, and then she picked up her fish and tore into it with her teeth, and everyone, myself included, laughed. I enjoyed her performance, and the fact that I was the only person in the world who truly knew her. Imagining Brian knowing her this way, or her crying in his arms the way she cried in mine that day over twenty years ago, is unbearable.

'She used to tell that story all the time,' I say to the girls.

187

We are back to the part of the beach that's populated with homes. People have brought down beach chairs and glasses of wine to watch the sunset. I search everyone's faces, looking for him, no longer sure I can be so giving and forgiving.

'Why did she stop telling it?' Alex asks. 'I've never heard it before.'

'I guess she got new stories,' I say.

The girls seem confused, perhaps stunned that their parents have done things they've never heard about.

'Like the one about streaking at Lita's wedding,' Scottie says. 'I like that story.'

'Or the one when the gorilla at the zoo reached through the bars and grabbed her,' Alex says. 'Or the one about beating a wild boar with her shoe.'

'Or how the back of her dress was stuck in her panty hose for the entire party and she wasn't wearing any underpants,' Scottie says.

'She thought all the men were whistling at her because she looked good,' Alex continues.

Now I understand why Scottie needed to create better dramas that were worth repeating. She was searching for a perfect offering, the promise of a legend. I look at my feet stepping on the sand. Nothing ever happens to me that's worth repeating. Except perhaps these past few days.

Sid catches up to us, and I know it wasn't a cigarette he was smoking. He's totally stoned. His eyes are heavy and he has a stupid grin on his face. It pisses me off that he doesn't even bother to hide it.

'What do you love about Mom?' Scottie asks me.

For some reason I look at Alex, as if for an answer. Her face is expectant.

188

'I love . . . I don't know. I love the things we love together. Just the way we are with each other.'

Alex looks at me like I'm weaseling out of something.

'We both love to go out for dinner, for example. We love our bikes.' I laugh and then say, 'We love the montages in romantic comedies. We admitted this to each other one night.' I smile and the girls look at me strangely. I wait for Scottie to ask me what a montage is, but she doesn't. She looks almost angry.

A couple ahead of us walk hand in hand.

'I love that she forgets to wash the lettuce and our salads are always pebbly.'

'I hate when she does that,' Scottie says.

'I mean, I don't like it,' I say, 'but I expect it from her. I'm used to it. It's her. It's Mom.' More thoughts come to me and I laugh to myself.

'What?' Scottie asks.

'I'm just thinking about the things we didn't like.'

'Like what?' Scottie asks.

'We didn't like people who say, "That's funny" but don't laugh. If something's funny, one should laugh. Or people who use the words "do" and "did" instead of the appropriate verb. Like "For lunch I 'did' a salad." We also thought men who went to nice salons were weird.' I could go on and on. The recollections make me giddy, almost. What fun we had. What laughs we shared. I thought I was marrying a young model, just as my friends married their secretaries, kids' nannies, and Asian women who weren't fluent in English. I was marrying a woman who was fun and easy, and she would raise my children and stay by my side. I'm happy to have been so wrong.

189

'Hey, I think that, too,' Sid says. 'About men who go to nice salons.'

'What are we talking about?' Alex says. 'This is fucking nonsense.'

The couple ahead of us turns slightly.

'What are you looking at?' Alex says to them.

I don't bother to reprimand her, because really, what are they looking at? I slow my pace and Alex punches Scottie in the arm.

'Ow!' Scottie screams.

'Alex! Why are we still on this pattern?'

'Hit her back, Dad,' Scottie yells.

Alex grabs Scottie's neck.

'You're hurting me,' Scottie says.

'That's kind of the point,' Alex says.

I grab both children by the arm and pull them down to the sand. Sid covers his mouth with his hand and bends over, laughing silently.

' "What do you love about Mom?" ' Alex says, mimicking her sister. 'Shut up, already. And stop babying her.'

I sit down between them and don't say a word. Sid sits next to Alex. 'Easy, tiger,' he says. I look at the waves crashing down on the sand. A few women walk by and give me this knowing look, as though a father with his kids is such a precious sight. It takes so little to be revered as a father. I can tell the girls are waiting for me to say something, but what can I say that hasn't been said? I've shouted, I've reasoned, I've even spanked. Nothing works.

'What do you love about Mom, Scottie?' I ask, glaring at Alex.

She takes a moment to think. 'Lots of stuff. She's not old and ugly, like most moms.'

'What about you, Alex?'

190

'Why are we doing this?' she asks. 'How did we get here in the first place?'

'Swimming with the sharks,' I say. 'Scottie wanted to swim with sharks.'

'You can do that,' Sid says. 'I read about it in the hotel.'

'She's not afraid of anything,' Alex says.

She's wrong, and besides, I think this is a statement and not something that Alex truly loves.

'Let's get back,' I say.

I stand up and wipe the sand off of me. I look at our hotel on the cliff, pink from the sunset. The girls' expressions when I told them about their mom made me feel so alone. They won't ever understand me the way Joanie does. They won't know her the way I do. I miss her despite the fact that she envisioned the rest of her life without me. I look at my daughters, utter mysteries, and for a brief moment I have a sick feeling that I don't want to be alone in the world with these two girls. I'm relieved they haven't asked me what it is I love about them.

# 28

We go back to our room empty-handed. I call the hospital, and they assure me Joanie's doing really well. I find myself getting happy before I remember that doing well, to them, means she's breathing. She's not dead. We order room service and watch a movie about World War II that is uncomfortably violent. Bloody bodies everywhere.

'The director's showing us how it really was,' Alex says in response to my complaining. 'I read that somewhere. He's making a statement against violence.'

We all fit on the bed. The girls and I are on our stomachs, and Sid is at the opposite end of me, sitting up against the headboard.

'I wonder what Mom's friend is doing right now,' Alex says.

'Probably watching pornos,' Scottie says.

Sid laughs. Scottie has a look of both innocence and calculation.

'Why would you say that?' I ask. 'Are you being funny?'

'Reina's dad watches pornos.'

'Do you know what a porno is?' Alex asks.

'Football highlights,' she says.

I look at Alex for a clue. Am I supposed to enlighten my daughter or let her think the wrong things?

'A porno is a movie of pretty women and ugly men having sex,' Alex says.

I can't see Scottie's face because she's looking down. 'Scottie?' I say.

'I know that,' she says. 'I was just joking around.'

'It's okay that you didn't know,' Sid says.

'I knew!' She turns to face me. 'I know what they are, I just thought they were called something else. Reina calls them masturbation movies. She plays them when her parents aren't home, and one time she invited boys so she could see if they grew down there. One did.'

'Reina sounds awesome,' Sid says. 'I'm digging her more and more.'

'Were you there?' I ask. 'Have you seen one of these movies?'

'No,' Scottie says.

'Scottie,' Alex says, kicking Sid in the ribs. 'Reina

192

is a fuckedup ho bag, and you need to stay away from her. I've already told you that. Do you want to end up like me?'

'Yes,' Scottie says.

'I mean the earlier me, when I was yelling at Mom.'

'No,' Scottie says.

'Well, Reina is going to be a crackhead, and she's going to get used. She's a twat. Say it.'

'Twat,' Scottie says. She gets up and runs across the room, saying, 'Twat twat twat twat twat.'

'Holy shit,' Sid says. 'This is some messed-up parenting. Isn't it?'

Alex shrugs. 'Maybe. I guess we'll see.'

'I don't get it,' I say. 'I don't know what to do. These things she does, they keep happening.'

'It will go away,' Alex says.

'Will it? I mean, look at how you kids talk. In front of me, especially. It's like you don't respect authority.'

The kids stare at the television. I tell them to get out. I'm going to bed.

*      *      *

It's almost midnight and I'm still wide awake. I get up to use the bathroom and see that the hall bathroom light is on and the door is slightly open. I'm suddenly afraid to catch Alex doing something bad, like snorting lines off the toilet bowl. I almost turn around but gently approach and peek inside and see Scottie in front of the wall-to-wall bathroom mirror. She's standing on top of the counter, her legs on either side of the sink. She slides into a stiff pose and holds it for a few seconds before finding another. She's modeling. I'm about to say something, to tell her she needs to go to bed, but then she pushes her arms against the sides of her breasts to form cleavage and I don't want her to know what I've seen. She looks in the mirror and then down at her body, as if the mirror's wrong. Then I hear her have a dialogue with herself: 'Why didn't you ever stop her? *I didn't know how.* You didn't notice, you bastard. Come here.'

She leans into the mirror and starts kissing it, openmouthed, her tongue on the glass. Her hands are pressed against the mirror. Then I hear, 'Ooh, baby. Put your junk in my trunk. Get your condom, baby. The one that glows.'

Oh God. I walk away as quietly as possible and lean against the wall and take deep breaths. Then I panic, thinking that she's imitating her sister and Sid, and I go to the main room to make sure Sid is sleeping on the foldout bed. I see a lump on the bed and wonder if it's really his body or if he put pillows under the covers. I rush over, my heart racing. His head turns and he looks right at me.

'Hey,' he says.

I feel foolish for being out of breath and standing over him. The moonlight cuts a line down my chest. 'Hey,' I say.

'Checking on me?'

'I couldn't sleep. Scottie. She's in the bathroom.' I stop talking.

'Yeah?' he says and sits up.

'She's playacting.' I don't know how to say it. I don't need to say it. 'She's kissing the mirror.'

'Oh,' he says. 'I used to do some messed-up things as a kid. Still do.'

I feel wide awake, which always makes me angry

194

in the middle of the night. I'm useless without sleep. I can't get myself to go back to my own room. I sit on the end of the bed by his feet. 'I'm worried about my daughters,' I say. 'I'm worried there's something wrong with them.'

Sid rubs his eyes.

'Forget it,' I say. 'Sorry for waking you up.'

'It's going to get worse,' he says. 'After your wife dies.' He holds the blanket up to his chin.

'What does Alex say about it? What does she say to you?'

'She doesn't.'

'What do you mean? I heard her say she talks to you.'

'No,' he says. 'We don't talk about our issues. We just . . . I don't know. We just deal with them together by not talking.'

'Do you have any more of that pot?' I ask. 'I can't sleep. I need to sleep.'

He lifts up his pillow and retrieves a joint.

'You sleep with it?'

He ignores me and lights it, then draws his knees up and hands it to me.

I look at the joint. Joanie liked it, but I never did. 'Never mind,' I say. 'I don't want it.'

'You can take it out to the patio,' he says.

'No,' I say. 'I really don't want it.' I think a part of me was trying to impress this idiot, and now I feel foolish.

He puts it out on a magazine on the side table. 'I don't want it, either. But thanks for letting me, you know, smoke. It helps.'

'Yeah,' I say. 'Whatever. I can't deal with all these things you kids do right now. It makes you moody, though, I've noticed. The pot.'

He drums his fingers on his quilt. I look around the room. There's a TV remote on the bed. I press a few buttons.

'What would you do?' I ask. 'If you were me. How would you handle my daughters? How would you handle the man we've come to get?'

'Notice how in movies, actors always overdo the whole smoking process?' he says. 'It's always so exaggerated. And they always pick something off their tongue. And try to talk while holding in the smoke. It's so lame.'

He imitates the actors and I see it. I see what he's talking about.

'First off, I'd kick the guy's ass. Boom.' He pantomimes a right hook and then slamming a body over his knee. 'With the daughters, I don't know. I'd take them on a trip. Or, no, I'd buy 'em shit. With your money, you can buy them all kinds of things. Alex told me about all the loot you're going to get.'

I look at him and wonder if this is why he's with Alex. 'Do you want some of it? Some money?'

'Sure,' he says.

'If I gave you a lot of money right now—tonight—would you leave?'

'No,' he says. 'Why would I leave?'

'No, Sid. I'm asking you a favor. If I give you money, will you leave?'

'Oh,' he says. 'I get it. Is that what you want? You want me to go?'

The hair on the sides of his head sticks straight out.

'No,' I say. 'I guess not.'

'I wouldn't know what to do with daughters,' he says. 'Exchange them for sons?'

196

'But then I could wind up with something like you.'

'I'm not so bad,' he says. 'I'm smart.'

'You're about a hundred miles away from the town of Smart, my friend.'

'You're mistaken, counselor,' he says. 'I'm smart, I can take care of myself. I'm an awesome tennis player, a keen observer of life around me. I'm a good cook. I always have weed.'

'I'm sure your parents are proud.'

'It's possible.' He looks at his knees and I wonder if I've offended him.

'Do they know where you are?'

'My parents?'

'Yeah, Sid. Your parents.'

'My mom's sort of busy right now, so she kind of wants me out of the way.'

'What does she do?'

'She's a receptionist at Pets in the City.'

'Our cat goes there. So, it's a busy time for pets?'

'No,' he says. 'She's busy getting the house together. Getting my dad's things organized. He died a few months ago.'

At first I think he's joking, that this is a prank like his retarded brother, but I can see that he's serious. He's doing the same thing I do when people talk about Joanie, trying to smile and look like he's okay with the whole thing. He wants me to feel at ease and is searching for a way to the next topic. And so I do for Sid what I wish people would do for me.

'Good night, Sid,' I say. 'Get some rest. I'll see you tomorrow.'

He leans back on his pillow. 'Good chat, boss,' he says. 'See you tomorrow.'

## 29

The next morning I go for a run on the beach, and he runs right toward me and then past me. He is looking at the ocean when he jogs by, and I am higher, near the houses, where the sand is dry and more difficult to run though. I turn around and follow him, heading down to the packed sand. I'm thrilled and nervous and somewhat mortified that we're doing the exact same thing at the exact same time. I run and watch the back of him, his calves, his neck. His T-shirt says STANFORD LACROSSE, which is just vile, and his shorts are the kind that serious runners wear, short and thin, with large slits on the sides. I imagine he's the kind of man who clips his phone to his belt. He's a fast little fucker, so I pick up my pace. There are only a few other people on the beach: some surfers checking out the swell, a fisherman planting his pole into the sand, a black dog sniffing in the bushes. The day is preparing itself for something promising, something grand—the gauzy light is beginning to sharpen, making the hammock of white sand flicker; the mists are lifting, dramatically and coyly revealing the bright sea and the blue-green cliffs.

I slow down, not wanting to get too close to him. I feel an incredible rush of energy and know it's fueled by rage and try to focus and remind myself why I'm here. I love Joanie and she loves this man in front of me and I am going to bring him to her. He has the right to say goodbye. He has given her something I couldn't. I'm like a cat dragging a rat to the doorstep.

A wave crashes onto the shore and he sprints away from it. I stay on course, letting the cold water splash up my legs. A little before the pier, he slows his pace, looks at his watch, and begins to walk up the incline. I stop jogging and watch where he goes. He walks on the beach for a while and catches his breath, then continues on toward the pier. I wonder if he's heading to his car in the lot. I begin to walk, not knowing what I'll do if he gets into a car. Am I ready? Can I do this now? Then I see him turn around and come back toward me, and I quickly face the water. I stretch, doing a twist that allows me to keep him in my sights. I twist to the other side and see him heading toward one of the small blue cottages that my cousin Hugh owns. I didn't think Hugh rented them out anymore, and I wonder if Brian knows Hugh. Brian walks up the porch steps and opens the screen door. He must know one of us, which isn't that much of a coincidence, since we're so prevalent here. Like cockroaches. I could ask Hugh if and how he knows Brian. I could get some information on this guy before I make my move. Or I could walk into this blind. Why do I need information? Here he is. I found him. Now I have to get him.

I look at the hotel on the cliff, wishing my daughters were here. I realize I'm afraid. The sun is getting warmer on my back, and I wish the air could stay the way it was moments before: the air of promise, the elements brewing but not quite cooked. Enough stalling. I walk toward the cottage, trudging through the deep soft sand, but as I get near, I see something that startles me. I see Brian disappear inside, but then he comes out and sits down on a recliner with a glass of water.

Following him are two children—one around thirteen, the other, I don't know, eight— and then from the screen door comes a beautiful woman in a white bathing suit and a large white sun hat. She's elegant. Radiant. Stunning. She's Brian Speer's wife.

# 30

I walk back toward the shore and sit on the beach. I wait to see if Brian and his family come down. I'm sure they will. It's what you do. He has put an obstacle in my plan. After seeing his wife and children, I can't bring myself to follow through. Not only would it be difficult logistically, but I don't feel right about it anymore. I begin to doubt the entire affair, even though I know that it happened.

I see my daughters and Sid walking on the rocks, making their way to the beach from the hotel. There's no path from the hotel beach to this one, just rocks and ocean, discouraging nonguests from entering or guests from ever leaving.

When they reach the bay, they look around until they spot me. Scottie runs to me and spreads out her towel.

'Alex ordered room service,' she says in a tattletale voice.

'Good,' I say.

Scottie never knows what will fly and what won't, and I think this is a good tactic. Her stings look better now. They're white and dry, like old scars. *What's happening to you?* I want to ask. *What can I do for you?* I think of her posing in front of the mirror last night, her hands pushing her breasts together. I never noticed that Scottie has little breasts, but she does.

She lies on her stomach and turns her head toward me.

'Do you get cable in your room at home?' I ask.

'Yes,' she says.

'What shows do you like?'

'*The Sopranos,*' she says. '*Dog the Bounty Hunter.* Wait, just on cable, or all shows?'

'I don't think you should watch any shows,' I say.

'I'd rather die,' she says.

Alex saunters toward us, Sid trailing behind her, smoking. I watch the men watch her until they see that I'm her destination, and then they look away.

'Any luck?' she asks.

'Oh yeah,' Scottie says. 'Did you find Mom's friend?'

I consider my answer. If they know I've found him, they'll expect me to act.

'No,' I say. 'No luck.'

Sid nods at me and I nod back. He has become a completely different person to me—a mystery, a rock. He must be strong. Or heavily drugged.

'Did you have a good breakfast?' I ask.

'Yup,' Sid says.

'Brought you a bagel,' Alex says, tossing me one with raisins in it.

'Wow,' I say. 'Thank you. I appreciate it.'

The sun has gotten even stronger, and it feels nice on my back. I have taken my tennis shoes off and press my toes into the cool sand. Sid and Alex are settling onto their stomachs, and Scottie turns onto her back. More people are on the beach and in the glassy ocean. People on either side of us have umbrellas and beach chairs, coolers, towels, sunscreen, hats.

'Do you guys have sunscreen?' I ask.

'No,' Scottie says. 'Do we have water?'

'Did you bring any?' Alex asks.

'No,' I say.

Alex pops her head up. 'Did you bring snacks for us?'

'We can walk to town.'

How do mothers manage to bring everything a child could need?

Alex props herself up on her elbows. She looks behind me. I follow her gaze and see the woman in white. She looks at us with a friendly expression, then down at the sand as she continues to walk. The two boys I saw at the cottage run toward the ocean, and she calls out to them, 'Stay in the zone, please.' They both crash through a small wave then settle like birds. They bob and drift. She walks a little closer to the shore and it's perfect because she's below us and I can stare openly. She takes the bags off her shoulder and pulls a towel out of one. She flicks her wrists, and the towel sails into the air, then floats to the sand. She has a green translucent wrap covering her bathing suit; she leaves this on, sits down on the towel, and takes a book from her bag. It's a thick hardcover.

Both girls are focused on the woman's every movement. I wonder if they're comparing her to their mother, or if they're looking at her the way one looks at something nice. I check behind me to see if her husband's coming, but I see only a man on a riding mower and some local kids cutting across the lawn with fishing poles.

Her boys ride the waves on their stomachs. Every

202

now and then she'll look up to watch, marking her place in the book with her finger.

'You guys should go swimming,' I say.

'Will you go in with me?' Scottie asks.

I don't really want to, but I don't want to say no because I know the woman can hear us.

'Sure!' I say too enthusiastically. 'Alex, you, too?'

Alex sits up. I never know when I'll meet resistance. Once I think I know the pattern with these girls—fun, intimacy, fight, unpleasantness, smooth again—they change the order.

'Sid? Want to join us?' I feel phony, like I'm pandering to him. Now he deserves my courtesy because his father's dead.

'Let's do this.' He stands quickly, runs toward the ocean, and stomps through the waves, then dives in. I don't see him for a while, and then I stop looking for him to surface.

The girls and I walk to the ocean, and I slowly sink into the water.

'Catch this one, Steven,' the older boy says to his younger brother. The younger boy looks back at the wave looming over his head. 'Go!'

We all duck under the wave, and I look toward the beach to see if the boy caught the wave. I see him in the distance. He caught the wave to shore.

'That was awesome,' he yells.

The older boy yells back, 'I told you.'

The older boy doesn't give Scottie a single glance. He's all business, watching for the next set, making false starts and slapping the water in frustration. What a little freak.

I can see their mother looking over the rim of her sunglasses at us. Alex and Sid have gone past the break. I see them heading to the floating green

203

raft. Scottie inches toward the boys and lines up to catch a wave.

'I got dibs!' the older boy yells at her. 'Go, Steven. This one's yours. Go! Go!'

I can tell Steven is shaken. He's out of breath, and the yelling is disorienting him. He glances at Scottie, then takes off, thrashing at the water, but the wave moves under him and he sails down its back.

'You're in the way,' the older boy yells at Scottie. 'Go find your own lineup.'

I watch Scottie respond with a hesitant, nervous look as though what the boy said was a joke.

'You're in an ocean, buddy,' I say. 'I think you can all manage to share an ocean.'

'I wasn't in his way,' Scottie says. 'He just didn't swim hard enough.'

*What are you going to say to that, little punk?* I stare him down and he backs off, perhaps because he sees his mother coming into the water. I soften my gaze and smile at the boy. 'Here comes a set that has your name on it,' I say. 'Thatta boy!'

Their mother nods at me. Her suit is modestly cut, and she has kept her sun hat on. It hides her face, so all I can see is her body plunging into the water. Her bronze hair splays out behind her like a cape as she glides toward her boys. Scottie seems enthralled. Joanie would have run into the water in a string bikini and behaved like the older boy, making a competition out of everything, urging everyone to go, go, go.

Mrs. Speer does a backstroke, her long arms windmilling behind her, the water falling off her fingertips. Her feet make tiny splashes in front of her. That she has left her hat on is somehow both silly and charming.

'Catch this, Mom,' the younger son says.

She looks at the small swell moving toward her and breaststrokes toward shore.

'Faster!' the boy says.

Scottie tries to catch the wave, too, her eyes still fastened on the woman. She sees Scottie and quickens her stroke to match. The wave is gaining height and it will reach its peak soon. Now I'm afraid, not for Scottie, because I know she's good at this, but for the woman, who seems so fragile, like something you'd put on a high shelf, spotlit with soft illumination. As she swims, she looks back, a grin on her face, until she looks up at the wave over her head and gasps. Then the wave spills down and she's gone.

I catch the next wave in and see both Scottie and the woman washed up on the shore. Scottie is already standing, but the woman is on her side in the sand, her long hair wrapped around her head, a strap of her suit down her arm and the bottom part hiked up and revealing her ass.

I run up to shore but remind myself that some women, such as my wife, don't like men helping them. I pretend to be concerned about Scottie and ask the woman while laughing, 'You okay?'

Another wave crashes into her, and she slides down the shore, receding with it; she's caught in a set and can't seem to get out. I look out at her boys, who are laughing hysterically. I go to her and swoop her up to standing. She steadies herself by placing her hands on my shoulders and then quickly moves them away. It has to be the strangest, warmest thing I have felt in months, possibly years: her hands on me. I can still feel them. I wonder if I'll always

205

sense them, like a tag burned onto my skin. It's not necessarily because of her but because she's a woman touching me.

'My God,' she says. 'I feel like I've gone through a car wash.' I laugh, or force myself to, because it's not something I'd normally laugh at.

'What about you?' she says to Scottie. 'How did you make out?'

'I'm a boy,' Scottie says. 'Look at me.'

Sand has gotten into the bottom of her suit, creating a huge bulge. She scratches at the bulge. 'I'm going to go to work now,' she says. I think she's impersonating me and that Mrs. Speer is getting an unrealistic, humiliating glimpse.

'Scottie,' I say. 'Take that out.'

'It must be fun to have girls,' Mrs. Speer says.

She looks at the ocean, and I see that she's looking at Alex sunbathing on the floating raft. Sid leans over Alex and puts his mouth to hers. She raises a hand to his head, and for a moment I forget it's my daughter out there and think of how long it has been since I've been kissed or kissed like that.

'Or maybe you have your hands full,' Mrs. Speer says.

'No, no,' I say. 'It's great,' and it is, I suppose, though I feel like I've just acquired them and don't know yet. 'They've been together for ages.' I gesture to Alex and Sid. I don't understand if they're a couple or if this is how all kids in high school act these days.

Mrs. Speer looks at me curiously, as if she's about to say something, but she doesn't.

'And boys.' I gesture to her little dorks. 'They must keep you busy.'

'They're a handful. But they're at such a fun age.

206

It's such a joy.'

She gazes out at her boys. Her expression does little to convince me that they're such a joy. I wonder how many times parents have these dull conversations with one another and how much they must hide. *They're so goddamn hyper, I'd do anything to inject them with a horse tranquilizer. They keep insisting that I watch what they can do, but I truly don't give a fuck. How hard is it to jump off a diving board?*

*My girls are messed up,* I want to say. *One talks dirty to her own reflection. Did you do that when you were growing up?*

'Your girls seem great, too,' she says. 'How old are they?'

'Ten and eighteen. And yours?'

'Ten and twelve.'

'Oh,' I say. 'Great.'

'Your younger one sure is funny,' she says. 'I mean, not funny. I meant entertaining.'

'Oh, yeah. That's Scottie. She's a riot.'

We are both silent for a while, watching Scottie sit on the sand and let the waves toss her around.

'Actually,' I say, 'they're both a little sad. Their mother is in the hospital.' I realize how uncomfortable this will make Mrs. Speer. 'She'll be fine,' I add after the obligatory 'Oh, no!' 'They're just worried. That's all.'

'Sure,' she says. 'That must be so hard. What happened? If you don't mind me asking.'

'She got into a boating accident.' I watch to see if she recognizes any of this.

'I'm sorry,' she says. 'Sailing? Or was she on one of those with motors?'

I laugh, and a red splotch blooms on her neck.

207

'One with a motor,' I say.

'Sorry, I don't know a thing—'

'No, I'm laughing because it was charming, that's all. You're charming.'

She touches her palm to her chest. I think this is as close as I'll ever get to cheating on Joanie, as close as I'll get to revenge. If Joanie was in love with someone else, why didn't she tell me? I wonder if she was really waiting for me to sell my shares to file for divorce. I hope she wasn't that cold. I'm grateful that I probably will never find out. Her silence lets me make her into whomever I want her to be.

Mrs. Speer looks at the ocean. I do the same.

'We saw John Cusack here yesterday,' she says. 'And Neve Campbell. They were surfing.'

'Oh,' I say. 'And who are they?'

'They're actors,' she says. 'Hollywood. They're, you know, celebrities.'

'Oh,' I say. 'Yeah, there's a lot of them here. What movies are they in?'

'Well, I'm not sure. I can't think of any.'

'Interesting,' I say.

'Silly,' she says. 'Talking about celebrities. Anyway.'

'No,' I say. 'It's fascinating, really.'

I give her a look of encouragement. She bites her thumb and looks down and then looks back up at me and says with a grin, 'I think you couldn't care less.'

I laugh. 'You're right. Actually, you're wrong. I do care! I can't stand celebrities. I can't stand how much we pay them, and those award shows, my God. It's absolutely ludicrous.'

'I know. I know. I get it, but I can't help myself.'

208

'You don't buy the magazines, do you?'

'I do!'

'Oh, no,' I say. I press my palm to my forehead and then see Scottie running toward us and realize I've momentarily forgotten who this woman is. She is Brian's wife. She isn't my friend. I'm not supposed to be laughing right now or enjoying life in any way.

'Your hat!' Scottie says. 'I found it.' She holds up the hat with the long and floppy brim. It's wet and resembles a strip of seaweed as Scottie wrings it out.

'Thank you,' Mrs. Speer says, reaching for it.

Scottie stares at her shyly, as though expecting an award. 'Do you want your towel?' she asks. 'You have goose bumps.'

I look down at Mrs. Speer's legs, the tiny bumps dotting her skin.

'I guess I could use a towel,' she says.

'I'll get it.' Scottie runs toward Mrs. Speer's bag, and I look at her apologetically, but she seems relaxed. She walks up the incline to the warm dry sand and sits. I follow her lead, running my fingers through the sand. I glance over at the bumps on her legs.

Scottie comes back to us and wraps the towel around Mrs. Speer's shoulders, then sits beside her. 'I shave, too,' Scottie says. The woman looks at Scottie's legs. 'Wow,' she says.

'I had to because I got attacked by a herd of minor wars. Man-of-wars, I mean.'

This is the line she wanted to use on her mother. I'm angry at how disloyal Scottie is. She has moved on, adopted a new form of mother so easily. She'd need only a day to fall in love with someone else,

209

but I guess this is what kids do. They won't mourn us the way we want them to.

'So you had to shave?' Mrs. Speer asks.

'Yeah. Shave off the poison.'

'Are you staying in the cottages?' I ask.

'Yes,' she says. 'My husband had to come here for work. We thought we'd make a little vacation of it. He knows the owner, so . . .'

'Hugh.'

'That's right.' She seems relieved that I know someone she knows.

'He's my cousin,' I say.

'Oh, I see. Oh. Okay. You probably know my husband, then. Brian Speer?'

I look straight ahead. I see Sid and Alex jumping off the raft, which lists back and forth. The woman's older son has drifted farther out. He could drown, possibly; he's unsuccessfully fighting the current to get back in. I could tell her everything. I could make her feel as bad as I feel, and we could talk about things more consequential than the ages of our children. We could talk about love and heartbreak, beginnings and ends.

'I don't know your husband,' I say.

'Oh,' she says. 'I just assumed—'

'Scottie, go tell him to swim sideways to get in.'

Scottie, surprisingly obedient, stands and walks to the ocean.

Mrs. Speer shields her eyes to look for her son, then stands. 'Is he okay?'

'He's fine. Current's just tricky. Scottie will help him.'

She looks at me, her face full of worry. I can read it clearly. She wants me to help her. Brian's wife needs me to rescue her son. I can't see the boy's

210

face, but I know what he's feeling. He's frustrated and embarrassed, he's both incredulous and mindful of the predicament he's in. He's alive. He has a simple desire: *Get back in, get back in, just get back to shore.*

*Get Brian, get Brian, just bring him to shore.*

I don't want to get wet. 'I'll get him,' I say.

'Thank you,' Brian's wife says. 'That's so good of you.'

# 31

I take the kids to dinner at Tiki's. The restaurant has a dark interior and woven mats hanging on the wall. It always looks closed, and there are no consistent hours or days of operation. The bar and the tables are stapled with a skirt of raffia that traps pieces of battered coconut. The service is slow, and the waitstaff always acts persecuted. Their food is made carelessly and greasily, and the way you order (baked, grilled, sautéed) is an unnecessary choice because it doesn't matter how you want your fish: You are getting it battered. Tiki's is my favorite restaurant on Kauai. My father would take me here. Sometimes after dinner he'd sit at the worn bar and I would stay at our table, listening to the ukulele club and coloring on the paper tablecloth. Now there's no tablecloth, just wood, and kids whose fathers sit at the bar carve into the tables with their steak knives.

The ukulele club still meets here to practice. They're here tonight, old Hawaiians who smoke cigarettes and snack on boiled peanuts in between their jam sessions. It's nice taking my kids to an old haunt, but I've also brought them here because I know Hugh comes in every night for pre-dinner cocktails. I want to ask him about his houseguests. I see him at the bar and tell the girls and Sid to get settled. Sid pulls out a chair for Scottie, and she sits down, then looks up at him as he pushes her in.

'Where you off to?' Alex asks.

'I'm going to say hello to our cousin.'

Alex looks over at the bar. 'Cousin Hugh!'

I check her face to see if she's being sarcastic. 'Are you joking?'

'No,' she says. 'I love Cousin Hugh.'

'Why?'

Sid looks at the bar and squints.

'He's just old and funny,' Alex says.

I look at the back of Hugh, his wild white tufts of hair, his broad upper body and skinny legs. For most of my life, he seemed a bit scary because of his big frame and sharp mind, but I guess people reach an age where scary becomes 'cute,' and I feel sort of bad about this.

'Okay, well. Order me something. It doesn't matter what. And be nice to the waitress. Talk pidgin. Don't talk, you know, English.'

They nod. They get it. Sid straightens up in his chair and peruses the menu as if he's the man of the house.

I walk to the bar. 'Hey, cousin,' I say, sliding up beside him.

'Eh!' he says, standing halfway up before collapsing back onto the stool. I sit down and make eye contact with the bartender. He stays where he is and purposefully looks at the other end of the bar. Hugh calls the bartender over and, in his raspy smoker's voice, orders me an old-fashioned, which sounds good. He pats my back and the bartender nods almost reverently. Hugh looks back over his shoulder to see who I'm here with.

'Is that . . .'

'Scottie and Alex,' I say.

'Big girls already,' he says and turns back around.

Sometimes I love that no one really cares about anyone else. If Hugh did, he'd say hello to the girls, ask questions about them and me, remember that my wife is in a coma. None of these things happen, and I'm grateful.

'I see you have some houseguests,' I say.

'What?'

'Some people staying in the cottage.'

'Oh, yeah, yeah. Determined son of a bitch. He's, ah, Lou's sister's—No, wait. Lou has a sister, and the sister's husband— Lou's brother-in-law—is cousins with that guy's wife.'

'Huh,' I say, not really getting it.

'No, wait. What cottage you talking about?'

Hugh is drunk. There are balls of sweat along his hairline: sweat balls. I remember them from childhood. Whenever he'd get drunk, he'd sprout them and try to put on the most serious expression, masking all the confusion skulking around in his head. He wears that expression now. 'You mean da cottage on the bay or da one back by da trail?'

'The bay,' I say. 'The guy with the wife and two boys.' The raffia brushes my thighs, and I look for ensnared pieces of old fish.

'Oh, sure, sure. Determined son of a bitch.' Hugh leans a bit toward me and talks to my chin. 'I'm doing some business with a guy, and this guy— in the cottage on the bay—is that guy's friend.'

213

'That's nice of you,' I say. 'To let them stay there.'

Hugh shrugs and suddenly grasps his bar stool, thinking he was falling, I suppose.

'So what's he like?' I ask.

'Who?'

'Never mind,' I say.

*'Hana hou!'* Hugh shouts at the musicians, who have just finished a song. They begin another fast song, and I look over at the old men singing, the small wooden instruments held close to their chests, their fingers strumming madly. One stands and lunges as he plays, as though his fingers need the extra push from his body. Their hands are all dark and gristly-looking. I look at my girls, watching them. Scottie's mouth is around a straw that's submerged in a fruity white drink.

The bartender keeps looking over at me, making sure I'm okay, as if to compensate for his initial rudeness. I nod and he looks toward the door at a couple entering. The man wears an aloha shirt and the woman wears a purple orchid lei around her neck, the kind that the hotel gives to guests on arrival. Sid threw his off the balcony and Scottie copied him. Alex tore hers into bits as she watched the movie. Mine is haloed around the bedside lamp. The man and woman look as though they want to leave but are afraid it may seem rude. They stand near the entrance, waiting to be seated, and then the husband finally walks over to the nearest table. I see his wife calling for him to come back, but she looks around and eventually follows. The bartender looks away from them. He punches his fist into his palm in time to the music.

'What's the guy like who's staying in the

cottage?' I take a long sip of my drink.

'He's lucky,' Hugh says. 'The bugga's lucky. His sister is married to the guy.'

'What guy?' This conversation is impossible. Hugh would be a good man to torture. He'd never tell because he couldn't.

'The guy I'm doing business with.'

'Who is . . .'

'Don Holitzer.'

'Don Holitzer? Well, shit, Hugh. I'm kind of doing business with him, too, remember?'

'That's what I said.'

A panic makes its way through my body. I feel like someone's playing a trick on me.

'That's what I said,' Hugh says again. 'Don's friend is staying in the cottage.'

'Right,' I say. There's no use fighting it. I try to take a few deep breaths without looking like I'm taking a few deep breaths. The same thought keeps repeating itself: *Don is Brian's brother-in-law. Don is Brian's brother-in-law?*

'Interesting,' I say. 'I guess he lucked out, having a brother-in-law like Don.' I feel I've had an epiphany and yet I don't know what the epiphany really is. I don't comprehend the luckiness or see how his family status would benefit Brian or Joanie. You don't become rich just because your sister's husband is rich. I suppose you get perks, but are perks the motivation behind Joanie's determination? I see only the bad sides: Brian's kids will play with Don's kids and will constantly compare inventory. *Why don't we have an Xbox iPod robot? Why don't we have a rock waterfall in the pool? Why don't we have new cars and a staff of childhood consultants?* Sounds like hell. Is this

215

what Joanie was aiming for? Giving her lover's brother-in-law another business opportunity? Was she so far past her own family that she was moving on to her potential in-laws? I look back at my children, frantic, as though they might have been kidnapped. I see my dinner waiting for me, which almost brings me to tears. They ordered for me. They took a guess on what I would like. They remembered me.

'He's a Realtor,' Hugh says.

I don't answer. Hugh looks at me like I've done something wrong.

'Great,' I say. 'I hope his business is booming.'

'It will be.' Hugh holds up his glass and looks at the liquid, trying to gauge something, though I'm not sure what. He shakes the glass and takes a sip. I hear the ice crash onto his face. He wipes his face with his sleeve.

'If we sell to Don, and that's what it's looking like right now— that's what you want, right?—then Don's going to redevelop and sell . . .'

'I know.' *Come on, get it out.*

Hugh waves his hand, indicating all of the dealings. 'And,' he says. 'And he's letting his brother-in-law be in charge of all the real estate transactions.'

The realization I'm supposed to have presents itself and settles in me like a strange sustenance. I get it. I finally get it. Brian is basically a Realtor with about three hundred thousand acres of commercial and industrial land, my land, as his client. Joanie wouldn't divorce me for a Realtor who lives in an average home, but she'd divorce me for a business partner of Don Holitzer, potential largest landowner in Hawaii. She'd divorce me for

216

someone she could mold.

Hugh whistles, a cartoonish sound indicating someone falling off a cliff.

The men play a slow song on their ukuleles and it sounds like an anthem, an ode to my loss. It's hard to love my wife right now. If she were perfectly healthy and I found this out, I'd wish upon her the fate she is currently enduring, at least momentarily. But I could ruin everything for Brian. I could choose someone else.

'There are still other bidders,' I say to Hugh. 'He may not get a thing.' *I can still win, Joanie.* I imagine her on the bed, her body still and gathering sores from lack of movement, the makeup on her skin settling into her pores because no one's there to wash it away. No one can care for her because she's refused it. No, I can't win. No one can win. Even Brian doesn't win because he won't have her.

I finish my drink. It has generated an angry heat in my chest that surges throughout the rest of my body.

'He'll get it,' Hugh says. 'We all want Don. You do, too.' He brings his glass down hard on the bar, then looks at me and smiles. His steely eyes are determined; I notice they haven't aged with the rest of him. They're not cute. They're young and smart, and I know he's telling me what to do. He's telling me my relations with my family will be damaged if I don't do what he wants me to do. I think of Racer breaking off his marriage to please his family, and I know I'm trapped.

'I'll see you tomorrow,' I say. Tomorrow's the day my cousins and I are meeting. Tomorrow I will need to please people I hardly know, yet people I'm undeniably and inexplicably bound and dedicated to.

'Next time stay longer,' Hugh says, his habitual farewell.

He edges off his seat, nods to the bartender, and raises his hand in farewell to the restaurant, keeping his gaze focused on his footing as though he's on precarious terrain. *'Hana hou,'* he yells toward the musicians, then puts on his cowboy hat and walks out.

I go to my table, to the food on my plate.

'This rocks,' Sid says.

'Totally,' Scottie says, coming up from her straw and then going back down again.

I could cry if I looked too closely at my daughters, so I don't look at them. I look ahead at the old men and wonder if I'll be an old man one day or if I'll die early. I take a bite of my meal, but it's hard to swallow—something anxious and sad is coursing through my body like a drug, and my throat feels swollen.

Scottie shuffles her food around. 'I ordered mahimahi, but I think this is just fried bread,' she says. 'They forgot the fish part.'

'That happens sometimes,' I say.

'Mine was so good,' Sid says. 'I love anything fried. Cheese, vegetables, fruit.'

Alex's plate is empty. She is relaxed in her chair, gazing at the musicians with a look of love. I bet she's not thinking about anything right now, and I'm glad for her.

The musicians strike the last chord with great fanfare, letting their strumming hands follow through to the sky. A few jump out of their chairs and hunch forward as though completing a race. The girls and Sid clap and cheer. Scottie stomps

218

her feet on the floor. I look down and shovel food into my mouth, trying to pat down the emotion that's threatening to spill over. I look at the tourist couple. I focus on them. My view of the man's hand is blocked by the raffia on the table, but I can tell it's resting on her thigh. She has taken off her lei. It hangs on the back of an empty chair. There are beer bottles on their table and glasses of ice with paper umbrellas. The woman has put one of these cocktail umbrellas into her hair. He tries to feed her a bite of his dessert—fried banana and ice cream—but she takes the fork and feeds herself, then cuts off another bite.

When our table's cheers wane, Alex gives me what seems to be a guilty look. I interpret it to mean that she knows her happiness is out of character, or that her happiness is out of place—we aren't supposed to be happy right now. I think we all know we should go home soon but don't want to. The musicians pack up their instruments.

'It's still so early,' Alex says. 'It feels like ten o'clock.'

'That's because we were in the sun all day,' Scottie says. She looks over at me and I nod.

I think of Brian's son. I brought him in from the ocean. I taught him something his father should have taught him: to swim sideways to shore if you're caught in a current, and never straight ahead. He had to place his hands around my neck while I tugged him to shore. I asked him, 'Do you take after your dad?'

'I don't know,' he said, his breath tickling my ear.

'Later tonight, maybe when you go to bed, tell your mother I'm sorry.'

'For what?'

219

I didn't answer. I couldn't go through with it. I saw her on the shore, the water rushing over her feet as she waited for me to bring in her boy. When we reached the shore, he slid off my back and I told him how to swim in the current. He couldn't look me in the eye. His mother ran to him, and when she reached to hug him, her face pained, he evaded her arms and sat down. I think of her thanking me, then rushing the boys back up to the cottage. I sat down to rest and saw Scottie drawing a heart in the sand with a stick. I LOVE . . . a wave rushed onto the shore and washed away her declaration.

'Who do you love?' I ask her now. 'On the beach—you were drawing in the sand.'

'No one,' she says.

Alex makes a hissing sound, meant to sound like someone peeing. 'Giraffe boy,' she says.

'Shut up!'

We all laugh and Scottie looks triumphant, perhaps proud of her trick to get close to the boy, or just proud to feel love. Because feeling love does make you feel superior. Until you find out you aren't loved back.

'That's not who it is, anyway,' Scottie says. She runs her finger on the table, spelling out somebody's name, perhaps. The true love.

'I love . . . you,' I say, throwing it out there. My girls look at me, unsure who's supposed to receive it. I don't think they want to know—both of them have never heard me say that before in a serious way. Most of the musicians have left the restaurant, but a few have stayed and are starting to play. We all look relieved. My abrupt love can diffuse.

'Here's to your father loving you,' Sid says, raising his glass of water.

Alex looks at me and then at Sid. I wonder if she knows that I know Sid's father is dead. She touches Sid's other hand, the one that's not around his raised glass. I raise my glass to Sid's and give it a solid tap. We lower our glasses. The tourist couple gets up, and the woman takes her purse and the orchid lei. The man counts bills and looks around, holding the check and the bills, then puts everything down on the table. The woman looks back at us and I wave goodbye and she waves and walks toward the door. The man looks down at the table and takes a few bills off the stack, then puts them in his pocket before following his wife.

I look at the musicians. Two men are playing guitars instead of ukuleles. The man with the ukulele sings Gabby Pahinui's *'Hi'ilawe,'* matching his guttural voice. The other two play slack key guitar and the sounds fill me like the alcohol— boldness and sadness, grit all sliding into me. Slack key. *Ki ho'alu.* This means 'Loosen the key.' It's what I'd like to do. Sit back and relax, loosen the key. If only we could stay here and never go home. But we can't. I have work to do.

I told the older son to tell his mother I was sorry. Now, if he asked, 'For what?' I'd say, 'For what I'm about to do.'


# 32


We walk on the road by the bay. Even though Alex made me remember that it's still early, I'm surprised by the soft light. The blood-orange sun is plunging into the ocean. Scottie is ahead of us, retrieving

221

flowers from people's yards. Everyone thinks we're going back to the hotel. Everyone thinks we have failed.

'Make sure she doesn't pick from people's trees,' I say to Sid. 'And tell her to head to the next beach access.'

He looks at me and then Alex, as if we're about to plot against him. 'Sure.' He jogs to catch Scottie and ruffles her hair when he gets to her. She punches his shoulder, then throws her bouquet into the air. Sid tries to catch as many flowers as he can.

I see Alex looking at him. Her bemused expression makes her seem much older. 'That woman today,' I say to her. 'The woman with the boys. That was his wife.'

'You're kidding me.' She stops walking and faces me. 'The hottie with the hat?'

'Yes,' I say. 'Sure. Hottie?'

'Someone who's good-looking,' she says. 'Hot. How do you know she's his wife?'

'I saw them both come out of the cottage with their children this morning.' I resume walking.

'Why didn't you say anything?'

I don't answer.

'I can't believe he has a family. What are you going to do now?'

I hear a car behind us. We both veer off the road, except Alex goes to one side and I go to the other. When the car passes, she walks back to me.

'I'm going to tell him,' I say.

'When?'

'Right now. That's what we came here to do. Tell him, right?'

'But what about her?'

I think of her delicate hat devastated by the

222

water. I think of her cold legs.

'You're just going to show up?' Alex asks. 'On the doorstep? Just knock on the door?'

'Yes,' I say. 'That's what I'm going to do.'

Alex has her mouth open, a glint of excitement in her eyes. 'Don't look like that,' I say. 'Don't look excited. It's nothing like that. This isn't fun at all.'

'I didn't say it was fun. Why would you say that?'

'I see it,' I say. 'Your look.'

She doesn't know the latest plot—the fact that this guy will have inherited more than my wife. He stands to inherit our entire past.

'He may come back with us on the last flight,' I say. 'To say his goodbyes. Are you ready for that?'

'No,' she says, looking ahead at her sister, bumping into Sid. Scottie hands him a branch of bougainvillea, and when he's about to take it, she pulls it away.

'Are you ready?' Alex asks.

'Not really,' I say. I'll never be ready. Yet at the same time, you always want to reach the end. You can't fly to a destination and linger in the air. I want to reach the end of this thing, and I feel terrible about it. The true end is her death.

'Will you come with me?' I ask.

'Me?'

'Yeah, you, Alex. You.'

'When you talk to him?'

'No. You can talk to her while I talk to him.'

'What about the flower child?' She points at Scottie, who is tucking a flower behind Sid's ear.

'She can come, too. You can watch her for me. The three of you can distract the others. I'll talk to him. I'll just tell him what's happening. I'll just . . . finish it.'

'Right now?'

'Yes,' I say. 'You know that.'

Scottie and Sid turn on the beach access and disappear. I notice Alex has slowed her pace. I wonder if this is all going to backfire. I shouldn't involve Alex so much. I should have other people in my life to depend on.

'What happened to Sid's dad?' I ask.

Alex takes a quick glance at me. 'What do you mean?'

'I know he died,' I say.

'Oh,' she says. 'Yeah.'

I wonder if this is why she likes Sid. Because he has a father who died.

'Car accident,' she says. 'He was drunk. So was the other driver. They were both drunk. But the other guy didn't die. A kid.'

I want to ask if Sid's okay, or if that's why he's here now, if they're sharing tragedy, or maybe she's trying to learn what it's like to have a dead parent. I guess I already know the answers to my questions.

'Is this helping Sid?' I ask. 'Being here?'

'I don't know,' Alex says.

'Is it helping you? Is he helping you by being here?'

'Yes,' she says.

I wait for her to continue, but she doesn't. We walk down the beach access, and at the end of it, she takes her shoes off. The sand is dry and deep. I feel my face. I haven't shaved in four days or so. I bet Brian will be showered and impeccable, his wife and kids, too, and it doesn't seem right to go into this with him looking better than me. I see Scottie and Sid ahead and call for them to stop. When we catch up, I tell them we're going to see the woman

224

with the hat and her kids.

'You mean the retard who almost drowned?' Scottie asks. The white fruit drink has dried in the corners of her mouth, and she looks rabid.

'Yes,' I say. 'Him.' I realize the boys could have been my daughters' brothers, and I almost wish it had happened—it would have been the ultimate revenge, sending Brian my furious girls. He would have been absolutely lost.

Alex walks ahead, brushing Sid as she passes him, and he follows her. I know she's telling him everything. He looks back at me, then puts his hand on top of Alex's head, a gesture that seems intimate and cold all at once.

I take Scottie's hand so she doesn't try to catch up with them. 'Did she invite you?' she asks.

'No. I just thought we'd pop in and say hello. I know her husband. I need to talk to him.'

Alex and Sid stop walking and let us join them.

'Good work,' Sid says.

'Right,' I say.

The tide has gone out and the beach is wide, a crooked line running along the sand, marking where the water reached earlier in the day. People have come down to watch the sunset, which is over, but they still sit in beach chairs and drink wine and beer. They peel their shoulders back as though still soaking in the sun. As we walk closer, I feel I'm walking the plank.

I look at Sid, for support, perhaps, but he's preoccupied. Whenever he's quiet, I think he's thinking about his dad, and it scares me to be around him. Part of me is almost angry. This is my time. I have a lot to deal with, and I can't be bothered by his problems. I also can't be bothered

225

by pornos, sea urchins, young love, but here we are.

The pier is ahead, and kids are running to the edge of the water, then running back up the slope. Scottie joins them. I wonder what the age is when you can no longer just join the other kids. As we get closer, I see that two of the kids are Brian's boys. I look higher on the beach to see if their parents are sitting on beach chairs, soaking in the night, but they aren't.

The moon is behind black clouds, and the bright glow behind the wisps of black make the moon and clouds look like an X-ray. I hear the water rush up onto the sand, sounding like someone shaking a container of broken glass. The kids playing on the sand run toward me, trying to catch a ball. The younger boy pounds the sand with his fist.

'Are your parents up there?' I ask him. He's surprisingly clean for a kid playing out here. There's black grime under Scottie's nails that I keep forgetting to remove.

'Yeah,' he says.

'Are they watching pornos?' Sid asks, coming up behind us.

The boy nods solemnly, the kind of nod that says he has no idea what he's affirming.

'Scottie, do you want to stay down here?' I call.

'Yeah,' she yells.

'Yes,' I correct.

Four boys rush toward her, gazing behind them at the ball in the sky. I almost yell to her to watch out, but she runs into the group of boys and jumps to catch the ball, which falls somewhere that I can't see.

'Sid? Will you keep an eye on her?'

Sid looks up at the house. The flower is tucked

226

behind his ear. 'Sure,' he says. 'I'll hang here.'

Scottie walks up the beach where the slightly older kids are hanging out. The older brother is explaining the rules to some kind of game. 'Wait,' he says to Scottie, thrusting his arm out to stop her. 'How old are you?'

'Ten and a half,' I hear her say.

'Okay, you can come in, but no one else!' he warns the others. Sid walks past them and lights a cigarette. All of the kids look at him, fascinated. I should tell him to put it out, but I don't care.

The older boy continues his speech. It's as though he's sending them out to fight a war.

'Hold fast,' I hear him say. 'I'm not responsible for you.'

Jesus. 'Hey there, son,' I say to the boy as Alex and I pass. 'You okay? You almost drowned today.'

His eyes dart around at his followers. 'I'm fine,' he says, and before I can say anything more, he lowers his voice and says, 'Let's begin.'

Alex and I cut through the hedge and walk up to the house.

# 33

We walk slowly. The small cottage looms ahead.

'What should I say?' I ask, immediately regretting it. I need to be the one in control. I need her to think that I know what to say.

'You should tell him that Mom is going to die soon,' she says flatly. 'Find a way to get him alone. I'm sure that won't be hard— he'll want to get you away from her once he finds out who you are.'

'I'm sorry for involving you, for letting you know

this about your mother. It's selfish of me.'

'I already knew everything about her,' she says. 'It's okay.'

She doesn't know everything. She doesn't know about her mother's campaign for Brian, for their life together. She doesn't know about Joanie's fear, or Joanie's strong love for her. She doesn't know everything, and neither do I.

Two heads appear in the kitchen window, and then Mrs. Speer backs into the screen door, carrying a platter of hamburger patties outside.

Alex nudges me. I'm afraid to scare her. It's bizarre that we're here. 'Hi there,' I call. Alex waves.

The screen door slams loudly and Mrs. Speer looks out at the lawn. I can't tell if she's happy to see us.

'Hello!' she says. 'How are you? I was hoping I'd see you guys again. We rushed away and . . . Well, here you are.'

We stand at the foot of the porch steps.

'I'm such an idiot,' I say. 'I do know your husband. I just put it together. We were walking back to the hotel from Tiki's, and I saw your boys down on the beach. I thought we'd drop in and say howdy to you. And to Brian.'

Alex looks at me and mouths, 'Howdy?'

'Come on up,' Mrs. Speer says. 'Actually, I was just telling my husband about meeting you but realized we didn't exchange names. After all that. I'm Julie.'

'Matt King,' I say. 'This is Alex.'

We walk up the steps. Julie seems too cute of a name for her. I say it silently to myself a few times.

'I thought you were mistaken when you said you

didn't know Brian. I figured you must have crossed paths. He's been so involved.'

'Yes,' I say. 'Really involved. I don't know what I was thinking. My mind was elsewhere.'

'For a while there, it seemed we never saw him. But I guess it's almost over. Would you like a hamburger?' she asks.

'We just came from dinner,' I say, 'but thank you.'

'That's right. You said that.'

I lean against the porch rail, and Alex stands on the edge of the steps, letting her heels drop. Then she stands on her tiptoes and lets them drop again.

'Are you exercising?' I ask.

'No,' she says. 'Sorry.' She walks across the porch and sits on a reclining chair. Julie holds a spatula in her hand, then balances it on the porch railing. I can hear the ocean and the children yelling.

'So, tomorrow, right?' she says. 'You'll know tomorrow.' She looks down. 'I'm sorry. I shouldn't have said that. There's a conflict of interest. That was stupid of me.'

'It's okay,' I say.

She laughs and leans against the railing and places her hands on her thighs and lifts her fingers to examine her nails. She's wearing jeans and a white T-shirt, and her hair is wet and piled into a bun on top of her head.

'Tomorrow it will be over,' I say.

'Yes,' she says. 'Thank God.'

We seem to be lodged into a dead calm. Waves crash on the shore, followed by a suction sound. I can see the kids and the orange glow of Sid's cigarette, but then it disappears.

'Would you like a drink?' Julie asks.

229

'Sure,' Alex and I say at the same time.

She pushes off the railing and the spatula falls. She gazes down at the dark grass. I move to retrieve it, but she waves for me to stay, and walks down the steps. I hear the screen door opening and see the silhouette of Brian behind the screen. Then he walks out and looks at my daughter and me.

'Hi,' he says, extending his hand. 'I'm Brian.'

Julie walks up the steps, blades of wet grass on her white tennis shoes.

'Brian.' I pump his hand vigorously, and when we pull away, he gives his wrist a tiny shake. 'We've met before,' I say, looking over at Julie. 'Matt King. My wife is Joanie; we met you at a shareholders' meeting, I think it was. This is our daughter Alex.'

His grin wilts. He looks briefly at Alex and does a double take, perhaps seeing her resemblance to his mistress.

'Matt's the one I was telling you about. He saved Christopher.'

Brian stares at me.

'I was just going to get drinks,' Julie says. 'And to wash this off.' She holds up the metal spatula. I can see rust on its underside.

'Good, good,' Brian says. He pats Julie on the back. 'Good.' He opens the door for her. You can tell that he never does this, because it takes her a moment to understand what he's doing.

'Do you need help?' Alex asks.

The screen door closes. 'No, no,' she calls.

As soon as she's out of earshot, I say, 'She's dying. I thought I'd give you a chance to say goodbye.'

His body tenses. The package of whole-wheat

230

buns in his hand looks ridiculous.

'I just came here to tell you. That's all I came to do.'

'My dad doesn't want to hurt your family,' Alex says. 'We're just doing what we think she would want, and she wanted you, evidently.' She eyes his face, then the buns he still holds in his hand. 'God knows why,' she adds and looks at me. 'Why would she want him?'

'That's enough, Alex,' and then I say, 'I don't know.'

'I can't,' Brian says, looking toward the door. 'I'm sorry. I never thought it would come to this.'

'You're sorry,' Alex says. 'That makes it all better. You're sorry to hear my mom's going to die, you're sorry you screwed my mom, or you're sorry you screwed my dad?'

'No,' he says. He stares at the space in front of him. 'Yes. I'm sorry for all of it.'

'There's a nine-fifteen flight out of here,' I say. 'I'm sure you can think of a good excuse to leave.'

'You must be good at that,' Alex says.

'Alex,' I say, though her remarks are lost on him. He's deep in his own thoughts.

'You can go to the hospital tonight or tomorrow morning,' I say. 'I'm sure you want to see her and say whatever you need to say. You'll be alone with her.'

'What?' he says.

'You can be alone with her.'

'Okay,' he says. 'Look.' He turns to the screen door, then faces me and lowers his voice. 'I can't have you here. You understand.'

Julie comes out with a glass of red wine and a soda for Alex. 'I hope this is okay,' she says. Her smile fades a little as she notices our expressions.

'Perfect,' I say and take a sip of the wine.

'Brian, no talking about business. I already made that mistake.' She looks at Alex and winks.

'What, Julie?' Brian says. 'What are you talking about?'

'Nothing,' she says. 'You all looked so serious, I just thought you were talking about . . . about the sale.'

'No,' Alex says. 'We were talking about love.'

'Well,' Julie says. She bumps her shoulder into Brian, who looks down at her, his brow still furrowed, a deep wrinkle running halfway across his forehead. 'What about love?' she asks.

No one answers or moves. Brian looks over Julie's head and frowns at me. I want to tell him that he doesn't get to frown at me.

'Are you in love?' Julie asks. 'With the boy on the raft.'

We're all standing except Alex. 'No,' she says. 'He's my friend. We have things in common, that's all.'

'Sometimes that's how it starts,' Julie says. She puts her arm around her husband's waist and presses her hand into him, something Joanie would do, signaling me to participate in the conversation.

'No,' Alex says. 'We have a friendship that we don't have to work on.'

'But I saw him kiss you,' I say, then realize I'm not supposed to add to this conversation. It's just a guise that Alex started and one of us needs to end. But I can't help it. I want to know.

'Oh, please,' she says. 'We're friends, but of course he's going to try to get laid. Every guy wants to get laid.' She looks at Brian.

'We're in for it, aren't we,' Julie says, looking up at her husband.

'What?'

'The boys. Our boys. Speaking of the boys, we should get them. Call them in for dinner.'

'They're fine,' Brian says. 'Just let them play.' He moves away from her. Her arm drops to her side. He places the buns on the table by a bowl that's filled with sea glass.

I hear a boy yell, 'No! Back off! Back off!'

We all look toward the ocean.

Alex gives me an urgent look and I return it: *What am I supposed to do?*

'I love this old house,' Alex says, looking at me again, urging me to do something.

'Yes,' I say. 'Great old place.' I look into the windows at the expanse of the parlor. 'I haven't been here in a while. My great-aunt used to live here, you know.'

Brian could be, at this moment, the angriest man alive. I could have called him. I could have done this differently, but his reaction is what I came here to see. 'I wonder if the inside has changed much. If they did something with that rough wood. We used to stay here a couple weeks in the summer as kids, and Cousin Hugh, he'd always get splinters from touching the walls.'

'I could show you around,' Julie says.

'Or, Brian,' Alex says, 'you could show my dad around, and Julie and I can talk about love.' The two women smile at each other.

'Hey, that would be great,' I say.

'Sure,' Brian says. 'But it's not like I live here. You're welcome to just . . .' He must have received a look from his wife, because he stops talking. He opens the door for me and I walk in. Alex shakes her head at me and I don't know what it's supposed to mean and not knowing makes my heart race. I look at the back of Brian as though an answer is pinned to his dark blue T-shirt.

'Here it is,' he says, sweeping his arm out at the open and warm room. The walls have been papered. The ceiling beams look lighter than I remember.

I walk to the far side of the room and have a seat in the koa rocking chair. None of the furniture in this house is comfortable. It all belonged to the missionaries, and our guesthouses all seem to be storage bins for the old settees and daybeds, the sewing baskets, the Hawaiian quilts and mosquito netting. The home across the street by the church still has the same stove and Dutch doors, a butter churn, bootjacks, and whale-oil lamps. The ceilings are low, the stairwell narrow and precarious, and the house has a roof like a pilgrim's hat.

Brian has his hands on his hips. It's amusing that he swept his arm out, displaying the room. I wonder if he's a funny guy.

'So, Brian. As I said, I understand if you want to talk to her alone. There's nothing I can do about the rest of it. So, I'm here. I'm telling you that I know about you and I know she loved you and that you were going to . . .' I wave my hand in the air, indicating whatever they were going to do after they left us. 'You're welcome to say goodbye. The doctor stopped artificial breathing yesterday. She has about a week, maybe longer.'

He looks like I've tricked him, like I really wanted to see the inside of this house.

'How did you meet?' I ask. 'I'm curious.'

234

'I can't do this,' he says.

'Believe me,' I say. 'Neither can I.'

'Did you come here for me?'

'Yes, I came to get you. I got everyone else who was important to her, and you were up.' I ask again: 'I can't very well ask her all of the details, so I need to ask you. I want to know. How did you meet?'

'I thought you said you came here just to tell me. That it was all you wanted to do.'

'I've changed my mind,' I say. 'How did you meet?' I was right. He is spotless. His hair is slicked back, the top strands thick with gel, and now I like the fact that I haven't shaved. I like that there's salt on my skin and hard alcohol on my breath. I wish I had one of Sid's cigarettes. That would look even better.

'At a party,' he says. After releasing the words, he sits down on the daybed to the left of me. I feel like telling him to get off the bed. It's my bed.

'What party?'

'Just a party. A Super Bowl party.'

I know exactly what party he's talking about. Last year's Super Bowl. New England vs. Carolina. But for me it was *State vs. Doreen Wellington.* Trial next day. I'd be up all night. Joanie home at six P.M., in a great mood, then by the end of dinner angry at me, impatient with Scottie. 'Must we always have fajitas on Sunday? I mean, really.'

I asked her about the party, wondering if something happened there that upset her.

'It was the best day I've had in a long time,' she said. 'I had a really good time.' She had a sad look on her face.

Why do I remember this? The sad face, the fajitas?

235

'The party at the Mitchells',' I say.

Brian nods, looking at me as though I'm an annoyance. 'Yes,' he says. 'That's the one.'

I rock the chair back and try to angle it so that I face him. I place my wineglass on one of the arms, something we were never supposed to do.

'Does that help?' he asks. 'Knowing that?'

'Hey,' I say. 'I'm doing you a favor here.' I take a sip of my wine. 'Get a better attitude.' He takes a drink of his wine. 'Do you have any beer?' I ask. 'I can't drink this.'

'Me, neither.' He gets up to retrieve something else. I rock in the chair. I have an upper hand that's so high. I close my eyes for a moment, feeling comfortable even in this hard and slippery chair. The air is warm but not stifling or humid, and in this house, I feel I have people behind me, Great-aunt Lucy, Hugh's grandparents and parents, people who loved me, though they're dead now. Brian comes back with the beer, and when he hands it to me, we look at each other and for a moment he's just a guy giving me a beer, and maybe in his eyes I'm just a guy taking a beer. I was planning on giving him my wineglass, but I set it on the floor instead.

'So then what?' I ask. 'You rooted for the same team? You liked the way she looked? You were amazed that a girl could be so cool, could watch football and know what she was talking about?'

'We're still on this,' he says.

'Some women dress sexy or get breast implants. Joanie watched football, raced boats. It was her way to get men to like her. It's not that amazing.'

He looks into his beer.

'How did you get the nerve to ask her out?'

He shakes his head.

'No, I'm serious. I really want to know what makes a person cross that line.'

He doesn't answer and I know he never will. He looks toward the window across the room. I follow his gaze and see his wife. Her expression is incredulous and thrilled, and then I hear my daughter laugh. Julie takes a sip of her wine. The sight of Julie talking to my daughter saddens me. Even though Alex seems to be truly enjoying herself out there, she's deceiving Julie. We all are.

'I've heard about your new business opportunity.' I keep my eyes on the window. 'Joanie worked hard to get me to like Don. Quite a plan you had.'

'It's not what you think,' he says.

'What do I think? How do you know what I think?'

'You think I'm ruthless,' he says. 'That I was plotting something. I think that's what you think. Me and Joanie. It just happened.'

'Nothing just happens,' I say.

'But it does,' he says.

'So, when you found out her connection to me, did you decide then to commit the adultery, or were you already committed? Did you ask her to sway me? Because, boy, she was hot for Holitzer. That doesn't just happen.'

He doesn't say anything. He looks at the window again, ignoring my questioning face. I take a long sip of beer. I see Julie opening the grill and poking at the burgers with the spatula. It occurs to me that she must have lit the grill, something that sort of astounds me. She doesn't seem so delicate, so foolish, anymore.

'Look,' I say. 'I'm glad she was in love, I guess.

237

I'm glad you made her happy. This must be hard on you. Finding out like this.'

He's still looking outside. Alex and Julie are standing with their backs to us, looking out at the bay. I realize his tactic—he's not responding, which makes me talk endlessly, backtracking and forgiving him without his having to sweat.

'Was she going to leave me?' I ask.

I don't expect him to tell me the truth, or even to answer, but he says, 'She would have. But it wouldn't have happened.'

'Why? Because of Scottie, or what? You were afraid to tell Julie?'

'No,' he says. 'I wouldn't leave Julie because I love Julie.' He leans forward a bit, and a new expression appears on his face. 'Please don't tell her,' he says. 'Please. I don't know what I've done.'

Here is the anguish I came to see, yet it's not over my wife or over my discoveries, and something dawns on me that I never considered.

'Did she love you?' I ask.

He nods and lifts his beer to his mouth. A watery circle has appeared on the leg of his pants.

'Did you love her?' I ask.

He takes a long sip and brings the beer back down, lining up the base of the beer with the halo of water.

'You didn't love her.' I need to say it again: 'You didn't love her.' I hear the surf collide with the shore, and a breeze full of salt and seaweed moves into the room.

'You just used her,' I say. 'To get to me.'

He lets out a sigh. 'No. I didn't try to get to you. It was an affair. An attraction. Sex.' He checks my face to see if I'm angry. 'She suggested everything

238

beyond that, and I went with it.'

His shoulders drop, and it's like we're playing charades and he's finally performed in a way that has led me to the right answer.

'And then you'd get rid of her after the sale,' I say. 'I guess things worked out great for you. Her lips are sealed, and you don't have to deal with dumping her.'

'I wasn't even trying to use her for a connection!' he says, standing up. 'She was consumed by it. I never asked her to help me. I never asked her for anything.' He walks the length of the bed, then walks back, looking up at the ceiling.

I can see this happening with Joanie. She takes on projects that aren't hers to take. She molds. I think of Alex and myself, even, her desire to make us over. I stand up, too, and walk toward the window but stop in the middle of the room. 'That poor girl,' I say. My wife was the fool. She will never know how bad it was. For the first time ever, Joanie seems weak to me.

I look at Alex's profile. She turns her head and sees me, and I get this chill. *That's my daughter watching me,* I think. *I made her, that girl there.*

'So I guess you don't need to say goodbye.'

'I love Julie very much,' he says. 'I love my family.'

'I love my family, too.' I walk back across the room. I hand Brian my empty beer bottle.

'Should we—' He gestures toward the screen door. 'Do you have anything else to say to me?'

I shake my head.

'Shouldn't you be with her?' he asks.

'Yes,' I say and walk to the door, passing pictures of my ancestors hanging on the walls, their creepy and moody daguerreotypes. I pass my great-great-grandfather, who looks affronted and merciless. As I pass, I imagine his somber dark eyes following me.

Brian goes to the kitchen to throw away the bottles and put the glasses in the sink. I swing the screen door open and exit the house.

'Thanks for having us,' I say to Julie Speer.

'Thanks for stopping by,' she says. 'I feel I know you so well after today and after Alex's stories.' She gives Alex a private smile.

'I feel I know you well, too,' I say. I look at Brian through the screen door, his face alert and searching. 'We have a lot in common, I think.' I take her hand and give it a little squeeze.

She holds on to my hand, her palm damp, then slides away gently. 'Bye, Alex,' she says. 'Maybe we'll see you on the beach tomorrow.'

'Have a good night,' Alex says. She walks down the steps and onto the dark lawn. The sky has filled with stars, the moon thin like a splinter.

As Alex walks away, I turn to Julie once more and kiss her. I lean in and part my lips and kiss her. Because I want to, because she is Brian's, because we've suffered a similar fate, because I want her to like it, because I want her to feel insulted, confused, annoyed, defenseless, happy. Because I want to.

I don't look at her eyes when I pull away, but I look at her lips, and the tip of her tongue peeks out to wipe me away. Without saying anything, I turn and leave her and her family behind. As I walk out to the beach, something in me loosens, and it's not because I'm relaxed. It's because something in me has given up and failed, returning with nothing to give.

# 34

The nine-fifteen flight is surprisingly full. Tourists have shopping bags of souvenirs to prove they were here. I imagine the hula-girl hood ornaments, the T-shirts and macadamia nuts, in their plastic bags. They'll have gold bracelets embossed with their Hawaiian names and will go home and name their dogs or their children Lani and Koa. I thought we'd have a man as our keepsake to take to my wife, but we have no souvenirs, nothing to show for all of this.

The girls' postures are collapsed. I swear Scottie has lost weight just in these past few days. She is sleeping next to me. The airline's gray scratchy blanket is over her head like a hood and she looks sickly beneath it. Like a crack baby, or Death. I need to remember to feed the children. I need to make sure they wash and brush their teeth and go to doctors and get books for school. I need to get them to take on a sport and to have good friends and to study and read for fun. I need to tell them not to smoke or have sex, not to get into cars with strangers or friends who have been drinking. They need to write thank-you notes and eat what's put in front of them. They need to say 'yes,' not 'yeah,' to put their napkins on their laps, to chew their gum with closed mouths. I need more time.

Alex asks, 'What happened?'

I point at Scottie and put my finger to my mouth to get out of answering the question.

'She's fine,' Alex says. 'Tell me. When is he coming back?'

Sid leans forward. I stare ahead and feel their eyes on me. I don't know what to say. This is like the problem I had with the shark story. I feel it's imperative to hoard some information, letting the girls have a better impression of their mother. Yet I'm not sure which impression is more favorable—the one of Joanie in love and loved passionately and recklessly by someone else, or the impression of Joanie as deceived and desperate. She'll never know the mistake she made, and I don't know if this pleases me or makes me feel cheated.

'He was shocked,' I say.

'Was he sorry?' Sid asks. 'I hope he was sorry, man. You could have told his wife, and you didn't. I hope he knows how lucky he is. I would have told her everything. She deserves to know. Or else she's going to be a dumb bitch for the rest of her life.'

'Calm down, son,' I say. 'No need to get creepy.'

Alex places a hand on Sid's leg, and I see his leg twitch. She's got a good grip on him. I wonder what he's so angry about. I remember, on the way over here, his concentration on the safety brochure. I take the laminated instructions out of the seat pocket, hoping to distract Alex and Sid. I look at the passengers getting onto a raft in an ocean with no land in sight. Their life vests are inflated. An Asian man has a slight smile on his face.

Alex looks over. 'Their clothes aren't even wet.'

I tap the picture of the plane floating in the sea.

'So, is he coming back to see her, or what?' Sid asks.

'I don't think so,' I say.

Weak, vulnerable, pining, used. I wonder if, in Alex's eyes, these things would make her mother more lovable, more human.

242

'I think he still loves Julie very much,' I say.

Sid scoffs: 'Too bad.' He looks the other way as he says this, out the oval window of the plane. 'If he loved her, he wouldn't have fucked your wife.'

'Sid,' Alex says, and her voice is surprisingly calm. 'Please shut up.'

'Yes,' I say, trying to match her patient tone. 'Please.'

A chunk of Honolulu floats into view, and I can see lights coursing up the hills, then a blank dark space and another long row of house lights. It's always strange to be reminded of other lives still moving along. For every light I see, there's a person or a family, or someone like myself, enduring something. I feel the plane dropping, and then a wisp of cloud obstructs the view and makes our speed tangible.

'I think you should go home,' I say to Sid. 'See your mom.' He stares out the window. 'Sid. Did you hear what I said?'

'I can't,' he says.

'Sure you can. She's your mother. She wants you home.'

'She kicked me out,' he says.

I try to make eye contact with Alex, but she won't look my way. Her hand is still on Sid's thigh, and the two of them together are absolutely impenetrable. The runways stretch out beside us. We're back to reality, miles and miles away from the slow and easy island.

# PART IV

# Wayfinding

# 35

I meet the cousins at Cousin Six's house. He's called Cousin Six because at one point in his boyhood, he chugged six beers and then punched himself in the nose. He is now around seventy, and like him, his moniker is still going strong. He sits in the living room, which is similar to mine—sliding glass doors open to the backyard. Every time I see him, he tells me how he'd give soldiers surfing lessons in exchange for access to his favorite spot, which was blocked off during the war, so I'm out by the pool, trying to avoid him. He tells me about the soldiers as though it's the first time he has ever told me, and it makes me sad and uncomfortable and a little angry.

I'm sitting at a table by the pool, with my pen perched over the documents and our statement to the press, but I haven't signed a thing. My mind is elsewhere, of course. Any day now I will be a widower. The girls are waiting for me at the hospital, making up for our one night and two days away. I haven't seen Sid since last night. I wonder what he expects from me. I thought of calling his mother, but then there would be another superfluous person in my life. There are so many people in my thoughts who shouldn't be there. I put Sid and the girls aside. Today I must deal with birthrights.

A few cousins want to take the highest offer, not caring about the Wal-Mart replacing the taro patch, but the majority wants Holitzer, our only local bidder. I don't like what's happening. I want all this land to go to a good home, and I don't like our decision, or any of the options in front of me, and neither would my father. Holitzer has won. Brian has won.

Other cousins are walking out to the patio. They wear shorts, Spooners, and rubber slippers and carry celebratory cocktails. Cousin Six's wife is passing around a bowl of mochi crunch, which makes everyone's breath smell like soy sauce.

'Eh, long time no see.' Hugh sits next to me with his documents. He carries a pen in his mouth.

'I just saw you last night,' I say. 'On Kauai.'

'Was that last night? Boy.' He looks at the chair. 'Will this hold me?'

I look at the well-worn seat made of plastic cords. I've sunk into my cords and can feel the impressions on the backs of my thighs. 'It should hold,' I say.

He sits in the chair and I can hear the plastic stretch.

'It's like an ass hammock,' he says, then begins flipping through the papers. 'Out of our hands.' He smooths the paper and presses the end of the pen so that it clicks.

It's all such a fluke, a stroke of luck. I look at the cousins standing around the pool. Their teeth are so white, their skin coloring like walnuts. What happened to me? Why am I not like them?

'Do you ever feel guilty about it?' I ask. 'All of this.' I hold up the papers.

'No,' Hugh says. 'I didn't do anything.'

'I know,' I say, and he's right. It's like feeling guilty about your eye color. The only thing I feel guilty about is that my wife thought she was going to inherit another sort of life. She should have been with somebody more charismatic than me. Someone more powerful and loud, someone who eats really fast and wipes his mouth with the back of his hand. I think of her entering Brian's house on Black Point, which makes me think of Julie. I can imagine Joanie eyeing their home, making fun of Julie's knickknacks or the art on the walls, perhaps planning the ways she would redecorate. I want to tell her to stop. It's Julie's home. Julie can light a barbecue.

'Joanie's not doing well,' I say to Hugh.

His pen moves across the first page, and I see his childlike signature. It's perfectly legible. He puts his hand over mine for a moment. His arm looks as though his skin has been pulled back. It's raw and spotted. 'She'll be okay,' he says. 'She's a fighter.'

'No,' I say. 'She won't be fine. She's going to die. We've taken her off the machines.'

I take a sip of Hugh's cocktail because it's there and I don't have my own. Hugh's the head cousin, the leader of the tribe, and he has always told us what to think and what to do. What we're building, what we're tearing down, and in this case, when we're selling and to whom. I want to hear what he has to say about this, about my wife dying. I put his glass back down on the table.

He looks at the glass, then at me. 'Have some more,' he says.

'That's okay.' I stare at the papers, the pen that says HNL TRAVEL. 'I can't sign,' I say.

He takes his drink and shakes it, then brings it to his mouth. He takes a sip and spits out an ice cube. 'He'll take over our debt,' he says. 'Just sign, go to your wife, done.'

'I don't want it to go to Holitzer. I don't want it

249

to go to Brian Speer. We can get out of our own debt. I want to keep it.'

He frowns. 'We need your approval to move.'

I shake my head. He's not getting my approval. No one is getting anything from me.

'I can't,' I say. 'I won't do it.'

I'm thinking of the princess. When she died, she wanted the land to be used to fund a school for children of Hawaiian descent. This was her spoken wish that she failed to put into a contract. I have no interest in this wish, in a Hawaiian-only school. There are already a few of them, and they're completely elitist, not to mention unconstitutional. But now I find myself not wanting to give it up—the land, the lush relic of our tribe, the dead. The last Hawaiian-owned land will be lost, and I will have something to do with it. Even though we don't look Hawaiian, even though our constant recombining has erased the evidence of our ethnicity, sharpening our flat faces, straightening our kinky hair, even though we act like haoles, going to private schools and clubs and not having a good command of pidgin English, my girls and I are Hawaiian, and this land is ours.

'Why are you doing this now?' Hugh leans on his forearms. I can see the pores on his red face, and his wild white eyebrows reach up toward his forehead, which is shiny and surprisingly smooth. A drop of sweat slides from his hairline down his nose and onto the table. Both of us look at the spot where it landed, then he grasps my shoulder in a way that's both affectionate and painful. 'What's the real reason?' he asks.

The princess, I think. My ancestors, but no, that's not it entirely. That's what I want the reason to be,

250

but there are other, less dignified ones: Revenge. Selfishness. A desire to see my daughters have the land. Let them make decisions about it. A desire to hold on, pass down, clutch something that was given to me. I don't want Brian to have a part of it. I don't want his sons to have it. I don't want their history to mix with mine. Kekipi rebelled, and so will I.

'It's just something I want,' I say. 'I haven't wanted something in a long time. This is what I want.'

He doesn't seem to believe me, or at least my answer is too ambiguous, too emotional. He lets go of my shoulder.

'This is our responsibility,' I say. 'This guy's going to come in here and rescue us. We've run our assets into the ground. We're Hawaiian—it's a miracle we own this much of Hawaii. Why let some haole swoop it up? We've been careless.'

'The hurricane ran our assets—'

'We did, Hugh. We've been paralyzed, and we're smart people. We can rescue ourselves. It's our problem.'

This angle works a little better. I think of Joanie, what she would say. 'Don't be a pussy,' I add.

Hugh has a delayed smile. 'You're going to make a lot of people angry,' he says.

'I could also make a lot of people relieved,' I say. 'We've moved too fast. Just think, I approve this buyer, then tomorrow—gone. Over. End of the line. Believe me, people will be relieved.'

He nods.

'Think about it,' I say. 'Sure, we'd make money, we'd have it easier not needing to run the business, but . . .'

251

'You want it,' he says.

'Yes,' I say. 'We own this.' I wave my hand in the air. 'There's nothing more powerful than this.'

Hugh brings his fingers to his mouth and blows. A sharp whistle cuts through the air, and the cousins stop talking and turn to look at me. It's as if they know.

*I'm sorry,* I'll have to say. *I know I wouldn't have done this if my wife weren't going to die, but the fact is, she is. She is going to die and she will be gone and my daughters will not have a mother. For some reason, luck of the draw, really, you need my approval. I know you understand the complicated nature of birthrights, how they're both fortuitous and undeserved. I've decided that you won't be receiving any money, but we'll all get to keep something, and we'll get to pass it on.*

I look at these people, my family, and I hope they'll understand.

# 36

There are new flowers—ginger, gardenia, tuberose. Joanie has had visitors since my cocktail party. Lots of roses, though none of them are red. I could see the husbands saying to the wives, 'But she'll never see the flowers.' It's something I would say, too. I'm glad we haven't been here these past two days. Scottie wouldn't have understood the visitors and their tears, and Alex and I got to avoid the discomfort that goes along with all of this.

I see an image of myself and my girls walking down the beach. I miss our hotel room.

'Dad,' Scottie says. 'What are you thinking about?'

'You,' I say. 'I'm thinking about you.'

Alex is off buying bottles of water, the only thing we can stomach, and I wish she would hurry back.

Joanie looks different. She's gaunt and pasty, vacant-looking. There is no tube coming out of her mouth. Scottie hasn't said anything about it, and I'm glad, because I still don't know how to tell her.

'What about me?' Scottie says. 'What were you thinking about me?'

'I was thinking about how you've grown so fast.'

'Hardly,' she says. 'I'm in the lowest percentile. Reina's in the lowest percentile, too, though. Reina says—'

'That's enough about Reina. Remember what we said about her.'

'Fine, but I want her to come back to the hospital tomorrow. Alex gets to have a friend, so I do, too.'

'Scottie. She can't come here tomorrow.'

'Why not!'

'Do you know what's happening?' Scottie walks to her backpack and rifles through it, taking out various things. 'Scottie, I asked you a question.'

'Yes, Dad, God!'

'What, then? Tell me why we're here. Don't tell me about Reina. Don't fuss around in your bag. Tell me why we're here and why you won't touch or talk to your mother.'

'Dad.' I turn to see Alex in the doorway. She gives me my water. Scottie is sitting in the chair at the back of the room, facing the wall. I want to hug her, but I can't. I feel committed to my anger.

'What are you yelling about?' Alex says.

'Nothing. Your sister was talking about

253

Reina, that's all. I got upset. I just want this to go smoothly, girls. I don't want to have to . . . manage you. Where's Sid, by the way? I'd like to have a word with him.'

'He's probably with other girls,' Scottie says. 'Last night those friends of yours were on the beach, and Sid went off with them while you were up at that house.'

'What are you talking about?' Alex says, and I see the hurt in her eyes.

'He probably orgied them,' Scottie says solemnly.

'I don't care,' Alex says, though it's quite evident she does. 'Oh my God.'

I follow her gaze to my wife's bed. Joanie's hand is raised as though she's taking an oath.

I immediately look at her face, but her eyes are closed. She does this sometimes, moves, but Alex has never seen it. I look at Scottie, facing the wall. 'Come here, Scottie,' I say.

I stare at Joanie's hand. It's pale and dry. Her nails are longer. She breathes loudly all of a sudden, as if she's trying to catch her breath.

'She can't breathe,' Scottie yells.

'Come here,' I say again, forcefully.

'Dad,' Alex says.

Scottie walks to my side with her head down.

'She can breathe,' I say. 'The doctor says that's just a reflex. She's not struggling, she's not suffering. Now, why don't you go hold it. Her hand.'

I see the faint hair on Joanie's arm, the wrinkles on her wrist. I take Scottie by the hand and pull her over to her mother. She resists me and Alex yells for me to stop, but I don't. I unclench Scottie's fist and stuff her hand into her mother's and then I make Joanie's hand grip Scottie's. Tears begin

254

to march down Scottie's cheeks. Her face has red splotches on it, which is what happens to me when I get angry or I'm having sex. Joanie continues to breathe roughly. It sounds like she's struggling. It sounds like she's suffering. I hold Scottie still.

'Dad!' Alex yells. 'Stop it.'

'Take the other hand,' I say to Alex, gesturing to the other side of the bed. 'Now. Do it now.'

Alex goes over to the side opposite me and looks down at her mother. She lifts the sheet and reaches for the hand with her eyes closed. Her face is puckered, as though she's about to eat something really bad on a dare. She frees her mother's hand and then sets it down and places her hand on top of it. And then she takes it. I see the force in her grip. Alex keeps her head down so I can't see her face. Scottie is shaking. I hold Scottie from behind, wrapping my arms around her as if we're going to crash. The girls need to do this or they'll regret it for the rest of their lives.

'Say something,' I say to Scottie.

'No,' she says, her voice full of torment. 'You're hurting me.'

I look at Alex. Her head is still down, her shoulders shaking slightly.

'Say something, Alex.'

'You say something,' she yells, and I see that she's weeping.

I bow my head and speak to Joanie softly. 'I'm sorry,' I say. 'I didn't give you everything you wanted. I wasn't everything you wanted. You were everything I wanted.' I'm mumbling as if I'm reciting a prayer. My head and throat pulse with heat. I'm trying to think of memories, key words I can say that will trigger entire moments, but I can't

255

think of anything. We've known each other since I was twenty-six and she was nineteen. Why can't I think of a memory?

'Every day,' I say. 'Home. There you are. Dinner, dishes, TV. Weekends at the beach. You go here. I go there. Parties. Home to complain about the party. Car rides home over the Pali before they put up streetlights.' I can't think of anything else. Just our routine together. 'I loved it,' I say, gripping her hand harder.

I never speak this way. I feel that she's smirking at me and glance up and see how uncomfortable Alex looks. Scottie, too, wears an awkward and fearful expression.

'I forgive you,' I say, and feel Joanie smirking even more.

Alex walks around the bed and pulls Scottie away from me. I still hold on and look at Joanie's face, the pleased expression. I try to read her, to understand her; it frustrates me to see her look so satisfied. I bend down so that my face is right in front of hers and say, 'He didn't love you. I love you.'

# 37

Why is it so hard to articulate love yet so easy to express disappointment? I leave the room without saying anything to the girls. To the left of the room is a thin glass wall, and I look through it at the dark husks of palms and the empty park benches. I see the huge monkeypod tree; its canopy seems to hover in space. Something glints from its branches, but I don't know what it is. I walk over to the row of chairs and sit down, practically collapsing. I close my eyes. When I open them, there's a young man placing a piece of paper on the seat next to me. He continues to the hallway, where he hands out more of his papers to people walking by. On the paper beside me, I expect to see an ad for a blowout sale or a menu for Chinese delivery. Instead, I see a list of burial options:

Be part of a living coral reef after you have gone!
Aloha burials at sea—be paddled off in a canoe
    and scattered!
Shoot your ashes into Earth's orbit!
Release ashes from a hot-air balloon to the
    four winds!
Go out as part of a firework display!

The last one doesn't have an exclamation mark. It says, *Have your loved one's remains mixed with the soil of a living and very beautiful bonsai tree. A bonsai tree that grows and will live for hundreds of years with simple care.*

At the bottom is a name, Vern Ashbury, and a phone number that I can call for pricing information.

'What's that?'

I turn to see Alex. She sits down next to me.

'I don't know,' I say. 'An ad for something.' I put it facedown on the other side of me so she can't see it. I close my eyes again.

'That was bad,' she says. 'You shouldn't have done that. Scottie's upset. She's just a baby.'

'She's not a baby.'

'She is now,' Alex says.

'I need to go home.' I sit up and open my eyes. 'I need to talk to Sid. I have things to do.'

'Why do you have to talk to Sid?'

'Why did he get kicked out?'

'You'll have to ask him,' she says.

'I'm asking you.'

'I don't know why,' she says. I believe her.

'We don't have time for him, Alex. I'm sorry he's hurting, but I don't have time for it. You tell him to stay out of the way, not to put his shit before ours. Especially if he's hurting your feelings.'

'Fine,' she says. 'Whatever.'

She reaches across my lap for the ad. I watch as she reads the options.

'Are you kidding me?' she says. 'Vern Ashbury. Christ. I guess I like the bonsai one. It's sad.'

'I know,' I say. 'What have you told Scottie? Does she know what's happening?'

'Just now, the hand. She thinks it means something. She thinks Mom might get better.'

'Okay,' I say.

'No,' she says. 'Not okay. Really not okay. You need to talk to her, Dad. You yell at her for not knowing, for not behaving properly, but she doesn't know what's going on. Don't put me in charge of her anymore. She needs you.' Alex stands and walks away.

'Where are you going?'

She doesn't acknowledge me, and I follow her, leaving the burial options behind. We pass the popular patient's room, and it seems even lonelier than the bare ones. The balloons are slowly shriveling; a few of the flowers in the vases are bowing toward the floor, and a lei hanging on a doorknob reveals its white string between the

258

withered plumeria.

A woman is standing at the end of the bed. 'I'm just a volunteer,' she says to the patient. 'I'm not allowed to touch you.'

Alex walks to the elevators across from the gift shop.

'I found you in there.' I gesture toward the shop, and it takes a moment, but then she sees the postcards.

'Great,' she says. 'Isn't that great.'

'I bought them and threw them away.'

'Thanks,' she says.

I look down the hall, hoping to see Scottie, but she isn't there. She's still in the room. I'll have to get one girl and leave the other one behind.

I choose Scottie, the baby, the one who shook in my arms. The elevator opens. A man shuffles out, hooked to an IV. I find myself wishing he'd hurry up and I think of Sid, his guilty impatience with slow people even when they're weak.

'Meet me at the car,' I say to Alex. 'I'll go talk to Scottie.'

\*       \*       \*

I'm embarrassed to see her. I know I should apologize, but she needed to do it. She needed to touch her.

When I near the room, I hear Scottie say, 'I have a really good eye.' I stop in the doorway. She is talking to her mother. I back away a little, but I can't walk away. I want to watch. I want to know what she says. I see her curled into her mother's side; she has maneuvered Joanie's arm so that it's around her. I catch myself thinking, *She's alive*. I

259

almost can't bear seeing Scottie in her mother's embrace.

'It's on the ceiling,' I hear Scottie say. 'The most beautiful nest. It's very golden and soft-looking and warm.'

I look up and see it, too, except it isn't a nest. It's a browning piece of banana, the remnant of our game still stuck to the ceiling. The game Joanie and I used to play, and now a game my daughter and I will play.

Scottie props herself on an elbow, then leans in and kisses her mother on the lips, checks her face, then kisses her again. She does this over and over, an exquisite version of mouth-to-mouth, each kiss expectant, almost medicinal, and I know she still has hope. I let her go on with this fantasy, this belief in magical endings, this belief that love can bring someone to life. I let her try. For a long time I watch her effort. I root for her, even, but after a while, I know that it's time. I need to step in. I need to teach Scottie the proper names of things. I need to tell her the truth.

I knock on the door. 'Scottie,' I say.

She stays under her mother's arm, her back toward me. I sit on the edge of the bed and lie down to put my head on her back and listen to her breathe. 'Scottie,' I say.

'What, Dad,' she says, and I tell her everything that's happening and everything that will happen, and I feel like the cruelest person in the world. But I fulfill my responsibilities as best I can, and when I'm finished, we stay there for what seems like a long time, her head on Joanie's chest, my head on her back, moving up and down with her short, sobbing breaths. Her little body is like a flexed muscle, tense and stressed, still resisting, and I know she doesn't completely believe it. How could she?

# 38

Tonight the girls and Esther and I sit together at the dining room table, something we haven't done in a long time, not counting Thanksgiving and Christmas. Esther has never sat with us before.

'How long has it been?' I ask. 'Since we've done this?'

'Christmas,' Alex says.

There's a story Alex wrote when she was young, and every Christmas Eve we read it aloud to the guests at the table and then reveal the author. The story is about Joseph, his perspective of the night Jesus was born. He asks the wise men and the farm animals how to take care of a baby, and they each have advice. By the end of the story, Joseph is ready for Jesus and even swaddles the baby, a trick he learned from the donkey. This past Christmas, when Joanie stood to read the story, Alex snatched it from her hand. I don't think any of the guests noticed that Joanie was about to do anything except our next-door neighbor, Bill Tigue, who thought she was going to read a prayer. He bowed his head and closed his eyes. Christmas was the time Alex saw her mother enter the home of another man. That shouldn't count as the real last time, and I suppose tonight doesn't count, either, since we aren't and never will be completely together.

'Well,' I say. 'Cheers.'

No one lifts a glass. Esther is having a beer. She grips her can with both hands and holds it in her lap.

'Doesn't Sid want to eat?' I ask. Sid is watching TV in the den, and no one has mentioned him, which makes me feel bad. I wonder if Alex has told him to stay away from me.

'He's fine,' Alex says.

We eat the dinner I have cooked: a salad, barbecued chicken, rice, and broccoli with hollandaise sauce. I keep waiting for someone to say the meal is good and have to hold myself back from asking. 'Well, we'll save some for him. If he wants it.'

Esther picks things out of her salad with her fork—the tomatoes, the avocados—and pushes them to the edge of her plate. The girls have drizzled shoyu on their rice. Esther's is topped with a pat of butter.

'Have you called their schools?' Esther asks. 'They been missing days.'

'Yes,' I say.

'Alex, when you go back?'

'She's not going back,' I say.

'Ay,' she says. 'You in trouble. I tell you. Pretty soon.'

'Could you please complete a sentence?'

She shakes her head. 'If only. If only.'

'Esther, what do you want to say? Do you want to stay? Why don't you just say that?'

The girls stop eating. Ever since I made them hold their mother's hand, they look at me in a way that makes me feel like a different man. They look at me like I'm their father.

'I want to stay,' Esther says. 'There. I complete a

262

sentence.' She puts her finger into the mouth of the beer can.

'Fine,' I say. 'Then stay.'

She gives me no indication that she's pleased. The girls seem indifferent.

'I want to get up now,' Esther says. 'I don't want to eat this way here.'

'Okay,' I say.

She starts to clear her plate.

'Just leave it,' I say. 'I'll clean up.'

'No, I still eat.' She takes her plate and her beer and pushes the swinging door of the kitchen. Moments later, we hear a crowd of people say, 'Wheel! Of! Fortune!'

A gecko croaks in the rafters.

'I'm not going back to HPA?' Alex says.

'No,' I say. 'You'll stay here.'

A termite climbs the ball of my rice. 'Ever notice how Sid's always putting things in his mouth?' I ask. 'His hair, shirt, wallet?'

'Like a toddler,' Alex says. 'I know.'

I notice another termite climbing up my water glass. They have found us. There's a blaze of light over our table. The girls pick them out of their food. Scottie fiddles with a few on the table, tearing off their wings.

'They look like maggots,' she says.

Our home has everything a termite could ever want: moisture, humidity, reservoirs of wood. If they keep coming, I'll have to fumigate the house, envelop it with a tent and let them inhale poison. Where would we go? I imagine us out on the streets. Alex flicks one from her rice and Scottie lifts one off her chicken; the red sauce has ruined its wings. I get up and turn off the lights, then turn

263

on the lights in the pool. They'll follow the light and drown.

I sit back down in the dark and we continue to eat. In the dark, I can hardly tell the girls apart. One of them burps. Both of them laugh.

I take a sip of my wine and the glass reminds me of my mother, what I did for her one Mother's Day when I was very young. I made her breakfast in bed. I placed lettuce in a red wineglass, then poured in granola and milk. I thought this was so sophisticated of me, something that a mother would truly want: cereal with an elegant garnish. When she saw her gift, she laughed, and at the time I thought she was laughing with delight. I watched her eat her granola in the pretty glass, green lettuce soaked in milk. When the girls were younger, I wondered what silly things they would get for me, how they would interpret my desires, but their gifts were always safe. Just cards, really.

'How come you've never made me crazy things for Father's Day?' I ask the girls.

'You don't like clutter,' Alex says.

'You don't like junk,' Scottie says.

'Well, I like it now,' I say. 'Just so you know. I like clutter and junk.'

'Okay,' Scottie says.

'This is good,' Alex says. 'The chicken.'

The compliment fills me with pride. I feel like Joseph in her story, like I have learned to take care of someone. At the end of Alex's story, Joseph burps Jesus, then rocks him to sleep. 'Don't cry, baby,' he says. 'I'm here.'

\*       \*       \*

While the girls clean up, I go to the den with a plate of dinner for Sid. When he sees me, he takes his feet off of the coffee table, and I notice he's on the phone. I turn to give him privacy, but then I hear him say goodbye.

'Was that your mom?' I ask.

'Nope,' he says. He looks at the plate in my hands. I hand it to him.

'Thank you,' he says.

'You could have sat with us,' I say.

'It's okay,' he says.

The lights from the television make his face blue then green then black. I think of turning on a light, but I see a termite walk across the screen and remember I have to keep us in the dark.

'Look,' I say. 'I appreciate you staying out of the way, but forget it. Just act like you normally do. It was better that way.'

He puts his feet back on the coffee table. I can see mud in the treads of his soles.

'Is everything okay with you and Alex?'

'Yeah,' he says. 'Why?'

'Scottie says you went off with those friends of hers.'

'Oh, please. Those girls are useless. I smoked them out.'

'Great, Sid. I'm so relieved you gave them drugs.'

'Sorry,' he says. 'I forget you're, like, a dad.'

'Why did your mom kick you out?' I ask.

'She didn't like what I had to say.'

'Which was?'

'That my father getting killed was the best thing that ever happened to us. I didn't mean it, but I said it.'

He looks at the food in his lap and picks up the

265

chicken with his hands.

'Why would you tell her something like that?'

His lips are red from the barbecue sauce. He chews, and I wait for him to swallow, but it takes him a long time.

'Want to sit?' he asks with his mouth full.

I sit beside him and stretch my legs out on the coffee table, which is actually a large leather ottoman, because according to Joanie, actual coffee tables are passé. 'Lara keeps a tray on hers. I like the way that looks,' she said.

'But it hardly holds anything,' I said.

'It looks nice,' she said.

I can't remember what else we said about the ottoman. I guess that's all.

I look at the television. In a crowded exercise studio, women step up onto benches and step down to the beat of music. The head woman says, 'And one, and two, now squeeze.' She points to her ass.

Sid changes the channel. Images appear and disappear until he lands on a picture of a bearded man painting a picture of a meadow.

'This guy's good,' Sid says.

'You know, Sid, Alex is having a hard time, too—'

He interrupts me before I can go on. 'No kidding.'

'Maybe you should look after her as much as she seems to be looking after you.'

'She's only with me because we don't have to comfort each other,' he says. 'Our shit cancels each other's out.'

I think of my relationship with Joanie. Do people ever fall in love anymore?

'You were going to tell me why you would say

such a thing to your mother who had just lost her husband.'

'No, I wasn't,' he says.

'Sid, I'm asking you to tell me.'

'Fine,' he says. He picks something out of his teeth and takes a deep breath. 'I have a friend, or I had a friend. Eliza. We were fifteen. Hung out a lot. She was one of the boys. That girl. I never messed around with her, even though I wanted to, and I think she did, too.' He wipes his mouth with the paper napkin, then balls it up and throws it toward the wastepaper basket. He misses. 'I'll get that,' he says. 'Anyway, she slept over a lot, Eliza. Not in my room. She'd crash on the couch in the living room. Dad liked her, too. They'd always joke around. This one time my dad gave us beer, and we were so excited because our life passion, basically, was finding ways to get beer. But he whispered to me that it was a joke, it was near beer, but we'd test Eliza to see if she pretended to be drunk. As we drank the beers, Eliza laughed a lot more, she said dumb things, she even stumbled on the kitchen step. When my dad finally told her, she got really defensive, saying she would have acted the same way despite the beer, near or not.'

'She was embarrassed.'

'Well, yeah. I mean, it was lame, when I think about it now. So, the next time she came over, my dad made it up to her and offered the both of us good old-fashioned Budweiser. We drank outside on the picnic bench. Some of Dad's friends came over and played poker. We went to my room and listened to music. We were both pretty trashed, which gave us a good excuse to make out, so we did. It was inevitable.' Sid smiles to himself. 'I

267

remember feeling this huge relief, like we could finally stop pretending we were just friends.'

I wonder if he feels this way about Alex. I wonder what they really are.

'So, we're going at it, I mean, not literally. We're just kissing, but you know, we're pretty passionate about it. Pretty urgent, you know what I'm saying, and then out of the corner of my eye, I see something. It's my dad standing in the doorway. She was on top of me on the floor, and we were fully dressed, but we were, you know, going through the motions. My dad was just watching, and when he saw me looking at him, it took him a moment to realize I could see him, because he was looking at the back of Eliza. I pushed her off of me, and he just sort of looked at us with this strange expression. Like he'd been caught. Eliza just sat there and I don't know. I don't remember what she did.

'Then my dad said, "Eliza. Better find your own place to sleep," and that's all, and he stood there until she got up and walked past him and went to the couch downstairs. When she left, he looked at me but didn't seem angry. He looked like he was the one who was embarrassed, who'd done something wrong. Then I went to bed. I was sort of happy but sort of bummed, too, because now he'd tell my mom, and Eliza probably wouldn't be able to sleep over. She wouldn't be just a friend anymore.'

Sid looks at the television for a while, and without ever taking his eyes away from it, he tells me the rest of the story in a flat, distant voice. It's a voice I've never heard him use. He doesn't use any slang or humor. He keeps his eyes on the painter,

268

whose voice is also hushed and hypnotic.

Sid tells me about his father coming downstairs to Eliza, passed out on the couch. He tells me how she woke to find his father on top of her, to feel him kissing her, moving on her. He tells me how she avoided Sid the next day and for weeks after and how he thought it was because of him. Then, to sum it up, Eliza finally told Sid. Sid got angry. He didn't believe her. Eliza didn't care if he didn't believe her. Then Sid believed her and hated his father, hated his mother for loving his father. His father died and Sid told his mother everything, about the beer, the kiss, about his father trying to take advantage of his drunk friend. His girlfriend. And that's the story. That's Sid's story.

'Alex doesn't know all that,' he says. 'She just thinks my mom kicked me out because she's upset.'

'Why haven't you told her?'

'She's busy,' he says. 'Like you said.'

'Why are you telling me?'

'Because you asked,' he says. 'And so you'll stop looking at me like I'm about to open fire.'

'Did your mother believe you?' I ask. 'When you told her?'

'Of course not.'

He goes through the channels once again. I see a giraffe, an animated sponge, someone welding, a bailiff giving a judge the thumbs-up.

'Why did you tell her? Why would you do it after he was dead?'

He settles on a station: a news anchorman reporting a deadly earthquake in Ethiopia, the ticker below reading, *Five days until the Oscars! Five days until the Oscars!*

'Because I respect her,' he says. 'He was never

269

good to her. He made our house tense all the time.'

'But you've ruined her life.' I think of Julie. I imagine the news literally breaking or damaging her in some way.

'I haven't ruined her life,' he says. 'She'll just know like I know. I still love my dad. We still have our life before the bad part. It doesn't make everything about him bad, right?' He looks at me for the first time. 'I'm not supposed to hate everything, am I?'

I try to fix my gaze on his, but I see his eyes watering. I'm not supposed to see him this way. Nobody is. I look at the anchorman.

'You're supposed to feel however you feel,' I say. 'You can miss him. You can love him.'

Out of the corner of my eye I see Sid look up at the ceiling. I stand up.

'Thanks,' I say. 'I appreciate you telling me all that.'

'No sweat,' he says and clears his throat.

I tell him to keep the light off because of the termites and say good night. I walk back toward my room, an uneasy feeling making me rack my brain for something more to say, something that will make everything okay. *Don't cry. I'm here.*

At the doorway I turn around. 'Are you warm enough in that room? There are extra blankets, you know. If you need them.'

'I'm fine,' Sid says. 'I'm good.'

'Anything you've noticed on TV lately?' I ask. 'Any keen observations, reflections?'

He rolls his eyes and holds down a smile.

'Go on, then,' I say.

'The cartoon diseases,' he says. 'The commercials make herpes, foot fungus, you know, all those

270

things, they make them into cartoon characters and have them yell and threaten and pillage the body. It's weird. Have you ever noticed those commercials?'

'I've noticed,' I say.

He locks eyes with me. 'They should just come out and say what they have to cure you. Those cartoons are disgusting. Just tell us how to get rid of what we have.'

He focuses on the TV again, and I leave him in the dark room.


# 39


Dr. Johnston walks into Joanie's room, and there's another man at his heels who is smiling at my children in a way that frightens me. Before I left the hospital yesterday, I asked Dr. Johnston for help. How do I tell my youngest child that there is no hope?

'You mean she doesn't know?' he asked.

'She knows,' I said quickly. I thought about Scottie kissing her mother and how it looked like she was trying to bring her to life. 'It's just that she still thinks there's a chance. Even after I explained it all. Joanie's hand moved, see. I guess I just don't know what to do now.'

He sat behind his desk and I could tell he was forcing himself not to look at me, as though I had done something wrong. His disappointment in me was clear. I even swallowed my pride and told him about the sea urchin and the man-of-wars, though not about the masturbation movies or her posing in

271

front of the mirror. He said he would talk to both of the girls and introduce us to a children's therapist whom some found to be helpful.

The therapist's eyelids are heavy, his mouth gently curled up. It's as though he has taken a bong hit. His face is tan and freckled, sun-beaten, and his features are soft, so there's not a lot you can really hold on to.

Sid sits on a chair under the window, flipping through a magazine. I can see a girl on the cover in a short red dress crawling across the hood of a Mustang.

'This is Dr. Gerard,' Dr. Johnston says.

'Hello, hello, everyone,' Dr. Gerard says, locking eyes with each of us in turn. 'You must be Scottie.' His voice is barely audible. He extends his hand, and Scottie gives him hers, but he doesn't shake it. He squeezes it and brings his other hand over it. Scottie pulls away a little, but he holds her there.

'And you must be Alex,' he says, letting go of Scottie and sidestepping over to Alex.

'Hey.' Alex reaches out her hand and shakes his vigorously.

He bows slightly to me. I notice he has a pen in his pocket; affixed to the pen is a rubber octopus. He notices that I'm staring at it and takes the octopus and makes a big show out of preparing to throw it to me and then tosses it my way. I let it land at my feet, and upon impact with the floor, the octopus lights up.

'It lights you,' he says.

Scottie retrieves it. The rubber toy flashes in her hand. 'My silly toy,' he says.

Scottie pulls one of its legs and then lets it go so that it snaps back.

'Such a funny creature,' Dr. Gerard says. 'With so many defense mechanisms. The ink sac, of course. I'm sure you know about the ink sac. She uses the ink as a distraction, a cloak of sorts, to escape from predators.'

Dr. Johnston is staring at the floor. Sid looks over the rim of his magazine, then ducks back behind it.

'They can also camouflage themselves to hide from predators. Some can emit poison, and some can mimic more dangerous creatures, like the eel. I guess I keep him to remind me of all our defense mechanisms—our ink, our poison, our camouflage to evade what hurts us.' He shrugs as though the thought has just occurred to him.

'What is this?' Sid says. 'Octopi 101?'

I try to hold down a smile; I'm grateful that Sid's back. He has an expression of disguised pride on his face and I know it's because of my smile, my endorsement of him.

'You're right,' Dr. Gerard says. 'Here I am, babbling on.' He brings his hands together into a steeple near the middle of his chest. 'The reason I'm here is to meet you girls. I've heard so much about you, and I'd love to talk with you if you'd like to talk with me.'

'What have you heard?' Scottie asks.

He places his chin on his knuckles and continues speaking, his voice quiet and casual. 'Well, I've heard you love the ocean and music and that you're a very wonderful and talented girl.'

Scottie considers this.

'I've heard that your mom's not doing too well, that she's going to die.' The girls look at me and I look at Dr. Johnston. It's such a simple and true

273

statement, but I'm alarmed to hear it. Has anyone said this so clearly?

'You're having an understandably difficult time,' he says. 'And I came to meet you and let you know that if you want to talk, then I'd love to face the present with you, without all our silly defense mechanisms. I'd like to help you own this time in your lives, and then I want to help you move forward. Not move *on*, but move *forward*.'

'Okay,' Dr. Johnston says. 'Thank you, Dr. Gerard.'

Scottie hands Dr. Gerard the octopus. He gives her hand another squeeze and mouths, 'Thank you.'

He walks toward the door and waves at Alex, who glares at him, reducing him to an octopus, a thing with no internal skeleton, a hideous freak. 'What was that?' she says when he has left.

Dr. Johnston looks apologetic, but he can't admit he's sorry. This is something he's supposed to support. 'Yes, well, Dr. Gerard is available to talk.'

'Yeah. He's got a degree in Squid,' Sid says. 'That guy's been tripping since Woodstock, man.'

'Yes, well.' Dr. Johnston looks behind him to a chair. He hesitates, so I nod toward the chair and he sits down. 'How is everyone doing?' he says.

Alex sits on the end of the bed. Joanie's face is discolored and her lips are dry and pale. Her chest moves sporadically, as though she's having a nightmare. She looks like an old woman. I pull Scottie toward me, hoping she has fully forgiven me for my force-fed affection to her mother. She slides into my embrace.

'I'm sure he's different when he's one-on-one,' Dr. Johnston says. 'That's his introductory speech. Try to look past it.'

274

'I liked him,' Scottie says.

'Good.' I rub her shoulders. 'We'll set up a time and talk to him, okay?'

I look at both Sid and Alex, making sure they don't say anything.

'Good,' Dr. Johnston says. 'And I want to make myself available, too. If you have any questions about what's going to happen, about why we're doing this. Anything.'

I feel Scottie's chest rising and falling. 'Mom will die for sure?' she asks.

To my surprise, Dr. Johnston says, 'Yes. We're doing exactly what your mother wants us to do. We're deciding to stop resisting what her body wants.' He looks at Joanie and seems deep in thought. 'We've been working hard, but we've found that major parts of her have broken down. They're dying or already dead.'

He looks at me for approval. I'm not sure if I should give it to him or not.

'Another doctor and I have determined that she's in an irreversible coma. Now, as soon as we determined this, your mother's living will applied. She has asked that we withhold and withdraw any treatment that might be considered life-prolonging or that artificially extends the dying process.'

'It's for the best, Scottie,' Alex says. 'She's not happy this way.'

'I know,' Scottie says. 'I know all this.' She tenses under my arms. 'She has no brain.'

'I want you to understand, Scottie,' Dr. Johnston says, 'and Alex, that we're not saying your mother is not of value; it's that medical therapy is no longer of value. My purpose is to heal, and I can't do that.'

'Do you understand?' I ask.

275

'Yes,' Alex says.

'Yes,' Scottie says.

'She didn't want to be kept alive in her state. Even if she were to come out of the coma, which is not at all likely—'

'She'd be a vegetable,' Scottie says.

'She doesn't want to live that way,' I say.

'I know everything already,' Scottie says.

'Your mom is receiving generous doses of morphine, so she's not in any pain whatsoever, but otherwise there's not much that we can do.'

*We're just waiting for her to die,* I think.

'Is there anything else I can answer?'

Alex shakes her head.

'What will you do with her body?' Scottie asks.

Dr. Johnston nods, and I take this to mean I'm supposed to answer this one. I give Scottie's shoulders a squeeze. How can I tell her that we'll burn her mother's body, that we'll reduce her mother to a gray, bony ash? How is it possible that this is what becomes of us?

'We're going to scatter her ashes in the ocean,' I say.

Scottie's stomach stops rising and falling and then it starts up again. 'When will she die?' she asks.

The doctor looks ready to launch into a speech but seems to stop himself. 'This is her third day on her own. Not much longer, I'm afraid. You still have time with her, though.'

We all look at Joanie on the bed.

'Some people say their goodbyes right away and then leave the hospital,' Dr. Johnston says. 'Though some stay to the very end.'

'What will we do?' Scottie asks.

276

'Whatever you want,' I say. 'It's your choice.'

Dr. Johnston stands. 'Please let me know if you have any more questions. Anything at all.'

I see a stain on his white coat, not blood but a tan smear that resembles peanut butter. I imagine him in the cafeteria eating a peanut butter and jelly sandwich, and this image comforts me somehow. Joanie liked to eat peanut butter on steamed tortillas; that was her comfort food. I wish she could eat something. I wish she could eat a grand last meal, like a prisoner gets to before the execution. Malasadas, shaved ice, plate lunch, grilled ahi from Buzz's, kiawe pork chops from Hoku's, a teri burger, and a Dreamsicle shake. These were her favorite foods.

'Thanks, Sam,' I say.

'I'm sorry,' he says, and he looks truly sorry, not just for us but for himself. I forget that death for a doctor is failure. He has been unsuccessful. He has failed Joanie and he has failed us.

'It's okay,' I say to him, which sounds strange.

'I'll let you have your time,' he says.

The room is quiet after he leaves. Alex sits next to me on the bed. Even though I think that Joanie's face is sunken, that she's getting smaller, I realize she really hasn't changed that much. Those are my expectations—that she'll age, she'll deteriorate, before she goes. But it's not true. She has been frozen in time. I can't help but think she's still in charge of us, silently managing us with an immense and unmatched force. Scottie's gaze is fixed in a way that tells me she's not looking at anything. She seems to be in a trance.

'Now what?' Alex asks.

'We're waiting for Uncle Barry and your

277

grandparents,' I say. 'They're saying goodbye today.'

'What are we going to do?' she asks. 'Are we going to wait until the end?'

Sid lowers his magazine.

'What do you want?' I ask. 'What do you girls want to do?'

They don't answer. I wonder if they're too ashamed to say they don't want to stay to the end. We've been saying goodbye for a long time.

I wonder what the end will look like. Will she just drift off? Or will she fight for life? Will her eyes open, her hand clutch our wrists? 'I don't think you girls should stay to the end,' I say. I don't want them to see her die. 'We'll pick a moment and we'll all say goodbye. If that's okay. If that's what you want. Or we can stay here or keep coming back until you feel it's time to go. You just let me know when.'

'Make sure you're ready,' Sid says. Alex gets off the bed and walks over to him, but he lifts his magazine, covering his face. I see the girl crawling across the hood. I want to ask her: *Why are you there? Get off the damn hood and go home.*

'I guess that's a good plan,' Alex says. 'We should each pick a moment for ourselves.'

'Do eyeballs burn?' Scottie asks.

I have no idea what will happen to her eyes and would never dare to ask. I think they burn. I just don't know.

'What?' Scottie says. 'Why are you all looking at me like that?'

'You'll have to ask the doctor, Scottie.'

'You shouldn't think about that sort of thing,' Sid says.

278

I wonder what they did with his father, if they buried him or cremated him. I wonder if Sid wondered the same thing about his father's eyes.

# 40

My heart races as though I'm on a stage. I can hear Joanie's mother.

'Joanie,' she calls. 'Joanie.'

I walk out to the hall. Scott has his hands in his pockets and is looking down at the floor, shuffling his feet like a kid. Alice is dressed nicely, or her nurse or Scott dressed her nicely, in a black sweater and a long red-and-white skirt. She has on her gold bracelets, and her hair looks like it's been done. I wonder if she knows where she is.

'Joanie! Joanie. Leper,' she says to a man who rolls by in a wheelchair.

The man looks at Alice, who keeps walking as though she hasn't said anything.

'Hi, Alice,' I say.

She keeps walking past me until Scott puts his arm around her and shuttles her into the room. 'Barry should be here soon,' he says. He looks at the bed, then goes to the window, lifts the curtain, and lets it fall again. He looks around and stands near the back of the room. It's as though he's shopping with a woman for lingerie. He doesn't know what to do.

'Scottie. Let Grandpa sit.'

'Hey, Bingo,' Scott says. 'I didn't see you there.' He looks over at Alex and Sid. 'There you are again,' he says to Sid.

279

Scott sits down and brings Scottie onto his lap.

Alice is standing next to the bed. She leans down and talks softly. I hear: 'What do you get when you cross an alligator with a child?' but I don't hear the answer. I keep wondering: *What* do *you get?* I suppose an alligator. Goodbye, child. For some reason her riddle breaks my heart.

*     *     *

Barry comes into the room holding flowers and what looks to be a photo album. He is crying. He makes the rounds to each of us, shaking his head, then collapsing into our arms. When I hug him I press my open palm onto his back instead of making it into a fist.

'Hi, son,' Scott says.

I take the flowers from Barry. He goes to Joanie's bedside and stands next to Alice.

'What did you decide?' Scott says.

'What's that, Scott?'

'What did you decide?'

'I think we're just going to see what happens. When we feel the time is right.'

'I mean what did you decide about the buyer? Who's your buyer?'

'Hoarder,' Alice says to the pikake leis.

My daughters seem curious, too. I can't bear to see their curiosity. They want to know how much. How much we will get.

'Is this really the right time to be talking about this?'

'How much are you getting?' Scott asks.

I look at Barry for a little help in shutting his father up, but all he says is: 'Dad, you can read all

280

about it in the paper, I'm sure.'

'I don't need to read about it,' he says. 'I can hear about it right here.'

'I'm not talking about this right now, Scott. It's hardly appropriate.'

'It's all the same to you, I guess. No big deal. A million here, a million there.'

'Is there a problem?'

Scottie looks petrified on his lap. He makes to get up and she gets off his lap, but then he settles back into his chair. He doesn't make eye contact. There's a cruel, teasing grin on his face. 'It's funny that Joanie happens to come into this misfortune at the same time you're coming into fortune.'

'It's not funny at all,' I say. 'There's nothing remotely funny about any of this.'

Yesterday the cousins gathered around Hugh as he broke the news, and I appreciated his delivery. It was flat and impartial, commanding. His tone was unwelcoming; no one balked or sighed dramatically. I know Joanie must have had something to do with it. They would have protested if she were healthy. Now they'll wait until some time has passed. Hugh made me sound bewildered though determined. He made me sound optimistic and brave. Ralph patted me on the back. Six said, 'Doesn't matter to me. I'll be dead soon.'

'You were selfish with her,' Scott says. 'She gave you everything. A good happy home.'

'Scott,' I say. 'What's the point?'

I look at Barry again, busying himself with Joanie, and I know he must agree with his father or else he'd be helping me out.

'We lived well,' I say. 'Better than well. You think she was unhappy because I didn't give her

281

enough? Are you actually angry about this?'

'She wanted her own boat.'

'I couldn't afford it! I don't have that kind of money at my disposal. Things are tied up. We live off of my salary. I will use trust money to pay for college, and I use it for Punahou, which is twenty-eight thousand for the two of them. Plus voice and dance, summer camp. The list goes on.'

The girls look startled and offended. That's the thing with privileged kids—they forget their teachers get paid. They forget that everything costs something: being in a play, making a bong in glassblowing. I'm sure poor kids are aware of what everything costs. Every little thing. I look at the wall over Scott's head and want to punch it. Why am I talking about tuition? Why am I defending myself?

'She should have had her own boat, something she really knew. Then she wouldn't be . . .' He gestures to his daughter.

'She wasn't driving in the first place, and you can't blame this on me. I didn't orchestrate this!'

'She deserved more from you,' he says, looking me square in the eyes. I can't believe he's saying this, especially in front of the girls, and I almost do it. The truth almost takes a swan dive off my tongue. I could tell Scott she was cheating on me, that I deserved more as well. I could tell him she broke all of our hearts.

'I know,' I say. 'She deserved more.' And I realize this is true, not just a statement to placate him. I take a deep breath, remembering he is her father. I couldn't imagine one of my daughters on that bed. 'You're right,' I say. 'I'm sorry.'

'For Christ's sake, take it easy on the man,' Sid says.

282

'Yeah, Grandpa,' Scottie says.

'Dad did the best he could,' Alex says.

I'm shocked, almost uncomfortable, worried that Scott might think I paid the girls to say this. Our united front feels strange, like we're some other family. One of those happy families I see occasionally. And then I think: *Are we?* Despite everything, are we on to something here? Yet wherever we are, whatever we are, it would exist only with Joanie's absence. This has all been made possible by her silence. I think of Sid telling his mother that his father's death was the best thing to happen to them, and I realize he didn't say it to be malicious or insolent. He said it because it was partly true, painful but true. How brave he must have been to say it.

I could tell Scott that money isn't going to make my life better; his daughter's death is going to make my life better. Deep within me, I know this. I don't want to be in this situation, I don't wish this upon her, but now that it has happened, now that I know what's going to happen, I am confident my girls will make it out and will become strong, interesting people and I will be a good father and we will have a better life than the one we thought we were destined to have. The three of us are going to do well, Joanie. I'm sorry about that.

'I didn't make a choice,' I say to Scott. 'I didn't sell.'

The girls search my face. Alex smiles. I'm not sure why, or what my decision means to her, but I'm so glad to have her approval.

'I'm keeping it in the family even though it's going to be a pain in the ass. I'll have a lot of work to do.'

283

'It's none of my business,' Scott says.

I want to shout that I'm holding on to it, that I'm holding on to everything, that life has taken me by surprise and I'm surprising it right back in my small way.

Scott stands and walks over to Joanie. He appraises the flowers as though looking at books on a shelf, and then he laughs. 'You must have pissed a lot of people off.' He seems almost proud.

'I did. And I probably haven't heard the end of it.' Even though what I have done is perfectly valid and protected by law, I'm not ruling out a jackass prosecutor finding some tiny rip in the seam that he can worm himself into.

Alice looks at Sid's magazine. Her eyes are huge, like an owl's. 'Are we ready to go?' she asks.

'No, Mom,' Barry says.

'Why not?' she asks.

'Because, Mom—'

'Yes, Alice,' Scott says. 'We're ready to go.' He holds his hands together and looks down upon his daughter. The girls look at me, panicked.

'Girls,' I say. 'Sid.' I gesture toward the door and they follow me into the hall.

'He's doing it now?' Alex asks.

'I guess so,' I say.

Out in the hall, we take a few steps in one direction, then turn around and walk in the other direction. Scottie is the only one who stands still and watches. After a while we follow her lead, yet glance down the hallway, perhaps trying to hide our interest in seeing how it's done. Scott is closing his eyes and touching her shoulder, but he isn't speaking. Barry is watching him, too, with both fear and reverence.

'Is he praying?' Sid asks.

'No,' I say.

Alice walks away from the bed and Scott glances up at her, then down at his daughter, and puts his hand over his mouth and squeezes his eyes shut. Then he opens his eyes and places a hand on Joanie's forehead, smooths her hair back, and lets his hand rest on top of her head. Then he goes to Alice, takes her hand, and walks toward the door. We all step back. He glances at me briefly before walking down the hall. It's a look I recognize—one that another attorney gives me when he loses to me. It's a look of annoyance that I seem to have gotten away with something. It's a look that's stupidly certain I am a lucky man.

# 41

Joanie seems different now that her father has said goodbye. It's as though his farewell pushed her a step closer to nonexistence, and it's hard to look at her, knowing that her parents won't ever see her again. Everything seems different. We stay out in the hall, letting Barry be alone with her.

'Does Grandpa even like us anymore?' Scottie asks, something I myself was thinking about. I wonder if he'll keep in touch with us, though I suppose that's up to me. I'll need to make sure he sees his grandchildren. I'll need to make sure he's taken care of. He's mine now, too, I guess. The tops of the girls' heads are identical. I notice this for the first time, a white flash of skin in the middle, the hair twisting to the right.

'Of course he likes us. He's just sad. We say things when we're sad.'

Sid keeps looking down the hall, toward the elevators, and it distracts me.

'I'm leaving, everyone,' Barry says, walking out of the room. 'Okay,' I say, catching myself from saying, *You're done? You're sure?* This is happening too fast.

'I might be back,' he says. 'I'm going to go and let it sit. If I feel there's more, I'll come back. But right now I'm going to go.'

'Okay, Barry,' I say.

He gives me a hug and then goes to hug the girls. 'We can do anything,' he says to them. 'We can act any way we want to, but we must not be angry. We can't be ugly.'

I recognize those words. I was cooking a roast and Esther was making empanadas and watching *Oprah,* and on the show a woman whose son was killed said the same thing to her family directly after his death. I remember actually stopping to watch this woman because she sounded so strong and smart and I really believed her, believed that she said this to her family, and I believed that saying this worked, but the words don't sound powerful coming from Barry. I'm not convinced they'll work for him. He's read so many self-help books, but they were about love, not death. I think grief and anger are going to come to him suddenly. They'll be undiluted and words won't work. We're all going to get hit and won't know how to hit back. I wish I knew the answers, how to help myself and the people who will hurt all around me.

'Well, girls,' I say. 'It's just me and you.'

'And you and me,' Scottie says.

'And me,' Sid says.

'Are you guys okay?' I ask. 'Should we go back in?'

Everyone looks in, but no one makes a move toward the room. 'This isn't working,' Alex says. 'I feel like we're just watching her. Waiting . . .'

'I know,' I say. 'I know.'

I see Sid looking down the hall and checking his watch and cell phone once more.

'You expecting someone?' I ask.

'No,' he says.

I can tell he's disappointed in me. He thinks that I should 'step up' and fight Brian who, Sid claims, 'couldn't bust a grape in a fruit fight.' He thinks telling Julie about the affair would make me feel better, and this is amusing to me, yet sad because he still doesn't get it. If anyone should know about the futility of revenge, it's Sid.

'Maybe we should get some air. Get some food? We could get a plate lunch.'

'Should we say goodbye like it's the last time?' Scottie asks. 'Just in case.'

I look into the room. 'No,' I say. 'It's okay. We'll be right back.' Saying goodbye like it's our last could become exhausting, so we leave. We just go, hoping she'll still be here and too afraid to admit that we could be wrong.

# 42

She was still there when we got back from lunch and she's still here this morning. And here we are again, another day sitting in the dark room, watching Joanie, waiting. Some of the flowers have wilted, the ginger and the pikake, though they still make the room smell good. The tips of Joanie's fingers are blue. I wonder if anyone else notices this. It has been five days since she's been on her own.

Joy appears in the doorway. I'm relieved to see her.

'Joy,' I say.

'Mr. King. Your wife has a visitor.'

I watched a father say a wordless goodbye to his daughter, yet this is almost more disturbing, Joy's graveness, the fact that she can't look me in the eye.

'Who is it?' I ask.

'A woman. I don't know her name. Should I send her this way, or would you folks like to be alone?'

I try to think of who it could be. Everyone I told has stopped in, though I could see Shelley coming back to check on us.

'Sure,' I say. 'Send her in.'

'Okay, Mr. King.' Joy walks away, and I wonder if she's sad for me or if it's that we're no longer clients; they're just waiting for us to get out of here so they can clear the bed for the next patient.

'Who is it?' Alex asks. She tucks her hair behind her ear and smooths her shirt. Only now do I notice how nice she looks. She wears black slacks and a crisp white collared blouse. Sid, too, is wearing a collared shirt, and jeans that aren't falling off him.

No one told them to dress nicely or respectfully, and I'm stunned though almost saddened that they didn't need me to guide them. Scottie, however, is still in my charge, which is evident from her extra-large T-shirt that hangs below her shorts so it looks like the T-shirt is all she's wearing. The back of the shirt reads FIERCE and has a picture of a pit bull foaming at the mouth and lifting his hind leg over a daisy.

'What if we don't want her in the room?' Scottie says. 'It's our time.'

'It's a little late for that,' Alex says.

'What if she's from the child protection agency?' Scottie asks. 'For what, Scottie? Why would they be here?' I look at her shirt, her hair, her nails.

'To take us away,' she says.

'But why would they do that?'

'I was only joking. Jeez, chill.'

Sid sits in the same chair and his foot taps against the floor; he seems nervous. Then his foot suddenly stops and he straightens up, a look of contentment brightening his face. I look at the doorway and see a huge arrangement of white roses, so large they cover the woman's face, but I immediately recognize the bronze hair and pale arms of Julie Speer.

*       *       *

She sets the vase of flowers on the floor and looks down at her light blue sweater.

'I've spilled,' she says. Water runs down her sweater, ironically forming a stain that looks a bit like a rose on its stem.

'Here,' Scottie says. She goes through the drawer

289

near Joanie's bed and brings out a hospital gown. 'Use this.'

Julie hesitates but then says, 'Thank you,' and quickly swipes at her sweater, then stops and looks at all of us and then at Joanie. I remember telling her that my wife was sick, but I can't believe she would come. Alex picks up the vase and places it on the shelf at the back of the room, since the counter near Joanie is full.

'It's nice of you to visit,' I say. 'I didn't expect—'

'I know,' she says. 'We just met, but I was thinking about you girls these past few days and I knew your mom was here. I just felt I should stop in.'

Her hands are shaking slightly. She brings one to her chest and takes a deep breath. I take her by the elbow and lead her to the chair by Sid. He nods at her.

'This is Sid,' I say. 'Sid, Mrs. Speer.'

'Julie,' she says.

He extends his hand and she takes it and for some reason says, 'Thank you.'

'Where are your kids?' Scottie asks.

Julie seems to consider her question carefully. 'They're still on Kauai with my husband. They're returning this afternoon.'

'Are you friends with my mom?' Scottie asks.

Julie studies Joanie as though the answer to Scottie's question depends on what she sees. 'No,' she says. 'I've never met her.'

Alex and I make perplexed faces at each other, something I've found we've been doing a lot lately. Whenever something is strange or annoying or funny, her face is the first place I look. *What is Julie doing here?* my face asks.

290

'We appreciate the flowers,' I say. 'We appreciate you coming by.'

'Alex,' Sid says. 'Scottie. Let's give them some time alone.'

'What?' I say. 'No, that's okay. You don't have to leave.'

Sid puts his hand on Alex's back and guides her toward the door. Scottie follows, and then he closes the door and leaves me alone with her. I need to tell Julie that my wife isn't going to get better, as I previously said. I need to tell her she should leave. I walk to my wife's bedside.

'I know,' Julie says.

She stands against the window, against the vertical blinds, the kind Joanie couldn't stand. I used to have them in the den. 'They're very starter-home,' Joanie said when she first moved in. They were there when I bought the house and I wouldn't have changed a thing—the floors, countertops, patio, garage, roof—until Joanie pointed out the flaws. She extended the front walk, planted three types of ferns, extended the roof, and put in large wooden posts so that the façade looked grand yet welcoming. She ripped out the carpet, tore down the floral wallpaper in the bedrooms, remodeled the kitchen, the bathrooms. She bargained with contractors, called in favors. She worked hard, and she made the old place into a beautiful home, and once I saw it, I couldn't imagine ever living in it the way it had been.

'Matt?' Julie says.

'Yes,' I say. 'Yes, Julie.'

'That's why I've come,' she says. 'Because I know. I've come because my husband wouldn't.'

I absorb this, searching my pants pocket, for

some reason. I finger a ball of something—lint or a worn wrapper. I wonder what it is.

'I know he was sleeping with her. I know she's . . . not well.'

'She's dying,' I say.

'I don't know what I'm doing here.'

'I'm sorry,' I say.

'That's not what I'm asking. I mean, why are you sorry?'

'I shouldn't have come to your house like that,' I say. 'I didn't know he had a family. I'm sorry.'

She looks at the foot of the bed, then up to Joanie's face.

'Joanie's beautiful,' I say. 'This isn't the way she normally looks.'

She nods. 'I feel awful,' she says, 'but I'm so angry.' She starts to cry. 'I'm so angry at both of them.'

'I'm angry, too. And it's really strange, a really bad thing to feel.'

She wipes the tears off her face.

'When did he tell you?' I ask.

She looks surprised. 'My husband?'

'Yes. Did he tell you after we left? Did something happen?'

'He didn't tell me,' she says. 'Sid told me. He called the house yesterday. My husband and I have been going crazy. You can imagine.'

'Sid,' I say. 'Well.'

'It's just that . . . ' She starts to laugh and begins fanning the air in front of her. I feel I should give her a moment alone, so I look up at the ceiling, but then I look back at her and can't mask my irritation.

'What are you laughing at?' I ask.

'It's all so terrible,' she says.

292

'Julie,' I say. 'I'm sorry for everything, really, but I can't do this now. I need to be with my wife now.'

'I know,' she says almost angrily. 'I thought it was awful that my husband didn't come here. I just came because I didn't think that was right. I wanted to tell your wife I'm sorry.'

I wonder if a part of her is satisfied somehow by my wife's fate. I don't like the way she looks, standing over Joanie; the contrasts between a healthy woman and a dying woman become pronounced. Julie's face is tan from her beach vacation. Joanie looks minuscule compared to her. I feel completely protective of Joanie, united with her, madly in love with her. I want to hold her hand and point Julie toward the door.

'He told me everything,' Julie says, either to me or to Joanie. 'I forgive you for trying to take him, for trying to tear my family apart.'

'Stop,' I say. 'Don't do that.'

She makes to say something else, something she has probably rehearsed, but I won't let her fight with a woman who can't fight back. Her grace and gentleness are gone. She has tricked herself into thinking she is doing something noble, but really, this is all about anger. She is feeling the same things I feel, I guess—the need to guard what's yours. This is a war. It always is.

I walk to the door and open it and wait for her to leave. She looks down at Joanie and I wonder if I'll have to remove her. She glances at her flowers, then turns away from the bed.

'He didn't love her,' she says.

'I know, but he didn't love you for a while, either.'

She pauses in front of me. 'I came here. I didn't

293

mean to act this way. I just love my family, that's all.'

'This is my wife,' I say.

She waits for me to continue, but I don't have anything else to say. I was going to say, *This is the love of my life. You can go home to your family. I can't.* But I don't want to talk to her anymore. These past few days have been about trying to weed everyone out. Go. Everyone, please go.

She hesitates, maybe wondering if she should shake my hand or hug me, but I make it clear that I don't want either. I think about how I kissed her, leaving my mark, just as her husband left his. I'm sickened by my trite revenge, and how Julie could be the last woman who kisses me back.

She walks out and I shut the door once again, and look at her flowers standing tall at the back of the room. And then I go to my wife, who looks like a ghost of a woman. I sit on her bed. I take her hand, which doesn't feel like her hand anymore. I touch her face, look at her lips, the lines in her lips. I rub my palm over her forehead into her hairline, just as her father did. I ask her silently to forgive me and then realize she isn't some kind of god and that I need to say it aloud.

'Forgive me,' I say. 'I love you. I know we did something right together.'

I have picked my moment. I don't want to hug her because I know I won't like the sensation of not being hugged back, and I don't want to kiss her because I won't be kissed back, but I do kiss her. I press my lips to hers and then I put my hand on her stomach because this seems to be the place where everything comes from, where I feel love and pain, anger and pride, and even though I wasn't

294

planning on doing it this way, I say goodbye. I lean over so my mouth is on her neck, our heads pressed together. Goodbye, Joanie. Goodbye, my love, my friend, my pain, my happiness. Goodbye. Goodbye. Goodbye.

# 43

I fix the gin and tonic and look over at the large window framing the mock-orange hedge, and below the window to the sofa, where Sid's mother sits. She wears slacks and a blouse, and I can tell she isn't used to dressing this way. She buttons her top button, then unbuttons it once again and fixes her necklace. I look away before she sees that I'm staring at her.

I figured that if Sid could do it, then so could I. He called Julie. I called his mother. That's the way it works.

I take the drink back to her. I like that she's having one. I'm having one, too, even though it's freezing and I don't want to touch the icy glass. It has been unusually cold all around the island these past few days, with hard rain, near-black clouds— the most perfect weather for now.

Mary cups her drink in her hands over her thighs. I realize I haven't given her a coaster and she's afraid to put the drink down on the wooden table. Her cocktail napkin is crushed in her hand, pieces of it pressed to the wet glass.

'You can put it down,' I say.

She looks at the long wood table in front of her, the heavy books: *Finding Paradise, A Sense of Place,*

*World Atlas*, and *Law in America*. She hesitates and tries to salvage the soaked napkin but stops and puts the glass down. Perhaps she realizes she can do anything and act any way she wants. She doesn't know my wife died two days ago. She, with her dead husband, her renegade son, is the winner here.

'I don't usually drink,' she says. 'Especially this early.'

'I know.' I can see Sid's resemblance to her: the sharp nose and large eyes that slope downward.

'Has he been okay?' she asks. 'Has he been good?'

I think of him smoking pot, cigarettes, slapping my daughter's ass, moping, running his mouth, ruining Brian's marriage, getting served, as Scottie says, by my father-in-law.

'Yes,' I say. 'He has been surprisingly helpful.'

'I can pay you,' she says. 'For groceries. For whatever he cost you.'

'Oh, no,' I say. 'Don't worry about that.'

She looks around at my house then through the screen door at the yard, the pool, the mountain. I look there, too, then ask her if she wants me to find out what's taking him so long.

'Did he tell you why I kicked him out of the house?'

'He told me his dad died. He told me he missed his dad.'

'His father was difficult to live with,' she says. 'But he took care of us. He loved Sid.'

'I'm sure he did,' I say.

'You must think I'm a horrible person for kicking him out.'

Her face looks tired. She looks older than she probably is.

296

'I don't think that. Children are hard. Sometimes doing something like that is the only thing that works. Especially with Sid. He's no walk in the park.'

'No, he isn't.' She laughs, and it's as though we're admitting that we have hard children but wouldn't want it any other way. I see that she has brought Sid one of those magazines he likes, the ones about girls on cars or girls on choppers.

'I need to tell him I believe him,' she says.

She looks behind me and I know he must be there, walking down the cobblestone corridor, past the pictures of us on the wall, past the table of sympathy cards, past the black Japanese planter that sounds like a gong when hit with a wooden spoon wrapped in a dish towel, which is the way Joanie would summon us to dinner. 'Dinner!' she'd yell after the deep gong. 'Dinner!'

'Hi, Mom,' Sid says.

She stands but stays where she is, in front of the sofa and behind the coffee table, protected. He's beside me. I stand and give him a look of encouragement. I can tell he doesn't want me to leave, but this isn't my problem, it's just a similarity we share, the need to come to terms with the dead and the people they truly were. We want to ascend, make our dead monarchs less powerful, stop them from directing our lives, even though I know this is impossible, because they've been ruling my life for centuries.

'Thank you for coming, Mary,' I say.

I walk away. I hear their voices. I want to think that I hear them embrace, but I'm sure I don't hear that. An embrace isn't audible. Alex is standing by the gong and I lead her away.

297

'Are they speaking?' she asks.

'I think so.'

We pass the pictures of Joanie. I don't look at them, but I know their sequence. Joanie on Mauna Kea with Alex on her shoulders, Joanie and me and friends dining at a rotating restaurant that made us all nauseated, Alex on her dirt bike riding through a banana plantation, Joanie on a boat in her bikini, Scottie leaning over the side pretending to throw up, Joanie in a canoe riding a wave, leaning over the ama to keep the boat from tipping.

\*     \*     \*

Scottie's on the daybed, under the quilt she has brought from her own bed. She's watching television; it's really all we've been doing these past two days. I take off my shoes and get into bed with her, and so does Alex. I lie back and watch a beautiful celebrity accept an award for playing an ugly woman.

I prop a few pillows under my head and pull up the covers. I could stay here forever. I notice that Scottie has taken up scrap-booking once again. Her book rests on her stomach and I pick it up and flip the pages. Time passes. Time passed. I see this from the photos—Troy at the club's bar on the day of the man-of-wars, Alex in the pool, screaming at Scottie, her first day home. There are countless pictures of Sid doing mundane things. Sid sitting by the pool reading one of his car magazines, Sid eating chips, Sid taking a nap.

'Is Sid going home?' Scottie asks.

'Yes,' I say.

'Are you still going out with him?' Scottie asks. 'Even though he went off with the skanks?'

'We're just friends,' Alex says, but in a moment of honesty, she adds, 'I don't know what we are. I think we're together now.' She points to the book. 'There's a lot of him.'

'He's photogenic,' Scottie says. She takes the book back and flips the pages, mesmerized with her work. She holds the album close to her and won't let me flip. It's like she's the warden of our relics. Our curator.

Next page. An old picture of me in my office, surrounded by cutouts of the things that define me: a briefcase, a beer.

I'll have to be there a lot now, the office, familiarizing myself with my own land, trying to make up for the years of neglecting the gifts bestowed upon us.

Scottie has placed me under my mother and father. Joanie is next to me, a picture from years ago, after her canoe race from Molokai to Oahu, taken before Scottie was born. It's a true picture of health—her teeth, her skin, the glow on her face. She is young and pretty, happy, and I realize this was taken before we ever met.

I ruffle Scottie's hair and she leans in to me.

'You're our keeper,' I tell her. 'Our family historian.'

'Mrs. Chun is going to say it's not really a scrapbook. I don't have fabric and words.'

'I like it just fine,' I say.

'Me, too.'

'What time are we going tomorrow?' Alex asks.

'Early,' I say.

'What if it's still raining?'

299

'We'll still go,' I say. 'We need to.'

The ashes are in a box. The box is in a purple satchel, and whenever I see the satchel, I think of expensive liquor and then think, *No. They're ashes. My wife's ashes.*

I'm still not sure how the girls said goodbye, what their moment was like, and I don't want to ask because it will hurt me too much to know. They each went in alone. They each said something, then walked out and searched my face for some clear answer. Then we left the hospital and came home. Scottie turned on the TV in the den. Alex went to her room. I went to my room, but I couldn't stay in that bed, so I went to watch TV with Scottie, and Alex was there lying next to her and I knew this was the best place to be. Joanie must have been waiting for us. After we all said goodbye, she died the next day.

Images of dead people who have worked in the film business flash on the screen. Some receive loud applause, others receive none.

Scottie's toes tap against my shin.

'Your toes are cold,' I say.

She presses her entire foot against my shin and I shiver. 'Stop it,' I say.

She lets out a hard laugh and I put my hand over her so that I'm touching the tops of both of their heads. It feels similar to the calculated and bashful move you make on first dates.

I remember walking with Joanie on the secluded beach in front of the Kahala resort. We'd just had lunch at Hoku's, and we'd each had a glass of wine. I remember walking close to her, purposefully brushing her hand with my own, hoping that it would stick somehow, and then finally putting my

300

arm around her and feeling so satisfied when she came in closer and stayed. The beautiful hotel was alongside us, and it felt as though we were on vacation, tourists in an exotic land. It's strange to think that we had ever been shy around each other.

'I'm glad you didn't sell the land,' Scottie says.

'Really?' I ask. 'Why?'

'Because then we wouldn't have it anymore,' she says.

'It will be yours one day,' I say. 'Both of you.'

'That's a lot to have,' Alex says.

Scottie flips to the last page of the book, and there are the two who started it all, Princess Kekipi and Edward King.

'Why are they at the end?' I ask. 'Shouldn't they be at the beginning?'

'I guess so,' Scottie says. She puts her hand on the princess's portrait. 'I'll do it later.'

'It's okay, though,' I say. 'I sort of like them at the end.'

It's funny that I think of them as the beginning, because they were also descendants of somebody, generations of prints on their DNA, traces of human migrations. They didn't come out of nowhere. Everyone comes from someone who comes from someone else, and this to me is remarkable. We can't know the people who are in us. We'll all have our moment at the top of the tree. Matthew and Joan. We'll be those two one day.

I drift off for a while. I don't know how long, but when I open my eyes, the Oscars are still on and Alex tells me that Sid has gone and this makes me a little sad. Whatever the four of us had is over. He is my daughter's boyfriend now, and I am a father. A widower. No pot, no cigarettes, no sleeping over.

They'll have to find inventive ways to conduct their business, most likely in uncomfortable places, just like the rest of them. I let him and my old ways go. We all let him go, as well as who we were before this, and now it's really just the three of us. I glance over at the girls, taking a good look at what's left.

# 44

I steer the small canoe and am doing a terrible job at it; we cut a crooked path through the ocean and the girls are tired from all the extra strokes. My Polynesian ancestors would be disappointed in me, in all of us. I don't have the gift of wayfinding, of using the sun, stars, and swells to navigate the open ocean. Those skills and instincts have been lost.

'Should we just put them here?' Alex yells back. She's in the first seat, and I can see the muscles rippling down her back.

'Swimmer, Dad,' Scottie says. 'Swimmer!'

I see a white bathing cap bobbing toward us, but then it floats toward the catamarans.

'Let's go past the break,' I say. 'Out of the traffic.'

'Go straight, then,' Alex says.

'I'm trying.'

'Try harder. You need to predict when it will turn, and don't overcorrect. You're too slow.'

Joanie could steer straight. I'm pretty sure that's what we're all thinking.

I try to use the orange wind sock as my target. I can see the reef poking up in spots like jaws. The sun is a fuzzy glow under gray clouds. The water is dark, and the darker shapes of the rocks on the ocean floor seem to move beneath us. My paddle grazes a chunk of reef that's pocked like a honeycomb, and I steer to the right to get us to deeper water. The ashes are in the bag and the bag is in my lap. Every now and then I'll look down at my lap and experience a feeling of injustice. It isn't right that she's in my lap like this. I can barely feel her. I think of those burial options: *Be paddled off in a canoe and scattered!*

Large swells move near the wind sock, yet they don't break. One moves under us, and the canoe glides to its crest, then comes down hard. The nose slashes through the water, and as we approach the next wave, which seems bigger than the last, I push the bag of ashes more snugly between my legs. Scottie stops paddling.

'Keep paddling,' I say, my voice taking on a nervous pitch. We need our momentum to make it over so that the wave doesn't take us back down with it. We climb the wave, spray shedding off it so I can't see, and then we sail down its curved back, landing hard so that we all fly up off our seats.

'Let's get out of here,' I say.

The girls are quiet and I can tell they're worried. They plunge their paddles in deep, moving as much water as their little bodies can manage. Their wrists are submerged and they take quick strokes. We paddle longer than we need to, so that we're far beyond the break. The water is even darker, and the rocks at the bottom of the ocean look like sleeping creatures. It seems too dark and cold and lonely to rest here for eternity, but I don't say anything.

The girls stop paddling. I look at the stretch of

Waikiki. It looks different each time I see it, though it hasn't changed that much: lots of people, aqua water, surfers sliding down waves, sand white like bone china. It just means something different to me each time I see it. Today it means Joanie. Joanie's beach.

I take the bag. It came with a silver scooper and I hold this in my hand, too, staring at it as if it's a joke.

I've thought about how we should do this.

'Alex,' I say. 'Come closer to your sister. Maybe sit on the ama.'

She turns around and steps over her seat and stands in the canoe, holding on to the sides for balance. She has piled her wet hair on her head so that it looks like a beehive, which makes me think of the reef.

'Here,' I say, holding the bag open and giving Alex the tiny shovel. She hesitates, then takes it, and her hand disappears in the bag. She brings out the sandy ash and some of it flies away. We watch the ash move like smoke, and then Alex points the shovel down so that the ashes fall densely in one spot, piling atop the water then slowly raining, darkening the ocean then disappearing.

Alex hands the shovel to Scottie, and I hold the bag open for her. To my surprise, Scottie takes the shovel and plunges it into the bag, moving it around as though searching for a prize. I would have thought she'd be afraid. She pulls out a mound of ash and flicks her wrist so that it flies through the air. We watch the water, and when we can't see anything more, the girls look at me. Scottie's teeth chatter, and there are bumps all over her skin. They both stand in the narrow canoe, catching

304

their balance as small swells move our boat up and down. I think of all the ashes that must be beyond the break of Waikiki, all the flowers tossed to the departed, and I wonder where everything goes. I lower the shovel into the bag and feel the weight of her. I toss the ashes in the sea, and this hurts me in a way that's almost physical. My throat hurts, my stomach and arms ache. Without my girls, I don't know how I would behave right now. I can't look at them without feeling light-headed. I know they're crying right now, and I can't look. If I look, I'll fall apart. I take the bag and turn it upside down, and so much comes out that the ashes actually make a sound when they hit the water. We watch them drown, the gray ashes that are like coarse sand. The girls toss four plumeria leis, and we watch them float for a while, and then it seems we are done with our ceremony. The leis race back and cling to the side of the canoe. Scottie reaches down for them, then tosses them over the other side. We stare at the water for a while longer and then begin to look at one another as if to say, *Now what? When is it okay to go back?*

Maybe when we can't see the leis any longer. That's when we'll go back. Alex sits down in the first seat, and Scottie sits on the edge of the canoe and leans against the ama. We face the shore and watch our flowers. Farther in the distance, I see people on the terrace having breakfast and wonder if we should do that, too, instead of running home to hide. When I look back to the water, the yellow leis are gone. I take my paddle, but then I hear a whistle and turn to look toward the horizon. I see a boat, a booze cruise, with a bunch of shirtless guys wearing pink leis around their necks, visors on their

305

heads, holding drinks in coconut shells. Isn't it too early for this? Scottie sits in her middle seat and Alex shields her eyes and looks toward the boat. A series of waves slaps against our canoe, making us list back and forth.

'Whoo-hoo!' I hear them yell. 'Whoo!' They wave frantically at us.

On the bow of the ship there are girls dancing. I hear the deep thumping of the music.

'Whoo! Yeah!' the boys yell. They hold up their drinks, as if in a toast to us.

We stare at them and they stare back, not understanding our quietness.

Alex starts paddling and Scottie follows, and the boys on the boat cheer wildly: 'Paddle! Paddle! Stroke! Stroke!'

A boy with a yellow line of zinc running down his nose takes off his lei and makes to throw it. 'Show us your boobs!' he yells, and everyone laughs.

I steer us around so we face away from them. The girls paddle. I don't know what they're thinking. I hope the last moment with their mother hasn't been ruined for them. I feel as if I'm deserting her by paddling to shore.

'I still love you,' she said one night.

This was right before her accident. We had just turned off the lights, but I was falling fast and mumbled 'Good night' in return. In the morning I turned to her, putting my head on her pillow, and I remembered what she'd said the night before and thought, *Still? Still love me?*

I believe her, though. I believe that despite everything, she still loved me.

'I'm sorry,' I say. 'The booze cruise. We had a nice last moment, though. I hope you guys are okay.'

306

'I think Mom would have liked that,' Scottie says.

'She'd probably show them her boobs,' Alex says.

Scottie laughs and I know Alex is smiling.

The girls paddle slowly, and Scottie stops and rests her paddle across the hull. Her back is hunched and she looks at her lap and I wonder if she's crying. She turns, holding up her hand. 'Mom's under my nails,' she says.

I look, and yes, there she is.

Alex turns and Scottie shows Alex her fingers. Alex shakes her head and gives Scottie this look that seems to say, *Get used to it. She'll be there for the rest of your life. She'll be there on birthdays, at Christmastime, when you get your period, when you graduate, have sex, when you marry, have children, when you die. She'll be there and she won't be there.*

I think that's what the look says; whatever it is, her quiet statement seems to warm her and her sister. The girls begin to paddle again, and the rhythm puts me in a trance: Blades hit the water, slide along the hull, then arc back to the top, a mist of water flying through the air. *Splash, thunk, hiss. Splash, thunk, hiss.* I think of last night, of Scottie flipping through her book, how she peeled the picture of her mother out, then planted her below my ancestors.

'I'll put her at the end,' Scottie said.

I looked at Joanie at the end. I didn't think Scottie meant anything by this order. There is no order to her book, really, and it's not a family tree. It's the scraps of a moment in our lives, picked up and assembled, moments we want to remember and forget.

'The end,' Scottie said.

'The end,' Alex said.

Scottie closed the book.

I think of my wife at the end, her small photograph, a reminder, a keepsake, evidence of a life. It does seem fitting that she should have the final say. *What were her last words?* I wonder. I hate that I don't know, but I suppose now, at the end, she gets the last word, whatever it is, and from her, my daughters and I will make our ascent.

I tell the girls to paddle faster, to get on this small wave that will carry us. They quicken their strokes and the wave picks us up and we glide over the reef and the dark shapes below. We must look like we're enjoying ourselves, and one day we will. And even though the art of wayfinding has been lost to me, I try to steer us to shore in as straight a line as possible.

# Acknowledgments

This novel is based on 'The Minor Wars,' a story from my first book, *House of Thieves*. I'd like to thank *StoryQuarterly* for taking 'The Minor Wars,' my first published story, and thank you to *Best American Nonrequired Reading* for reprinting it.

Many thanks to Kim Witherspoon and David Forrer for your support and hard work; to Laura Ford and everyone at Random House, I am so grateful for your enthusiasm and guidance. Dr. Frank Delen—thank you for your wisdom on coma patients and their families. I hope I got it right.

To my family in Hawaii, and to my reader and husband, Andy, whose wisdom on everything from wills and trusts to motorcycles helped me write this book. Thank you for your encouragement, counsel, and sense of humor, which always seems to make its way into my work.

Finally, a note on Hawaii's present and past. I was inspired by historical facts and current events, yet this book is a marriage of reality and fiction, and fiction wears the pants in this family.